LAURA

the Cursed

BURNING EMBER PRESS

This is a work of fiction. References to real people, events, establishments, organizations, or locales are intended only to provide authenticity, and are used fictitiously. All other characters, and all incidents and dialogue, are drawn from the author's imagination and are not to be construed as real.

A Burning Ember Book
Published in the United States by Burning Ember Press, an imprint of Lavabrook Publishing Group.

THE CURSED. Copyright © 2014 by Laura Thalassa
www.laurathalassa.blogspot.com

To Alison,

Best friends for life.

Chapter 1

"*Please, help me.*"

The night air nipped at Ana Gabor's skin, but she could barely feel the sting. The voice she'd woken up to called out to her, beckoning her away from her home.

"*Please, find me,*" the voice whispered.

She passed the row of houses she'd lived by since the day she was born and left her neighborhood. Still the voice pleaded with her, and she was no closer to finding it.

The blocks of houses thinned out as she walked to the outer edges of the city, ignoring the growing pain in her feet as sharp stones and pieces of glass nicked at them. Soon the paved road narrowed, and asphalt gave way to dirt.

Ana sighed as her feet squished into the muddy street,

the pain somewhat lessening. She couldn't remember how long she'd been walking, but the moon had already crossed the sky and dipped below the horizon.

"*Help me.*"

The voice came from the woods that pressed up against the side of the street. She hesitated for a fraction of a second. Those woods had always made her skin crawl. Something unnatural lurked within them.

Yet now she placed one foot in front of the other, turning off the road and moving into the forest.

The damp underbrush crackled beneath her feet and her breath hitched. She didn't want to be here, but she couldn't turn away. Not when someone called out to her and begged for her help.

The trees twisted unnaturally, contorted as though they were in agony. She shivered as cold wind brushed past her, and she rubbed her arms. In the distance Ana could see the flicker of lights. Humanity—and maybe the woman in need.

The trees around her opened up into a small clearing, and the voice that had pleaded with her finally fell silent. Her steps faltered for an instant.

A dozen individuals waited for her, cloaked in scarlet robes, their faces obscured by hoods. One stepped forward holding a white garment in her arms.

"Change into this, then come back," the voice instructed. The same voice from earlier. Only now, it didn't plead, it ordered.

Ana glanced uneasily at the cloaked figures. Her brain was telling her to run, but her body calmly walked her a short distance away, where she changed behind the cover of a tree. Not that anyone could see her through the dark forest.

Her teeth chattered and she couldn't stop shivering as she walked back into the clearing. Bare feet and thin fabric offered her little protection against a winter's night in Romania.

She fingered the soft material of the gown as she faced the robed individuals.

"Come forward."

She did so, noticing the way the group parted for her. Beyond them rested a stone altar. Vines—some dead and some living—wrapped their way up the sides. Her shivering escalated at the sight.

"Don't be afraid," the voice said. "Go ahead and rest your weary body."

Ana's footsteps dragged as her body carried her up to the stone altar. At least the cold ground had numbed the pain in her feet. She slid herself onto the stone slab, and her shivering somewhat subsided. Someone had draped a velvety cloth over the altar, so her skin wouldn't touch the cold stone beneath. She rubbed her fingers anxiously over the material. They were the only part of her that appeared agitated.

Her breath billowed out around her as the cloaked figures clustered around the altar.

Someone fastened a noose around her neck, and she winced as it tightened, cutting off her air supply. She blinked frantically. *This couldn't be right.* Hadn't she been trying to save a woman? Had she just imagined it? Why

3

couldn't she think? Why couldn't she act?

"Don't fight it," the voice soothed her.

Fight what? She pinched her eyes shut. *So confused.* The only thing Ana knew was that she couldn't remember things she should be able to. And deep in her gut this situation felt wrong.

But even as that thought crossed her mind, black spots clouded her vision. She watched them spread. In the distance she heard chanting.

Focus. That's what she needed to do. For a moment— just a moment—the blackness receded enough for her to see the glint of metal above her.

She had only time to recognize the blade of a dagger pointed at her heart before her vision clouded and the world fell to darkness.

"MOVE FASTER." ANDRE'S voice taunted me from behind.

I ducked and dove left to avoid his hit, tucking my body in on itself as I somersaulted. This was a lethal dance, our bodies bending and twisting with each move.

Andre was on top of me in an instant, his hand going for the throat—the quickest kill. "Faster. You need to be faster. And think like a predator."

I moved to slam my palm into his nose, but he caught it before I had a chance to land the blow. I was moving faster than the human eye could follow. Even so, Andre was still far quicker than me.

"That's the best you got?" he growled.

Using my free hand, I punched Andre in the kidneys,

once, twice, three times—until his grip loosened. He may not have used his kidneys in seven hundred years, but they could still cause pain if injured.

Andre made a move to grab my free hand, and I used the distraction to throw him off of me.

It didn't work so well. For a split second his grip loosened, and then he placed his full weight on top of me, pressing me into the ground. I tried to ignore my body's very non-combative response to that. It grew pliant under his.

"Damnit, Gabrielle, if your opponent is bigger than you, you cannot let them take you down," Andre said, grabbing my wrists and holding them above my head just to further prove his point.

Unfortunately for him, it was proving another point entirely. My eyes dropped to his lips and my fangs descended.

"You are one of the only beings stronger than me," I said.

"But the devil is another, and he is after you." Andre said the words fiercely, even as his fingers absently stroked the skin of my hands. I wondered if he realized he did that whenever he got me into a compromising position. Like he couldn't help but caress me.

I exhaled, staring into his eyes. "I'm not going to be able to outrun or outmaneuver the devil, Andre," I said, resigned. My eyes moved away from him to take in Bishopcourt's training room. Ever since Samhain, Andre had been training me in grappling, knife throwing, and sword fighting (yeah, supernaturals are majorly old school)—

5

preparing me to hold my own when I saw the devil again. The problem was, not in a million years would I be able to go toe-to-toe with him. He'd proven that on Samhain.

Once I died, I was doomed.

Andre let go of my wrists and caught my jaw. He turned me to face him. "If you think that I'm going to just let you give up, then you don't know me very well, soulmate." His eyes flashed. He'd been like this since Samhain—ferocious, determined. It was kind of hot, but mostly scary. Andre was intense enough as is. I guess the prospect of having his soulmate face an eternity as Satan's unwilling mistress really pushed his limits.

I swallowed and nodded at his words.

His eyes dipped to my lips, and his nostrils flared. A wild, spicy scent rolled off him, and my skin started to glow. His forehead creased, and I felt his whole body shudder. This was happening more and more often. We were soulmates; this was *destined* to happen. Fighting it was impossible. But boy did Andre try.

He made a pained sound at the back of his throat, and then he lost his internal battle. His lips met mine, and I tasted heaven on them.

His tongue parted my lips and I wrapped a leg around his and ran my fingers through his hair, reveling in him. The kiss was savage—two tortured souls desperate to become one. I'd never get over this. He was mine and I was his. Soulmates.

I clutched him closer to me. More, I needed more. My skin flared, and I broke off the kiss. Or maybe it was Andre.

We both panted. Andre's eyes shone so brightly that I cupped his face and smiled at him. His expression was one of anguished beauty.

"Don't have dark thoughts, Andre." I didn't always know where he went when he wore that expression, but it usually had something to do with me.

He looked away as he stood up. Taking me hand, Andre pulled me up alongside him and wrapped his arms around me. His lips skimmed my forehead. "I'm not going to let anything happen to you, Gabrielle. I'll die first."

I WATCHED LEANNE shove clothes into a duffle bag the following day. My lips drew down into a frown.

"Don't be sad, Gabrielle," Leanne said, not looking at me. "You have an exciting week ahead of you."

"You know, you're super creepy when you do that," I said. My powers weren't the only ones growing. Leanne's had been intensifying as well, and she was quickly becoming the queen of cryptic messages.

Leanne laughed and finally glanced over at me. "Look who's talking, my little vampy consort."

"Point made." I turned back to my desk and picked up a letter I received in the mail. Judging by the familiar cream stationary and the lack of a return address, I knew exactly who the sender was. Cecilia, my childhood nanny and one of three fates.

If Leanne was the queen of cryptic messages, then Cecilia was the inventor of them.

Happy birthday, tesoro, she wrote along the edge of the

envelope. I blinked back my surprise; I kept forgetting that today was my real birthday. Thanks to my forged birth certificates, March instinctually felt like my birthday month, not December.

I ripped open the envelope and pulled out the card. On a cream colored sheet of paper she'd written five lines in that loopy scrawl of hers. Five lines, and nothing else.

Daughter of wheat and grain,
Betrothed to soil and stain,
Your lifeblood drips,
The scales tip,
But will it be in vain?

Goosebumps broke out along my skin. A dark riddle, that was my birthday gift, and it probably held all the vital clues to how I'd survive the future. I pocketed the poem; I'd best keep it on me. Chances were, I'd need it.

The door to my room burst open, distracting me from Cecilia's strange letter.

"Someone's going to get laid tonight! Someone's going to get laid tonight!" Oliver chanted as he flittered into my room. A gift box was tucked under his arm.

He looked at me and waggled his eyebrows.

My cheeks flushed. "Stop giving me that look."

"No way, Sabertooth. Leanne have you foreseen it? Fifty pounds says she's a nasty freak in the bedroom."

"Oli-ver." The flush was creeping up my neck.

From across the room, Leanne paused in her packing. Unlike Oliver and me, she was going home for the holidays. "Oliver, I don't spy on my friends future sex lives—something you should be thankful for."

"I've got nothing to hide," he said, touching his hair. "I am a sex god. Better than porn."

Ewwww.

Leanne pinched her eyes shut. "I'm going to pretend I didn't hear that." She took a deep breath. "Anyway, even if I did see ... you know ..."

"Andre pillaging that virgin treasure? Stealing the booty? Deflowering our little cherub?" Oliver said, walking over to me.

I raised my eyebrows. "Thanks, Oliver. Descriptive, as always."

"I'd still never tell you," Leanne finished.

Oliver pouted. "You're no fun." He turned to me, and his pout morphed into a sinful little smile.

"Guess what I have?" He held up the gift in his hands before I could answer. "Your birthday present!" he squealed. Oliver shook the box, and I could hear the swish of material rubbing together. Not that it took heightened hearing to guess what Oliver had given me.

"A present? For *moi*?" I said, surprisingly touched at the thought.

Oliver handed me the box. "Open it."

I did so, tearing away the Christmas paper Oliver had wrapped it with and lifting the lid. A dozen sexy pairs of bras and panties were nestled in tissue paper.

I tried not to laugh as I lifted one up. The netted material was fringed with lace. It looked like whoever had made it had run out of fabric.

"Wow, this is—" *going into the back of my drawer, where I'll never touch it again,* "uh, really sexy." I wasn't going to ask how he knew my size.

Oliver smiled smugly. "It's about time you replaced all those hideous cotton panties you have stashed away."

And just like that, Oliver managed to spoil a good moment. Fairies.

"My panties—"

"Needed to be burned," Oliver said. "Lucky for you, I've already taken care of that situation."

I blinked a couple of times at Oliver, trying to make sense of his words. Then I squinted suspiciously at him. My gaze darted to my dresser. I was up in an instant, pulling open my top drawer.

Empty.

"All my underwear is ... gone."

"Happy birthday!" Oliver squealed. I could hear the glee in his voice.

I turned around, my fangs descending. "You are so going to—"

Leanne stepped in front of me and handed me another box, this one much smaller than Oliver's.

I took the small package from her, still staring at Oliver. "I can't believe you just pillaged my underwear drawer."

"Upgraded it, sweets," he said from behind Leanne.

"Just shut up, Oliver," Leanne said, "or she's going to drink you dry, and I want her to open my gift before she does that."

She winked at me and leaned in close. "I promise you can have at him as soon as we're done," she whispered.

"Hey, I heard that!"

I smiled at her, and she nudged the present in my hand. Taking the hint, I ripped off the wrapping paper and opened the box hidden beneath it. Inside was a bottle of perfume.

When I reached for it, Leanne's hand shot out and she stopped me. "Wait. Before you put it on, you should know that this is magical perfume—it repels ... er, *suitors*."

My eyebrows shot up. "No fucking way?" I said, reappraising the perfume bottle. Now that my powers were intensifying, the siren in me was growing, which meant that I had an increasing amount of unwanted attention. "This will scare them off?"

"Well, it won't *scare* anyone off—you'll have to flash some fang for that—but it should dampen some of the lusty looks and the creepy stalkers," Leanne said, shaking her head.

I set the bottle aside and tackle hugged Leanne. "You. Are. The. Best."

"Hey!" Oliver said, "what about me?"

I opened my arms. "You too Pixie Sticks, even if I haven't fully forgiven your for burning my undies."

Oliver huffed but stepped into the embrace.

"I can't believe I had to buy my friend boy repellent," Leanne said.

Oliver shook his head. "Sometimes life just ain't fair."

I rolled my eyes at them. "Where did you even find that?" I asked Leanne. "I didn't know that sort of thing even existed."

"Yeah, it does, but it's sold in the 'Hexes and Curses'

section of supernatural shops."

There was a thoughtful pause as the three of us considered this, and then we fell into hysterical laughter.

"Why didn't you throw in a bottle of hair loss shampoo or some aging cream while you were at it?" I asked when I finally caught my breath. "I'm offended."

Leanne flashed me a wicked smile. "I was tempted."

Man I was going to miss her.

THAT EVENING I exited my dorm, pulling my jacket tighter around me as soon as I walked outside. My body thrummed long before I caught the gaze of the dark being in front of me.

Andre pushed away from his car, his body seeming the gather the shadows around him. He looked for all the world like the prince of darkness he was.

He sauntered over to me, power snapping off of him. The thrum of energy built upon itself until he stood in front of me. Then the noise fell silent.

"Happy birthday, soulmate," he said, a smile tugging at his lips as he spoke. He leaned in and kissed me gently.

Loose strands of his hair tickled my face as his mouth glided against mine. Fire simmered through my veins as the kiss escalated. Our lips parted, tongues touched, and I closed the remaining distance between us until our bodies were flush with one another.

He sighed and pulled away, looking regretfully at my lips.

"What's wrong?" I asked.

He glanced at his watch. "As much as I enjoy that mouth of yours, we have a boat to catch."

"A boat ... to catch?" I asked, not sure whether I'd heard him correctly. "I thought we were going out to dinner."

"We are," he said, "out on the open ocean."

THE FROSTY OCEAN air whipped my hair about and tugged at my coat. Not even this chilly evening could prevent me from enjoying the open water. The volatile siren in me had relaxed now that I was surrounded by it.

A warm chest pressed into my back as the boat left Douglas harbor.

"Are you sure you're not too cold out here?" Andre's lips tickled my ear as he spoke, and his hair grazed my cheek. We stood on the deck of his yacht, watching the land grow smaller and smaller.

My fangs slid out, and heat rushed to my skin. "I'm good." He was doing plenty to keep me warm and flushed already.

"How did you know?" I breathed. There was no place I'd rather be than out here, with nothing but water stretching out around me on all sides.

His lips skimmed my ear. "How could I not?"

I smiled and leaned into him, and for a while we remained like that. That was, until Andre kissed the exposed skin behind my ear. I swiveled around to face him.

His gaze was heated, and his eyes dropped to my lips. Was Oliver right? Was all that held Andre and me back from doing the deed just my age? And if that was so, where was tonight going to lead?

The thought made me excited. And nervous.

"What are you thinking about?" Andre asked, his voice low.

"Nothing," I said a little too quickly.

"I think you're lying." His lips quirked and his voice dropped even lower. I remembered too late that, for a vampire, smell often dominated even our excellent vision. He probably knew exactly where my mind was.

And just as soon as I thought the night might get *really* interesting, he backed off. His eyes grew troubled. "I have to leave again tomorrow for Romania."

Romania. I was starting to hate that place without ever visiting it. Andre had been going there every couple weeks. That was where his coven was holding the hearing against him for crimes he'd committed on the night of his birthday.

"I'll be gone for a few days, as usual. Until I get back, remember your training and keep yourself safe."

Chapter 2

"I HAVE ONE more surprise for you," Andre said.

I stared at him across the dining room table in his yacht, my food and his wine long since gone. "Andre, you really didn't have to." He was going to give me unrealistic expectations about birthdays if he kept this up.

"Gabrielle," he said, his eyes smoldering, "this gives me joy, so do me a favor and go with it."

"Bossy vampire," I said, a smile spreading across my face.

He came around the table and took my hand, tugging me to my feet. His head dipped to my ear. "And you like it."

Before I could respond, Andre led me into the boat's lounge. I took a seat on one of the couches and crinkled my brow, not sure what to expect from Andre. Oliver's earlier words ran through my mind, and my cheeks flushed.

A sculpted eyebrow rose as Andre sat down next to me, his body dwarfing the couch. I wanted to cringe that he could smell just how hot and bothered I was.

He reached into his coat pocket and pulled out a small box—the kind that contained jewelry—and my pulse began to beat loudly in my ears. A ring? Oh God, a ring?

He took my hand, his thumb rubbing slow circles along my skin. "It's not what you think it is," he said.

I felt a surge of relief course through me, but underneath it was a small sense of disappointment. That second emotion confused the hell out of me.

Andre's face remained unreadable as he passed me the box. I took it from him and rubbed the velvety surface of the box, and then I raised the lid.

I sucked in a breath as I stared at the ring inside. A large ruby sat at its center, encased in a band of gold. It glinted in the dim light of the lounge.

"How is this not what I think it is?" I asked, glancing up from my gift.

Andre's gaze was intense when he responded. "There are no strings attached to this ring, Gabrielle. No promises, no commitments, nothing. It's just a piece of jewelry that's dear to my heart, and I wanted to give it to someone who's dear to my heart."

So much more was behind his eyes when he spoke. In them I could see all the things he wasn't saying—that he was making me a promise, that he'd always be mine.

Andre took the ring out from the box, then took my hand. "May I?" he asked, nodding to my fingers.

May he put it on. My hand. He's putting a ring on my finger.

"Mm-hmm," I murmured, not trusting my voice for the moment. My heart was slamming in my chest.

He slid it first on my index finger, but the ring was too small. Then he tried my middle finger. Again the ring got stuck halfway on.

Andre removed it and paused, staring at my ring finger. We both were. He lifted the ring and slipped it on. It fit. Perfectly.

As though it were fated.

"I don't want to be a child bride, Andre."

Happy laughter bubbled out of him. "I promise that won't happen, soulmate. We can wait until you look more like a mummy than a vampire before we get married."

I swatted him. "Look who's talking, Father Time." Then, when the rest of his words sunk in, I raised my eyebrows. "You want to marry me? Eventually?"

Andre's gaze focused on me, and the humor drained from his face. "You're wearing my mother's ring," he said by way of answer.

My eyes widened. I wore something in my hand that predated Andre. "And you're giving it to me?"

Andre nodded.

I ran my finger over the face of the ring, the weight of the gift falling on my shoulders. This was a piece of jewelry that had over 700 years worth of personal value to Andre. And now it was mine.

My gaze drifted up from the ring. I badly wanted to tell him that I couldn't accept something this valuable, but when I met his eyes, they were full of guarded hope. I'd throw myself in front of a bus before I dashed that hope.

"It's incredibly beautiful," I said. "Thank you for giving me something so meaningful."

Sometimes I managed to say the right thing. Now was one of them. Andre's face crinkled into a full-blown smile, making me forget for a moment that he was anything other than the man I loved. "I'm glad you like it," he said. "I want you to always have a part of me, even while I'm away."

Andre looked up from the ring to my face, his expression heated. I had only a moment to notice that resistance that always shone in his eyes melt away. And then his lips met mine.

The kiss was slow and scorching, and it progressed quickly into something more. Andre gathered me to him, and I twined myself around his torso. This was the problem we constantly ran into—fighting the physical attraction between us. Andre usually did a much better job of it than me, but not at the moment.

My fingers slid through his silky hair before trailing down to his shoulders and arms. Our bodies were flush with one another, and despite the layers of clothing that separated us, I could easily feel every dip and curve of his muscular torso.

Andre lifted me from the couch and moved us down the hall. My skin felt feverish as he carried me into one of the bedrooms.

Was this happening?

He set me down on the bed and peeled off his own jacket. I scooted forward, reached a hand out to his shirt, and glanced at him. His eyes were heated. I guess that was permission to continue.

I began unbuttoning his shirt, my hands trembling. He cupped the sides of my face, placing soft kisses over every inch of exposed skin he could find.

He released me only long enough for me to slide the shirt off of his shoulders. As I did so, I relished the feel of his coiled, sinuous muscles.

This was too much. The siren in me was already moving to the surface. I fought against her, closing my eyes and taking a deep breath to push her back.

When I was under control again, I leaned back and drank Andre in. "You're so pretty."

Andre narrowed his eyes. "*Pretty?*" he said incredulously. "I've fought in crusades, held dying men in my arms, led a coven of vampires for over seven centuries. I'm many things, soulmate, but *pretty* is not one of them."

I bit the inside of my cheek. The truth was, Andre was pretty the way a panther was. Beautiful, but lethal. And right now his eyes glittered dangerously. I grabbed his hand and tugged him forward until he joined me on the bed.

A whisper of a smile graced his lips, and I traced it with my thumb. My mouth followed my finger, and I kissed him, tentatively running my hands over his naked torso.

He rolled on top of me, and inner Gabrielle squealed with delight. My skin shimmered on and off like a strobe light as the siren and I battled for control.

Andre broke off the kiss, and I heard his husky laughter.

"Are you laughing at me?" I asked indignantly, my skin losing its ethereal shimmer. I pushed him over and he let me, his laugh building on itself. I rolled on top of him and straddled his torso. "That's not very nice."

"I'm not a very nice man," he said, trying to stifle it.

"It's hard to control that thing, and you don't exactly make it any easier."

"What a difficult cross to bear," he said sympathetically, running a hand down my arm.

It was my turn to narrow my eyes. "You're not doing so well in the boyfriend department right now. And let's not even talk about the future-husband one."

He laughed again, and I fought a smile. "I cherish you so much, Gabrielle."

In response I leaned down and brushed my lips against his, and then we resumed where we left off.

That is, until I yawned.

I wasn't bored in the least. Far from it. But each passing day made me a little less human, and my sleep cycle had been off for a while.

Andre's eyes honed in on my yawn. "You're tired."

"No—*no*," I said, desperate to not mess this up. Since we'd been dating, Andre had been policing the physical nature of our relationship like a nun.

He brushed back my hair, flashing me a smile that crinkled the corners of his eyes. "Ah, to be young," he said, discreetly reminding me of our considerable age difference. I gave him a look.

He kissed each of my eyelids. "You are gorgeous even when you pout," he said, pulling away from my face to take me in.

"I'm not pouting," I said, aware of the obstinate note in my voice even as I spoke. Dang it, he was the sourpuss, not me. I was all for where things were leading.

He wrapped me up in his arms. "And I'm not leaving. I'll be right here. But you should try to get some sleep," he said, his eyes moving over my face.

I yawned again without meaning to, and my eyelids drooped. They fluttered open before falling shut again.

There was something incredibly comforting about falling asleep curled in Andre's arms. I'd gone on for so long thinking that I was a lone traveler in my life; it was nice having someone to share it with.

"Sweet dreams, soulmate."

SNOW COVERED THE ground up to my ankles. It frosted the trees that stretched out around me, making the place both beautiful and bleak.

What forest had I wandered into?

The silence surrounding me was deep and pure. I stepped forward, my boots crunching into snow. The sound raised the hairs along my arm.

A familiar sense of unease slithered through me as I walked along what appeared to be a path. Now that snow covered the ground, only the extra wide space between trees indicated that it was manmade.

My breath clouded around me. But other than that, nothing moved. Nothing made a sound. Unease became dread the further into the woods I walked. My body seemed to know more about my surroundings than I did.

Ahead of me, beyond the gnarled branches, I caught a glimpse of something. The thick woods opened up.

My breath froze in my chest. Fear coursed through my veins and begged me to leave. But I couldn't move. Instead I stared, transfixed, at the stone castle in front of me.

It seemed to grow out of the rocky earth, raw stone transitioning to quarried, polished blocks stacked one on top of each other. Icicles had formed along the castle's ledges and along the faces and wings of gargoyles that watched me.

I'd seen this place before, when snow and ice hadn't covered it. When I'd almost sold my soul. And now I was back.

"Welcome back, Gabrielle."

I shrieked before I could stop myself and glanced around, looking for him. The devil.

He stepped out from the woods to my left, looking just as beautiful and terrifying as he always had.

I stumbled back. "Why can't you leave me alone?" I asked, my voice unsteady. Now I remembered why my body had been signaling for me to leave. It knew on a primordial level that this was an unholy place.

He ignored my question and stepped towards me. For each of his steps forward I took one back, until I bumped into a tree.

He closed the remaining distance quickly. "Little bird," he said, the back of his hand grazing my face. I flared my nostrils at his touch, "I will never leave you alone. Not until you agree to my terms."

I flattened myself against the tree, trying to put space between us when there was none. The tree I was butted up against groaned as it leaned away. It too was trying to distance itself from the being in front of me.

The devil picked up a lock of my hair and rubbed it between his fingers. This close to me, our breath was intermingling. It felt much, much too intimate.

He placed the lock of hair back against my chest, his fingers lingering. I whimpered at the awful sensation, then bit my lip as his gaze moved to my mouth.

Gabrielle, the forest echoed.

The devil cocked his head at the voice, and I used the momentary distraction to slip away from him. Using my supernatural speed, I sprinted down the snow-covered path.

The earth quaked as I ran, snow shaking loose from the trees around us. I threw a glance over my shoulder. The devil's face had contorted into something ugly.

Gabrielle! This time the voice was more insistent.

I lost my balance and pitched forward. The moment I should've hit the cold, frozen earth, the world around me vanished.

"Gabrielle!"

My eyes snapped open and the room came into focus. I was still on Andre's yacht. Safe.

Andre leaned over me. A frown tugged at the edges of his lips and a line formed between his eyebrows. I ignored the way his closeness hitched my already ragged breath.

"Did you dream of him again?" he asked.

I opened my mouth to speak, but my throat was dry. Instead I nodded.

Andre's thumb moved to my face, and he stroked away a tear that must've slipped out in my sleep. The crease between his brows hadn't smoothed out. I could read his thoughts; he was wondering how he could save me from something as slippery as the devil.

"You can't protect me," I said.

"That's what you told me shortly after we met," Andre said, his gaze flittering across my face.

I swallowed. "I remember."

"The thing is," he said, his eyes intense, "you're my soulmate, not his. That means that it is my job to look after your wellbeing, and it's his job to leave you the hell alone."

That made me quirk my lips. The devil following the rules? Not likely.

I rubbed my arms as I sat up. "He's not going to stop Andre," I said. "Until he gets what he wants, I don't think he ever will."

I WOKE UP the next morning to the sound of my phone ringing. I stretched and glanced out the window. Rain came down in torrents, and the wind had blown away some of the Christmas garlands that had decorated Peel Castle's walls. In the middle of the grassy lawn, the evergreen Christmas tree shook violently, the ornaments making a tinkling noise.

I smiled to myself, remembering my evening with Andre. It drooped a little when I realized that it might be days before I saw him again.

Beside me, my phone continued to ring. I snatched it up, noticing the caller ID. *Hellhole*, a.k.a., the Politia.

"Hello?" I stared at the ring Andre gave me, trying to absorb some of him through it.

"If you have any plans today, cancel them," my boss, Inspector Magdalene Comfry said on the other end of the line. "We need you to come in."

"What's going on?"

"A girl was murdered overseas, and the Politia has requested your expertise on the killing. Congratulations Gabrielle, as our lead demonologist, you and your partner have been assigned to the case."

Chapter 3

I ENTERED CASTLE Rushen, the Politia's headquarters, from its back entrance, mostly to avoid stares. Since Samhain, I'd become infamous for spending an evening with the devil and living to tell the tale. Those who saw me as a victim stared at me with fascination, wondering what I'd experienced that night. And those who thought I was evil, they often glared at me like they wanted to douse me in holy water.

I shoved my hands in my pockets as I walked down a back hallway. Here the smells of mildew, grime, and blood assailed my nostrils.

I passed the training rooms, half tempted to stop and work on my knife-throwing skills. Between my supernatural reflexes and my training with Andre, I had developed wicked accuracy.

Later, I promised myself.

A side hallway branched to my left, and I couldn't help the spooked glance I gave it. The cellblock. The cells were officially called neutralization tanks because they were enchanted to strip a being of their powers. That is, if the being could be parted with their powers and live. For some beings, like me, their magic was intrinsically tied to their life force. Neutralization meant death.

I held my breath as I passed the hall, reminding myself of a childhood game I played with my friends when we passed graveyards. *Don't catch your breath around the dead, lest you want to lose your head.*

The truth was, the cellblock smelled even worse than the morgue—the permanent stench of fear and anger lingered there, overlaying the more common smells of bodily fluids. I couldn't stand it.

I made my way to the lobby, where the smell of coffee masked the castle's less savory scents.

I chewed on my lip, worried that whatever assignment I was being called in on would wipe out my winter vacation. Because I was considered an adult in the supernatural world, they could place me in a fulltime position if they wanted. Then poof, there would go my holiday break. And knowing the Politia, they just might do that now that I'd acquired the title of demonologist.

Once I crossed the lobby, I entered the break room. I poured myself a cup of coffee and peered at a discarded newspaper someone had left. On one of the side columns of the front page, my name jumped out. I picked up the newspaper and skimmed the article.

"Let me save you the pain of reading that," a familiar voice said from behind me. "Today you've been called the devil's consort, queen of the damned, and—my personal favorite—the tainted one."

I glanced up from my reading. Caleb stood in the doorway of the break room. Despite his dimpled smile, I could read the turmoil all over his face. Since that night at the Braaid, something—maybe everything—about our relationship had changed.

I dropped the newspaper back where I found it. "Have you heard any details on this case?" I asked.

He shook his head. "None."

The slap of boots against the linoleum sounded in the hallway outside the break room. "Sergeant Fiori, Sergeant Jennings," Maggie said, poking her head in, "what the hell are you two doing down here? Move it. You're late, and the chief constable needs to fill you both in before you head out."

Head out?

CHIEF CONSTABLE MORGAN sat on the edge of his desk. "Two nights ago, a young nephilim woman by the name of Ana Gabor was found dead in the woods outside of Cluj-Napoca, Romania," he said.

My ears perked up. Romania, Andre's homeland and the country where a group of vampires were currently gathered. A tight ball of unease coiled itself in my stomach. Could this murder be a result of having too many vampires in one location?

"Nephilim?" Caleb asked.

"Of angelic blood," the chief constable said. He grabbed two file folders from his desk and passed one to me and the other to Caleb. "Our victim's throat had been slit and her body drained of most of its blood."

This all sounded a bit too familiar. "Was it a vampire?" I asked.

The chief constable honed his attention in on me. "That's for you to figure out."

I swallowed delicately. I'd been given the title of resident demonologist after the Samhain murders. It was a title that encompassed everything of dark origin, including vampires. No doubt they gave me the title begrudgingly—after all, most of my colleagues had studied for years to earn the same status. I guess when evil shit threw itself at you, you either died or became an expert real quick.

I flipped open the file. Paper clipped to it was an image of a beautiful girl with blonde hair, her arms folded across her chest, a noose made of twine wrapped around her neck. Below it her throat was slit. The only other injury appeared to be a stab wound to her heart.

"You two will be working directly with the Romanian branch of the Politia per their request. You'll be reporting to Inspector Grigori Vasile. He's the director of international affairs, and he will be your liaison for the duration of your investigation.

I swayed a little on my feet. This was really happening—they were giving me a leadership role I didn't want. Oh holy shitballs. Please no.

Chief Constable Morgan turned his attention to Caleb.

"Despite the fact that Gabrielle carries the title of demonologist, as her partner you are fully expected to participate in the investigation."

Caleb nodded his head eagerly.

The chief constable looked between the two of us. "This is a high priority case, and it could potentially be dangerous. Caleb and Gabrielle, you both have shone remarkable teamwork and talent. Now it's your chance to shine and prove your worth to the Politia. Think you can handle it?"

No. I didn't think I could. Not at all.

"Yes," Caleb responded for us.

The chief constable's eyes flicked to me. "Chief Constable," I said, "I don't know if I'm ready to take on this kind of responsibility. I've only been a part of the Politia for a few months ..."

I stopped talking when I heard Caleb hiss in a breath. This was an opportunity for both him and me, and I was ruining it.

The chief constable's gaze had me shifting my weight. "I'm glad to hear you voice your concerns, and I appreciate your honesty," he said. "You do not have to take the case, but that decision will likely affect your continued employment here."

I sucked in my cheeks.

"We cannot just deny a branch of our institution access to one of our experts because she doesn't feel she's qualified to do work she's been given a title for."

My heart pounded in my chest. If I agreed to this, I'd be willingly immersing myself in the darkness that already sought me out. But if I didn't, I could kiss my job with the Politia goodbye.

I glanced at Caleb, whose eyes pleaded with me. My decision affected him too. Damn.

Finally, reluctantly, I nodded. "I can handle it," I said.

"Then congratulations," Chief Constable Morgan said. "Until the Romanian branch releases you, you are both now officially on the case."

I could smell Caleb's excitement. My stomached roiled. I was going to fuck up big time, I just knew it.

The chief constable glanced at the clock in his office before grabbing another stack of papers littered on his desk. "These are your plane tickets and itineraries—the Romanian Politia's covered all of your expenses. Inspector Grigori Vasile will pick you up at the airport in Romania to take you to your lodgings, where you will stay for the duration of the investigation. I suggest you spend the next few hours packing. Your flight is this evening."

So MUCH FOR my winter break. I spent the next several hours in Peel Academy's main library, Xeroxing supernatural maps of the area and as many pages of demonic and angelic folklore as I could find.

I checked the time as I slogged back to my dorm. I had under an hour to pack everything I needed for my trip.

When I opened my door, Oliver was sprawled out on Leanne's bed, flipping through one of her old diaries. I snatched it out of his hands. "Nosy much?"

"Geez harpy woman, I just miss her."

I dropped Leanne's diary on her desk and moved over to my bed, pulling my suitcase out from underneath it.

"Wait, what are you doing?" Oliver asked, noticing the suitcase.

"What do you think I'm doing? Packing." I began emptying my "upgraded" underwear drawer.

"But I thought you were staying here for winter break."

"Unfortunately, I'm not," I said. "The Politia put me on a case in Romania." I walked over to my closet and grabbed a section of clothing and threw the items into my bag, hangers and all.

"Oh, unh uh, girl. That is *not* how you pack a suitcase." Oliver crept over to my bag and began removing the hangers from my shirts and folding them. It was actually pretty endearing, until I realized he was screening out shirts he didn't approve of. "And *Romania?*" he said skeptically. "There's, like, a whole body of water that will separate us."

I exhaled. "I know." I dropped a couple of coats into my bag.

"You're leaving me all alone!"

"You have Rodrigo." Rodrigo, the poor werewolf who decided to not go to Brazil so that he could spend winter break with my commitment-phobe friend.

"But he's so *clingy*," Oliver complained.

I snickered. "You find relationships clingy."

"Plus," Oliver added, ignoring my comment, "things are bound to get interesting where you're involved."

I looked up from my packing so I could give him the stink eye.

"What?" he said. "It's not like it isn't true." Oliver muttered to himself, "I just wish those incubi would come back."

I shuddered at the thought. But what I didn't tell Oliver was that, though the incubi were gone, their leader haunted my dreams.

Just like Leanne, I was getting better at keeping secrets.

"NICE TO MEET you Inspector Vasile," I said, shaking our liaison's hand in the airport terminal. It was late evening by the time Caleb and I landed in Cluj-Napoca and met up with the inspector.

"Please, call me Grigori," he said, inclining his head. "It's an honor to meet the Politia's youngest demonologist." If only he knew how ill-deserved that title was.

"I'm glad to be here," I lied.

"Well, we are indebted to the Isle of Man for letting us borrow you and your partner for this investigation." Grigori's attention moved to Caleb. "Ah, and you must be Inspector Jenning's son. We've heard about you even all the way over here. A lot of officers are excited to see another shapeshifter on the force."

Caleb's face flushed. He rubbed the back of his neck and extended his hand. "It's nice to meet you too. I, uh, look forward to working with you on the case."

"Good, good." Grigori nodded and took one of my bags. "Well, let's get going. We'll get you settled tonight and begin the investigation tomorrow."

We headed to Grigori's car and loaded our belongings before getting in and pulling out of the airport. It was only then that I got my first close up look of Cluj. The city appeared to be nestled at the foot of a sloping mountain range, and everywhere I looked, old European architecture blended with more modern buildings.

Andre's somewhere out there. This was not exactly how I'd imagined visiting his home country for the first time, and it felt strange being here without him by my side.

"A snowstorm is heading our way within the next few days, so I hope you planned to stay for awhile," Grigori said to us, his accent rolling the words. "Air travel will likely be stalled during that time."

"Fantastic," I said, suppressing a sigh. Caleb and I would be stuck here even if we managed to solve the case in record time.

Eventually we pulled up to a small inn that sat on the outskirts of the city and made our way to the inn's front desk.

"Sergeant Fiori," Grigori called, following Caleb and me inside.

"Gabrielle," I corrected him, glancing over my shoulder.

"Before you and your partner retire for the evening, can I speak to you both for a moment?" he asked, gesturing to a sitting room across from the front desk.

I glanced at Caleb who flashed me an excited look. We were really doing this. I nodded to Grigori. "Of course."

I dropped my luggage, and Caleb and I made our way to one of the couches facing the inn's stone fireplace.

Grigori took a seat across from us. "How much do you both know about the crime?"

"Not much," Caleb replied, "other than what was given to us in the file earlier today."

"Do you know why we called a demonologist in to investigate?"

I paused. "Not exactly."

Grigori nodded to himself. "I figured as much. You see, we called you in because we feel that there are some glaring similarities between this murder and the Samhain murders."

I jolted in my seat. "Similarities?" I repeated, my voice weak.

"After the Samhain murders, we've been watching our ley lines in case a copycat decided to mimic those killings."

I swallowed. I knew what was coming next.

"Our victim was killed on one such ley line."

I closed my eyes. No wonder they wanted me here.

"If you've looked at the case file on this murder, then you've seen the photos. Our victim, Ana Gabor, wasn't simply killed. There are details that indicate this was premeditated, ceremonial."

I grimaced, remembering the photos.

"Here's what we know," Grigori said, leaning forward in his seat. "Whoever killed our victim dressed her in a white gown, then proceeded to inflict three separate, lethal injuries: she was suffocated, stabbed through the heart, and her throat was slit. One of our psychometric officers got a read from the body; it appears that the wounds were inflicted simultaneously."

"Was the psychometric able to pull any other information from the body?" Caleb asked.

Both of us knew from working under Maggie, who herself was a psychometric officer, that certain bodies produced more information than others. Some of it had to do with the victim's state of mind at the time of death, some of it had to do with the perpetrator's, and some of it had to do with the psychometric's own ability to read the information.

Grigori shook his head. "Nothing helpful." He rubbed his jaw. "We do know that once our victim was dead, her blood was then collected," Grigori said.

"Collected, rather than drank?" I clarified.

"Yes."

I exhaled. The perpetrator could still be a vampire, but now at least I didn't have to assume that he or she was one.

Grigori looked between Caleb and me. "Do either of you know the properties of angel blood?"

I glanced at Caleb. He looked just as confused as I felt. "No," I said for the both of us.

"If willingly given and ingested, angel blood is said to cleanse the soul of wrongdoing."

I stilled at the thought. Many, many people would kill for that. But if it were true, then it would be paradoxical to kill someone with angelic blood unless they agreed to it beforehand.

Grigori rubbed his cheek. "This is all conjecture, since no angels have willingly given their blood to another within the last several centuries and written records before that time were ... poor at best.

"In addition, the folklore on angel blood only discusses

angels, not their offspring. So we don't really know what the killer's motivations were. But, celestially speaking, it's a significant loophole in the system."

"Are you saying that you think the killer murdered the victim and drank the blood to cleanse their soul of the murder?" Caleb asked.

Grigori inclined his head. "Precisely."

We all sat silent and let that sink in.

I cleared my throat. "You said that an angel's blood had to be willingly given. How do you know that it was?"

Grigori assessed me. "We don't know whether the folklore is true—that the blood must be given, not taken. However, there were no signs that the victim was under duress, save one."

He opened a briefcase he'd brought with him and pulled out a photograph and placed it on the coffee table. The image was so zoomed in that at first I wasn't able to recognize what I was looking at. Then I began to make out toes and two heels. Feet. I was staring at feet.

I pressed my lips together tightly. Across the victim's feet the skin had been sliced open. Dozens of angry-looking, open wounds—some of which still had rocks or shards of glass imbedded in them—had shredded up the bottom of Ana Gabor's feet. Bloodied twigs and leaves had then cleaved themselves to the sticky blood.

"What could've caused this?" I asked, touching the photo. I was caught between grief for the victim and a kind of horrified curiosity.

"Walking a very long distance barefoot," Grigori said.

Grigori tapped his fingers to his lips. "There is one

more thing you should know. The victim was found in Hoia Baciu forest."

When he didn't say anything more, I spoke up. "What about it?"

Grigori watched me, his gaze intense. "Whatever did this to her—whatever brought her to those woods—we're not sure it was wholly human."

Chapter 4

After Grigori filled us in on tomorrow's itinerary, I made my way to my room. I was in the middle of unpacking my clothes when my phone rang. I snatched it up from where it lay on my bed.

"Hello?"

"I can die a happy man, now that I've heard your voice tonight."

Andre.

I smiled and fell back on the bed. "You need to save the panty-dropping comments for in-person visits. They'd be much more effective that way."

"Don't tempt me, soulmate. It's hard enough as is."

"That's what ... she said?"

He chuckled, throaty and low, and it physically made me ache for him. "I miss you and your dirty mind already," he said. "How's life been since I last saw you?"

I ran my fingers over his ring. "Busy," I said.

"Busy?" Andre asked. "You're on vacation."

I stared up at the wooden beams overhead. "Not anymore."

The lightness that was in Andre's voice a moment ago vanished. "What's going on?" he asked.

"The Politia put me on an investigation."

"What kind of investigation?" Andre's words were slow and deliberate, which meant that he was trying to control his emotions.

"The kind where people show up dead." I glanced out my window at the dark night. The thin crescent moon did little to drive out the night's darkness. Below it the mountains stained the horizon an even deeper shade of black. This was a wild, mysterious place.

"Gabrielle," Andre said, much too calmly. "Are you still on the Isle of Man?"

"No."

"Where, exactly, are you?" His voice was sharp, his words clipped. Andre was losing control of his emotions. Oh goody.

"Cluj-Napoca, Romania."

The line fell silent.

"Andre?"

"You're in Cluj-Napoca?" The name rolled smoothly off his lips, reminding me that he spoke Romanian.

"Yes."

Another pause, then, "I'm coming over."

Coming over? I could hear him moving into action on

the other end of the line.

"What hotel are you staying at?" he asked.

"Whoa there, Andre. You're not thinking about meeting up with me, are you?"

"Of course I am."

How close could he possibly be to consider visiting me right now?

I rubbed my eyes. "I'm about to go to sleep, and you have a trial to worry about."

"You don't understand, Gabrielle," he said. Something awfully close to fear laced his voice.

"Understand what?" My skin prickled. This was one of those moments where I recognized how little I knew about this supernatural world.

"Cluj-Napoca was the small Romanian village I grew up in." The phone slipped a little at this new piece of information. Somewhere in this region, 700 years ago, Andre had grown and nearly died. This was where the devil had cursed him. "It's also the place where my current trial is being held," he added.

"You're *here*?" My eyes fluttered, and I sat up, twisting his ring around and around my finger. "In the same city?"

"Yes."

I swore. This was just too coincidental.

When Andre spoke again, his voice was grim. "Something's brewing, and I fear you're at the center of it. Again."

I LAY AWAKE in my bed, staring at the wooden beams over

my head. I was supposed to be asleep—I'd even managed to convince Andre to put off visiting me for that very reason. However, as soon as I turned the lights off, my thoughts took off.

My pulse skittered along. Two months ago, I'd solved my first case, and when it began, I'd assumed it had nothing to do with me. Since then, I'd learned that the fates were dabbling in my life, and the devil desperately wanted me. Though I had no idea why these beings took an interest in me, I now knew the signs. Whatever was going on here, I might very well have something to do with it.

My thoughts moved to the case and the young victim. The torn flesh of the girl's feet bothered me. Why would someone walk until their feet bled unless they were under duress? And if they were, then they wouldn't willingly give their blood, would they?

I rubbed my temples.

"*Siren.*"

My head snapped up at the voice. Was that just my imagination? I strained my ears and sat in the silence of my room.

"*Come face me.*"

The voice sounded like it was coming from outside. I threw off my covers and changed into a pair of jeans and a sweater. While I tugged on my boots, I heard the voice speak again.

"*If you dare.*"

I left my room and strode down the hallway. No one was in the lobby any longer, but the remnants of the fire crackled in the fireplace, now mostly dying embers.

I crossed the lobby and gazed out a window near the inn's main entrance. In this section of the city only a handful of dim lights lit the street. That, combined with my ever-improving night vision, allowed me to study the landscape outside.

A shadow flashed between a cluster of trees. I squinted, trying to make out what I saw, but whatever had moved was beyond even my range of sight.

I reached for the handle of the inn's front door.

"Where do you think you're going?"

I jumped at the voice and whipped around.

Caleb stood behind me, his arms folded. He didn't look pleased.

I put a hand to my heart. "You scared the crap out of me." He shouldn't have been able to sneak up on me. Either I'd been more absorbed in the strange voice, or he was getting better at disguising himself.

His eyes flicked from me to the front door. "Going for a midnight stroll?" He sounded accusing.

I glanced back outside. "I heard something, and I wanted to check it out."

"There's a killer out there somewhere."

"I'm also a killer," I reminded him.

He flinched. "You could get hurt." I could smell the adrenaline as it hit his veins. Normally that meant that he was just excited to talk to me, but right now I suspected he was angry.

I rolled my eyes. "Melodramatic much?"

His lips drew down. "No, not really, considering how every time you go rogue you end up putting your life in danger."

"That's not fair," I said, even though his words were absolutely true. But what he'd forgotten to mention was that I often found myself without good alternative choices.

His gaze moved over my face, and he sighed. "Honestly?" he said. "I get it. I get that there are a lot of things in your life that just aren't fair. I'm not trying to make you feel bad about them. I just don't want to have to do this every night—babysit you on an official investigation."

Babysit? I slitted my eyes. "Were you watching me?" A thought blossomed. Had Caleb been in the room with me—or out in the hall—in some other form?

I walked up to him. "Were you watching me?" I repeated.

Caleb stood there obstinately, his arms still folded over his chest. "You really think that little of me, Gabrielle?" he asked, cocking his head. I could see a flash of hurt in his eyes.

"You followed me out here," I challenged him.

"To make sure you weren't running headlong into trouble, like you have a tendency to do."

I clenched my fists. "You don't know the first thing about my tendencies."

Caleb stepped in closer and his jaw tightened. "You are a siren, Gabrielle, a type of supernatural cursed with misfortune and untimely death—and that's not even the worst of your problems."

His face lost some of its anger. "Do you know what it's like to worry that one night your friend might just be gone—taken?" he whispered. "Taken by your worst nightmare." His eyes glittered with some emotion as he gazed at me. "Because that happened to you on Samhain, Gabrielle, and now that's what goes through my head, over and over."

"That's not going to happen again," I said softly.

"I'm not stupid, so don't lie to me to make me feel better," he snapped. "I heard the fate that night. It *will* happen the next time you die."

I winced at his words.

He stepped forward, getting in my face. "But more than that, don't lie to yourself, Gabrielle," he said, his eyes boring into mine. He'd make a great interrogator one day; he already had me squirming. "Just because we're no longer at the Braaid doesn't mean this is over. Far from it.

"I don't know everything that happened to you that night, but I can tell you this: the more reckless you are, the sooner you'll have to face that horror all over again."

Chapter 5

THE NEXT MORNING, after we'd showered and eaten breakfast, Caleb and I loaded ourselves into Grigori's car. The
first event on today's agenda was visiting the crime scene.

I wouldn't look at Caleb, and he seemed fine with that.
We'd parted on uneasy terms the night before. I didn't
know what to make of him anymore. The boy who once
had deep feelings for me now seemed to hate that he
cared for me. It made me feel angry and incredibly guilty
to think that I somehow did this to him.

We pulled out of the inn. Now in the light of day, I
could see that we were in fact on the edges of the city.
The inn rested on a hill, giving me a panoramic view of
Cluj-Napoca.

Everywhere I looked I saw red roof tiles, domes, and
spires. The city was a thing of the past, at least to my Cal-

ifornia-grown eyes. The closer I looked, the more modern architecture I saw tucked away between rooflines. But the effect wasn't lost. No wonder the supernatural world so easily made its home here. Everything about the place seemed a little fantastical.

The car ride took us further and further out of the city, until trees replaced buildings. A short while later Grigori pulled off the road.

We got out of the car, and Grigori passed Caleb and me each a pair of latex gloves. "Use these once we enter the woods. Anything in there could potentially be a part of the crime scene."

I removed my knit gloves to put on the latex ones. As soon as I did so, I could practically feel my warmth leaving me through my fingertips.

I could be enjoying hot chocolate right now in the comfort of my dorm room.

Grigori's gaze moved from us to some distant point in the woods. "I have to warn you," he said to us, "this forest will play tricks on your senses."

Already I could feel some ominous presence press down on me. I wondered what Leanne would think if she were here. I smiled sardonically. She wouldn't come within ten miles of this place ... unless it was to protect me. My smile fell from my lips. I shouldn't be here, I didn't want to be here—especially after talking with Andre last night—but that didn't stop me from following Grigori and Caleb into the forest.

A chilly fog hung low in the woods; it dampened my jeans and made my surroundings appear all the more sinister. The trees around me stood straight and tall, their branches bare of leaves.

I saw no woodland creatures, but I heard scuttling and saw barren trees rustle. If I listened hard enough, I could make out the quiet heartbeats of the animals that lived here. Haunted or not, at least something lived in Hoia Baciu forest.

We trekked through the woods for ten minutes before I glimpsed the crime scene tape. Beyond it was ... nothing extraordinary. It looked like every other square foot of forest I'd passed. Barren trees, fallen leaves, some scattered rocks.

My nostrils flared. While I hadn't seen anything unusual, my nose picked up the sickly sweet smell of blood and decay.

Next to me I noticed Grigori scent the air. I furrowed my brows, wondering what kind of supernatural he was. Something with a good sense of smell. If I had to guess, I'd place money on a therianthrope—a were-creature.

When we reached the tape, Grigori lifted it so that Caleb and I could duck through. Once the three of us crossed the barrier, the smell of blood and carnage became sharper and more complex. I closed my eyes to better focus on the scent. Something pure overlaid the tangy, fetid smell of death.

Angel blood.

So many residual scents flavored this most overpowering smell, but before I could read further into them, Caleb's breath caught. I let my eyes flutter open.

We stood in the middle of a small clearing. The trees

around us contorted into unnatural shapes. But that wasn't what had caught my partner's attention.

In the center of the clearing rested a stone altar. Vines twisted up its sides, some dead, some living. The victim's scent was strongest there.

"What is a stone altar doing in the middle of forest?" I asked.

"We don't know," Grigori said, his voice frustrated.

I crept closer. A maroon stain had dried on the altar's surface. Nausea rose at the sight. I put the back of my hand to my mouth and collected myself. A stone altar resting along a ley line—that couldn't be good. It looked as though it had grown up from the ground, as though the earth itself demanded payment for its magic.

Behind me a twig cracked. I threw a glance over my shoulder, thinking Caleb was behind me. I was wrong.

Something shifted between the trees, but then it was gone. The tempo of my heartbeat increased. It felt as though the whole forest was watching us.

"Have you seen anything like it before?" Grigori asked. If he felt foolish for asking a teenager such a question, he didn't show it.

I turned back and stared at the altar, seeing it even as a different image played out in my mind's eye. One where the altar was located in a cathedral made of bones. On it my friend lay, unconscious, and then later, dead.

"Yes," I said solemnly, remembering the things that had crowded around that altar. "I have seen something like it once before."

I felt Death's finger draw down my spine.

"And ... ?" Grigori prompted.

I took a deep breath. "I saw it on the night of Samhain, when the devil took me."

I glanced at Grigori, just to make sure that he knew what I was talking about. He nodded. "I have heard the story of your abduction.."

"One of the places he took me to was an ossuary," I said. "When we arrived, my friend's doppelganger lay unconscious on an altar not so different from this one." I swallowed the lump in my throat before I spoke again. "The devil ordered her killed, and ..." I worked my jaw, "a group of beings the devil commanded slit her throat."

Both Caleb and Grigori were silent while they processed my words. "Did they drain her blood?" Grigori finally asked.

"They didn't," I said, "but I don't know if they were planning to. The ossuary ... *exploded* right after this."

A grim silence descended once more as we turned our attention back to the crime scene. Dread and something like acceptance cloaked me. This murder might very well be the work of the devil.

I CIRCLED THE altar, eyeing its bloodstained surface.

"Do you know what the beings were that stood around the altar in the ossuary?" Caleb asked.

I glanced up at him, thinking about the robed things that had killed my friend. They'd seemed to be made of shadow.

I shook my head. "I have no clue."

I closed my eyes and breathed in the smell of the crime scene again, picking out the scents. It was hard to discern the fainter smells under all the blood, especially now that a crime scene unit had trampled through the area. I focused on picking out the strongest scent other than the victim's. Something sweet and burnt lingered just beneath the smell of blood.

A frustrated sigh escaped me. It could very well belong to the killer, but it could also belong to the team that had analyzed the scene. There was no way to know for sure.

ONCE WE LEFT the crime scene, we headed to the Politia's offices. The Romanian branch was centered in Bucharest, but each city with a large supernatural population had a station, including Cluj. And right now, Cluj's housed our case's evidence.

Grigori pulled the car into a packed parking lot in the middle of Cluj, and I caught my first real glimpse of what the Politia looked like outside of the Isle of Man.

The building was white with red rooftiles, just like many of the surrounding buildings, and it appeared weather-worn and fairly old. However, unlike Castle Rushen on the Isle of Man, this building didn't seem to hold any supernatural cultural heritage. It was just ... a building.

Caleb and I followed Grigori inside. A smile tugged on my lips when I noticed the similarities between the Politia here and the Politia on the Isle of Man. The same smell of coffee and pastries permeated the air, as did the buzz of activity.

Grigori nodded to people or briefly exchanged words with them in Romanian as he led us down to the basement.

I ignored the stares from people who recognized my face. I'd become infamous in the last several months, and it didn't help that the siren in me drew people in. Too bad I'd forgotten to pack the perfume Leanne had given me.

"Gabrielle, you have a good nose on you, right?" Grigori asked as we followed him down the hall.

"Um, yes."

"Good, good. I wanted to see if you could pull any smells from the evidence."

I gazed at him curiously as we walked into a sterilized room. I might have a good nose on me, but so did he. What insight could I possibly provide that others couldn't?

Some demonologist I was.

Inside the room rested a table, and on it, a cardboard container filled with plastic baggies.

Evidence.

Grigori grabbed a pair of latex gloves from a dispenser next to the door and walked over to the box. "I've had Evidence pull some of the items found on our victim to see if you might get a read on them."

Caleb and I peered over his shoulder at the plastic bags. I recognized the twine rope and the white gown the victim wore. Both were drenched in blood.

Grigori reached into the box and grabbed the bag that contained the clothing item. "See what scents you smell from this." He opened it up and placed it below my nose.

I forced myself not to stumble back as the smell of

blood and rotting gore hit my nose. It overpowered all the other smells.

Remember what Andre taught you. Scents came in layers. If I could separate them, then I could distinguish them.

I slowed my breathing and let this first smell invade my senses. The scent of blood contained something other-worldly—divinity. Once I'd familiarized myself with the smell, I noticed something below it.

"Ash," I said out loud, my eyes meeting Grigori's. Caleb glanced between the two of us as Grigori nodded. "Our inspectors noticed the same smell, but we've been unable to identify the being it belongs to. We were hoping you might know."

What he was really saying was, *We were wondering if the devil's peeps smelled like this.* Some dark beings had that smoky, my-soul's-been-frying-in-Hell smell to them. But this particular brand of damned? Nope. I hadn't come across it.

I shook my head. "Sorry, but I don't recognize it."

THAT EVENING I was rifling through my notes on the case when I felt the first thrum of energy. I glanced up from the desk in my hotel room. A set of headlights flashed across my room as a sleek black car swung into the parking lot.

Andre had found me.

I set my notes aside and left my room, trepidation prickling my skin.

By the time I'd reached the lobby, Andre was already there, chatting with the woman behind the front desk. A lock of hair fell over his eyes, making him look roguish.

Based on the woman's bubbly laughter and the way she kept touching her hair, my guess was that Andre had done his magic and gotten her to fall in love with him. He had a knack for that.

His gaze slid to me, and though his friendly smile didn't waver, his eyes got a hungry look to them. He said something to the woman in Romanian and pushed away from the front desk.

The way he walked toward me made me half tempted to make a run for it, but I forced myself to stand my ground and face him.

He closed the distance between us and cupped my jaw. I only had enough time to blink before he took possession of my mouth. He kissed me roughly—angrily—and when he finally pulled away, his jaw clenched and unclenched. "You and I are going to go for a little car ride," he said. His tone left no room for argument.

So, naturally, I argued. "I'm not going anywhere."

"Soulmate, you do not want to test my mood this evening."

"Then ask nicely."

His hand twitched, and I swore he was battling his natural instinct to haul me over his shoulder. Neanderthal.

He lost the battle.

I squeaked as he scooped me up into his arms and crossed the room. The woman at the front desk watched us with wide eyes, especially once I started pounding on Andre's chest. "Put me down, Andre."

In response, he kicked the front doors open. I shivered

as the cold evening air hit me. Andre's arms tightened around me and he pulled me closer to his chest.

"Are you really doing this?" I asked.

He ignored me.

I sighed. "Andre, really, it's called manners. You ask. I answer. We both win."

He carried me to his car and placed me in the passenger seat. As soon as he closed the door I lunged for it and yanked.

Locked from the outside. "*Andre!*" I bellowed. "Let me out!"

In the next moment, he was in the driver's seat, turning over the ignition.

"Andre," I warned. He wasn't going to do this, was he? Memories of our first, horrific date surfaced.

Damnit, he was.

He shifted the car into first, and with a squeal of burning rubber, the car peeled out of the parking lot.

"Oh my God," I said, glancing back at the inn. My mouth was opening and closing. "You can't just—just *abduct* me!"

The muscles in his jaw were clenched tightly.

"You know, sometimes you scare the crap out of me," I said, watching Andre's expression flicker between fear and anger.

Andre's hands flexed around the wheel. "You have the same effect on me," he said. He drove down the city streets, completely at ease here in this strange country.

I rubbed my temples. "So, where are you taking me?"

"The airport."

The balls of this man. "Andre, I'm not leaving this place in the middle of an investigation."

"You already know who's behind it," Andre said, glancing over at me. "Case closed."

I swallowed. The devil.

"Andre, my hands are tied," I said, my voice dropping low. "If I walk away from the investigation, I'll lose my spot on the Politia."

"Better than losing your life, soulmate," Andre said.

It dawned on me, what this was. Panic. Andre was panicking.

"I'm not leaving, and you can't make me get onto that plane—not if you want to continue dating me."

Andre looked at me, frowning, and pulled the car to the shoulder of the road.

He shifted the car into Park and bowed his head over the steering wheel. "There's more than one reason why I want you to leave Romania."

I stilled at his words and waited for him to continue.

He sighed. "I can't shield you from the coven's justice system if you're here."

My brows pinched together. He'd been shielding me this whole time? "But I thought that ..."

"That the trial was solely against me?" he said. He shook his head. "It is, but you're a vampire as well, and victim or not, you were involved."

I bit my lip. I hadn't thought much of Andre's trial. If I was being honest with myself, I thought it was a joke. Andre was the king of the vampires; I assumed that gave him complete power over his subjects.

Clearly I was mistaken.

"How did you manage to keep me away from the trial all this time?"

He didn't say anything, which was answer enough. Bribing and threatening—that was how he did it. That, and making sure I never left the Isle of Man. Between him, Peel Academy, and the Politia, I was almost untouchable. Almost.

"Why didn't you tell me?" I finally said.

Andre reached out to me and ran a thumb over the skin of my cheek. "Because I knew that if I told you, you'd somehow get yourself involved."

"No, you don't know that," I said heatedly. "You never gave me the chance to decide for myself what we should do."

His hand dropped, and it tightened into a fist. "I'm still not giving you the chance."

I wanted to scream in frustration at him. "I'm not going to the airport." I'd glamour him before that happened.

"They will learn of your existence here," he said. "There are eyes and ears everywhere; it's only a matter of time before someone on the council learns of your arrival in Cluj. And once they do, you will be called in."

"And what is so wrong with that?"

Andre growled. "You are asking to be subjected to some of the cruelest beings that walk this earth. I can assure you, most of these men and women were not good people in life, and they've had centuries to wipe away the last of their humanity. If they learn the truth about what happened that night at Bishopcourt, they will kill you, and not even I will be able to stop them."

What he wasn't saying was that he'd been lying to them to protect me. Lying to his coven about what happened that night. Which meant they still didn't know about the prophecy. Because if they did, he was absolutely right, they'd kill me to save themselves.

I believed him. God help me, I believed every word he said. But it wasn't enough to make me leave this place, not yet.

"Andre, I'm not leaving Romania tonight."

"Gabrielle ..." His voice was full of dark warning.

My lips spread into an amused smile. "Are you trying to intimidate me with that voice of yours? 'Cause it ain't gonna work."

"Don't make light of the situation," Andre said.

"I'm not. I'm going to help solve the investigation and get the hell out of here before one of your friends eats me."

"No one's going to eat you, Gabrielle."

"Okay, fine—stake me, draw and quarter me, roast me over an open spit, ..."

"Leave Romania," he whispered.

Persistent vampire.

"No."

"Please, Gabrielle." This was the closest he ever got to begging.

"Quit and go back to the Isle of Man," Andre continued. "I won't let anything happen to you." Oh, I bet he'd love me quitting. He'd probably throw a party in my honor the day that happened.

"Much as I appreciate the offer, I want to go to school and lead a normal life for as long as possible," I said.

"You call this a normal life?"

I gave him a look. "You know what I mean."

Andre closed his eyes. "If you don't leave here, this place might kill you." He talked as though Romania itself wanted my blood.

I gave a hollow laugh. "I'm destined to die in about a year anyway, so what's the difference?"

Andre thumped his palm against the steering wheel. Hard. Metal crunched as it bent under the force of his blow. "Damnit Gabrielle, it makes a difference to me!"

He pushed open his door and got out. I tried my door handle again, intent on following him. Still locked. Damnit.

I crawled over the center consul and exited the car on the driver's side, barely noticing the light white flakes that drifted down around us.

Andre strode away from me, his coat flapping in the chill breeze, and I could see how tension coiled itself in his muscles.

"Why are you so upset?" I yelled after him. He ignored me, his sinuous form moving further and further away. "This is my fate, not yours!"

Andre stopped. "No, it's not," he said.

"What?"

Andre turned around, and even though it was nighttime, even though it was starting to snow, and even though he was some distance away from me, I could clearly see his grief. "It's not *your* fate," he said. "It's *our* fate."

He began walking back to me. "What do you think happens to me once you die?" he said. "I'm not going to just get over you." His voice broke. "It doesn't work like that with soulmates."

My lungs constricted. Of course it didn't. On an instinctual level I knew that, but consciously I'd never thought it through. If I died, part of Andre would die along with me—maybe all of him if we were indeed physiologically connected.

The thought of hurting this man or of him simply ceasing to exist, that was just as terrifying as what waited for me on the other side of death.

Andre stepped up to me and cupped my face. "If the devil tries to take you again, I don't know if you'll come back to me as a vampire. I don't know if you'll come back at all."

His eyes searched mine, and they shined in the dim light.

"I'd come back," I whispered. "For you, hell couldn't hold me. I'd come back."

Chapter 6

I WATCHED THE buildings blur by as we drove back to the inn. I'd won the battle of wills tonight, but the discussion wasn't over.

"So, you have a house here?" I asked, glancing away from the view and down at our entwined hands. I couldn't remember when our hands found each other, or who initiated the touch. Our connection was growing stronger.

"Yes." Almost absentmindedly, Andre brought my hand to his lips and kissed the back of it.

"The one you grew up in?"

He smiled. "That's a cute thought. No, the house I grew up in is long since gone. But my current home is one of the oldest buildings in the city."

"And this city, Cluj-Napoca," my tongue stumbled over the name, eliciting another smile from Andre, "is the place you consider home?"

His eyes slid to mine. "I think you and I both know exactly where home is these days."

Warmth pooled in the pit of my stomach. Within the last four months I'd gone from the girl that couldn't be loved, to the girl that pushed it away, to the girl who hesitantly embraced it.

My ring caught the light of a streetlamp. "You're wearing my gift," Andre said, surprised.

"Of course. I haven't taken it off."

He took his gaze off the road to look at me, his eyes filled with longing and something deeper. Love. We hadn't ever said those three important words, but lately I'd see it in his expression, or the way he touched me—I'd find it in the details.

I cleared my throat. "I am not going to get to see your home, am I?" I said, getting back on topic.

Andre's expression looked agonized. "If I'm to keep you away from this trial, then no. Vampires visit my place on a regular basis."

I made a face. My experience with the vampire community wasn't great. Other than the bossy one sitting next to me, the only other vampire I'd gotten to know had tried to kill me.

I rubbed away the condensation on my window and glanced outside. The weather here was different from the Isle of Man. Here the chill had nothing to do with rain and ocean mist. It seemed to emanate from the very earth itself.

"If you're not going to change your mind about leaving,

then at least promise me one thing," he said.

I worked my jaw, then nodded. "What is it?"

"Don't tell anyone we're soulmates."

"Who would I tell?" I asked, glancing at him.

"Well the coven, for one."

That shouldn't be too difficult, considering I was supposed to avoid them at all costs anyway.

Andre took his eyes off of the road to meet my gaze. "More importantly, you can't tell Caleb."

I peered at him curiously. "Why shouldn't he know?" I already had my own reasons for not telling Caleb about Andre and me, but I was interested to know his.

"Caleb's in the Politia's pocket. They would eventually learn about us through him."

I furrowed my brows. "I'm still not seeing what's so bad about that. They already know we're dating."

Andre squeezed my hand. "Having a soulmate is one of the most revered bonds in the supernatural world. It's unbreakable."

I smiled a little when he said that.

"Unfortunately," he continued, his face darkening, "because of the bond's very nature, it can be exploited. For seven hundred years I've been the thing supernaturals fear. I wielded too much power, and I couldn't be controlled. But now I can." His gaze landed meaningfully on me.

I realized what he wasn't saying. The ruthless vampire king had a soulmate. For someone like Andre, someone who lived by the sword, love was a weakness, a devastating one.

"Anyone could use me to get to you," I said, my eyes wide.

Andre grimaced. "And they would. Especially the Politia and the coven. They wouldn't hesitate."

"COME TO ME."

Sonja Antonescu slid out from under her sheets and left her room. She wiped the sleep from her eyes as she left the luxury suite she shared with her roommate. Her bare feet padded down the five flights of stairs standing between her and the ground floor of her apartment complex.

She needed to find that voice.

Sonja crossed the lobby and opened the front door. Outside the winter storm had already rolled in, though the weather report had insisted it wouldn't arrive until tomorrow evening. She stepped out into the storm, her flannel pants slapping against her legs.

"*Please, find me.*"

She rubbed her arms and followed the voice down the street, and then down the next and the next, until she reached the edge of her town. In front of her the Romanian wilderness dared her to enter.

"*Come closer.*"

Sonja took a deep breath and pushed forward into the inky blackness of the forest. It had been awhile since her feet had fallen numb, but the voice sounded closer than it had before. She was almost there.

Her feet pressed into the thin layer of powdery snow

beneath her, and she wandered through the snow-covered woods.

"*Follow my voice.*"

Torchight flickered in the distance; it seemed to be where the voice came from. Sonja stepped through the trees and the forest opened up.

A group of cloaked figures stood in the small clearing. A few carried torches, the source of the light. Goosebumps broke out along her skin as the firelight made their cloaks flare scarlet, the same shade as spilled blood.

Sonja blinked several times; she felt like she was surfacing from a terrible, terrible dream. "What's going on?" she asked.

She took a step back and several heads turned, tracking her movement.

"Come closer," said a feminine voice.

And just like that, Sonja was dragged back under. She walked over to the cloaked woman, all the while her muscles twitched, as though they knew on some instinctual level that she shouldn't be here. She couldn't see the woman's eyes, but she saw her luscious smile.

The woman handed her a folded dress. "Put this on."

Sonja took the bundle she was handed and began to strip in front of the crowd. Her stomach felt sick, like she shouldn't be doing this, but she couldn't stop herself from removing her clothes and pulling the thin linen gown over her head. Her body trembled from the cold and her numb hands fumbled, but eventually she managed to get the dress on.

"Lay down your tired body," the strange woman said,

gesturing to a wooden altar behind her.

Now that she had mentioned it, Sonja was tired. So, so tired.

Sonja passed the woman and approached the altar, ignoring the stares that seemed to bore into her skin. She paused, for the briefest of seconds, murmuring a prayer under her breath, and then hoisted her body onto the raised platform.

The cloaked figures fanned out around her, their presence making her breath hitch.

Another woman's voice began to speak, chanting some incantation in a language that Sonja's bones recognized, even if her brain didn't.

A twine rope slipped over her head and someone tightened it around her neck. The skin squeezed in on itself, crushing her windpipe. Her hands twitched, compelled by instinct to remove the force.

"Don't fight it," the woman said, brushing Sonja's hair away from her face. "Find peace in the moment."

Sonja's muscles loosened at the command. She stared at the cloudy sky and the snow that drifted down. The ache of her feet, the chill of her skin, the spasm of her lungs, these sensations were all remote things to the calm that had come over her. She welcomed the darkness that spread over her vision, and she never felt the knife that pierced her heart, nor the one that slit her throat.

I STOOD IN the middle of a snowstorm. Small white flakes blew around my body as I looked around. On either side of me dark evergreens were largely hidden under snow.

Something about this place tugged at my memory. Hesitantly I crept forward, and out of the snowstorm I made out gray and white stone.

The falling snow heightened the unsettling silence of the place, and as my heartbeat sped up, it became the only sound ringing in my ears.

I climbed up a short staircase, my steps faltering as a sense of déjà vu washed over me. It was right on the edge of my mind, that memory. But the moment I tried to focus on it, it dissolved. A wisp of smoke carried away.

I stared at the large door, dread soaking through my skin.

Evil lurks within.

The thought had only just crossed my mind when the door creaked open on its own.

That thought was all it took for me to stumble away.

"Wait." The voice was rich and deep; the kind that came along with a beautiful face.

I knew that voice.

Even though every muscle screamed at me to run, I froze. I saw his almond-shaped eyes first. They glittered as though they were lit from behind. Then his chiseled features came into focus. The deep shadows threw his high brow, square jaw, and cruel lips into sharp relief. He looked even more sinister than I remembered.

I backed away from the devil, never taking my eyes off of him. Dangerous creatures were better out in the open than hidden in shadows.

"You do not need to fear me," he said.

My teeth chattered as a shiver racked my body. "That's what you said on Samhain," I said, "right before you beat the crap out of me."

He left the shelter of his castle, and his hair ruffled in the storm. It was such a human detail that, for a moment, it felt ridiculous to fear him. Then I remembered who I was dealing with, and I did what I wasn't supposed to do: I took my eyes off the devil to turn and run down the stairs.

I flew down the steps, my hair whipping around me as the wind blew it about.

He materialized at the bottom, arms crossed, and I yelped.

He cocked his head. "Why you haven't learned is beyond me, but you. Can't. Escape. You can't outrun me. You leave when I say you do."

There was nowhere for me to go. I couldn't get past him—not without brushing by him. The thought repulsed me. My only other option was up.

"I'm not going to let you go until you take a tour of the castle," the devil said. "If you remember, I never got the chance."

I pushed down my nausea. "I'm not going in there."

"Yes you are."

I curled my lip. "Over my dead body."

He flashed me a cruel smile. "We can arrange that."

The devil's hand shot out and snatched my wrist. My skin crawled at his touch, and my stomach twisted in knots as I felt his presence wash over me. Evil was very much a physical sensation when it came to the devil.

A scream bubbled in the back of my throat, and terror had my heart jackknifing in my chest.

"Come, consort," he said, approaching the staircase and yanking my arm.

"Let go of me," I whimpered, tugging back on my arm.

As if he couldn't help it, the devil closed his eyes and leaned in, breathing me in. "Your fear smells so damn good. I can practically taste it." The devil's eyes opened, a smile blossoming along his face. "I am going to enjoy devouring you piece by piece."

Fuck. My. Life.

I spoke through my terror. "You really know how to charm a lady," I managed to bite out.

He ran a hand down my hair, and I shuddered at the sensation. "Don't worry, little bird, I'll make certain you enjoy it as well."

I made a small sound at the back of my throat, and his gaze flicked to my lips.

No. Oh please, no.

I swallowed and leaned back as he leaned in. His gaze crept back up to mine and he smiled at me again. "You make this too much fun." He ran a hand down my arm, and I yanked against the wrist holding me. His grip tightened. "It's only a matter of time until you're mine, but how I hate waiting."

My gaze moved between his eyes. He looked so human. It was such a stark contrast to the ungodly chill creeping over my skin.

"Come, consort," he said, tugging my arm.

"No."

"Hard way it is." He yanked me forward.

I stumbled and tripped on the slick steps. The devil lunged to catch me, and I had a split second for the sight to strike me as funny—the devil was trying to accommodate me.

My head struck the sharp stone staircase, and I jerked awake.

I sat up in bed, my breathing labored. *Just a dream. It was just a dream.*

Then again, when in my life had a dream ever been just a dream?

OUR FIRST STOP the next morning was the morgue. I stifled a yawn as I followed Grigori through the Politia's offices, only barely managing to resist the scent of brewing coffee. I knew from experience that coffee and corpses didn't mix well.

I rubbed my arms when we dipped below ground. Down here the air had a deep chill to it. It didn't help that the smell of mildew and rot assaulted my nose.

Grigori opened the door to the morgue and Caleb and I filed in. I'd seen several bodies since the first time I stood in the morgue with Caleb, but I never got over the nausea that accompanied them. The decaying bodies, the scent of chemicals and death that filled the air—it overwhelmed my senses.

The pathologist greeted Grigori in Romanian, and Grigori gestured to us, presumably explaining who exactly we were. The pathologist's eyes widened, lingering on me.

70

And then he crossed himself.

I guess my reputation preceded me.

Next to me Caleb snickered, and I covertly flipped him off, which only made him chuckle louder.

"Let us go see the body," the pathologist said, his accent thick. The three of us followed him across the room, where he'd already laid the body out on an examination table.

I breathed through my mouth as I approached the victim. She had been beautiful once—angelic. But in death even the most beautiful faces looked grotesque, and hers was no exception.

The pathologist drew down a paper sheet that had covered most of her body. He pointed to a deep knife wound across her neck and spoke to us in Romanian.

"This is one of three lethal injuries that killed the victim," Grigori translated.

The pathologist pointed to a deeply bruised swath of skin just above the neck wound and spoke again. "Here's the second," Grigori translated, "the discoloration indicating where the noose was tightened around her throat."

The pathologist pulled the paper sheet down further, revealing a third lethal injury. I grimaced when I saw the stab wound through the victim's heart. In all the photos, her stained dress had obscured the wound itself, but now I could see the split skin.

Bile rose at the back of my throat. *Don't vomit on the victim. Don't vomit on the victim.*

The pathologist spoke, this time in English. "All happened at roughly the same time. All contributed to death."

For the next twenty minutes the pathologist went over the details of the open wounds—both made by a dagger, both done in a single stroke, both made while the victim was still alive. Given the fact that both wounds happened simultaneously, that meant that two knives were used.

"So, unless the killer was extremely dexterous, ..." I said.

Grigori finished the sentence for me. "We have more than one killer on our hands."

As my eyes moved over the victim, a familiar smell wafted off of her. Ash. Beneath it was an even fainter smell of something floral. The body had been dead for too long and exposed to too many people to know for sure that this scent belonged to the killer. But it was enough to develop a theory.

Grigori's phone chirped. He fished it out of his pocket and answered it, walking to the other side of the room to talk.

Caleb walked around the examination table and he whistled low. "It's hard for me to believe that the victim wasn't under duress," he said, staring at the victim's feet.

I came to his side and studied the feet. They'd been cleaned of blood and debris, and it was easy to now see just how severely they'd been sliced up.

I had to agree. People didn't just willingly injure themselves this way. My eyes drifted back to our victim's face.

Her feet were the only evidence of duress. There were no broken nails, no scratch marks or bruising that would indicate our victim fought back. It was as though she'd chosen to walk barefoot until her skin was raw. As though she'd agreed to be murdered.

Very strange.

The click of Grigori's shoes drew my attention up to him.

"Gabrielle, Caleb," he said, clasping his phone in his fist, "we need to go. There's been another murder."

Chapter 7

I SCOWLED AT the snowy scenery we drove past while Caleb chatted with Grigori. We had a serial killer on our hands—oh, excuse me, serial killers. There were at least two of them. And it was my job to capture these sickos. In the middle of a blizzard. While bloodthirsty vampires were holding a trial I needed to stay far away from. Happy fucking holidays to me.

My cellphone vibrated as a text from Oliver came in.

What address are you staying at, Sabertooth? I want to mail you your Christmas present. Long distance bosom hugs for my favorite consort in the world. Muah!

My lips twitched as I read Oliver's message. I sent him my address before setting the phone aside. God I missed my friends.

The car slowed as we approached a line of parked vehicles, and I glanced one final time at the map of Romania resting on my lap. I'd snatched it up back at the station when I'd learned that the second murder scene was located in an entirely different region of Romania. One that had taken us over two hours to get to.

Two areas had now been circled, representing the two crime scenes. The latest one had occurred in Bistriła-Nłsłud County, located northeast of Cluj.

I set the map aside as Grigori parked the car along the side of the rode, and then the three of us hopped out.

Caleb, Grigori, and I followed the stream of inspectors into the forest. Like the last crime scene, this one was also located in the woods. By the time we arrived at the small clearing where the second body was located, investigators and crime scene technicians swarmed the area.

An inspector approached us, greeting Girgori and eyeing Caleb and me. Just like the pathologist, his eyes lingered on my face, and I saw a mixture of lust and repulsion within them.

Ah, infamy, thou suck.

After exchanging a few more words, the inspector handed Caleb and me a set of gloves and motioned for us to follow him.

I tugged on the gloves and weaved through the throng of officers and forensic technicians. My breath caught when my gaze landed on a wooden altar. The victim still rested on it, a thin film of snow now covering her body.

I couldn't look away from the peaceful expression on her face. Laying there, she reminded me of Snow White.

Dark hair, pale skin, delicate features.

The group of us approached the altar, each focusing our attention on the latest victim.

Unlike the last altar, which seemed to grow out from the earth itself, this one was made of polished wood and intricately carved. Had it been set up specifically for this murder? If so, that took an amazing amount of time and organization.

I crouched down and studied the designs cut into the wood. Flowers and fruit were carved along the edges of the altar, and inside them were a series of images broken into frames. In one, a female figure knelt in a field of flowers. In another a man held a screaming woman. In another a different woman stood alone, a desolate expression on her face. The images were sad and disturbing, and I couldn't make sense of them.

I pushed myself up and stared down at the body laid out in front of me. The twine noose cinched tightly around her neck was still there, now discolored with her blood. I pressed my lips together as my eyes moved to the severed skin below it, where her throat had been slit. Just like the first victim.

My eyes traveled down. She wore a white gown marred by a deep crimson stain above her heart. A third wound— probably a stab wound to the heart—again, identical to the last victim.

My nose flared at the smell of blood. She smelled heavenly. Literally. The scent hit the back of my throat and I could taste holiness in it. It should've been impossible to sense, but I could, just like I could feel evil. I knew that if

I had a sip of her blood, I'd taste God in it.

Another angelic victim. The similarities between the two deaths were so precise. So organized.

I circled the body, wanting to get a look at her feet. Would that detail be the same too? Could the killers really have replicated the first murder so completely?

As soon as the victim's feet came into view, my mouth thinned. Blood and grime stuck to them, just like the last victim.

My eyes moved back to the white shift she wore. No one wore an outfit like this in the winter, which meant she'd changed—or someone had changed her. And the exposed skin along her hands and arms was unblemished. She hadn't fought her attackers either.

None of it made any sense.

Finally, my gaze landed on her face. Death had already turned her loveliness into something disturbing. The snow that came to rest on her forehead, nose and mouth didn't help. No living person would lay in the same position long enough to collect that much snow.

A gust of wind blew through the trees. I bit the inside of my cheek as I watched a few strands of the victim's hair stir in the breeze. She'd never again be able to brush that hair from her face.

I closed my eyes. Now was not the time to think of her as a human. Not if I wanted to keep it together.

I breathed in and out in an effort to calm myself. Instead, my back went ramrod straight as a smell caught my attention. It was the same smell I noticed back in the morgue. The smell of ash and something else, something floral.

I almost jumped out of my skin when a hand landed on my arm. "What is it?" Caleb asked.

I'd been so hyper focused on the crime that I'd forgotten about the people around me.

My eyes moved to his. "I think I know our killer's scent."

CALEB'S EYES WIDENED. "Could you follow the scent to its source?"

I chewed the side of my lip. "I could try."

Caleb nodded, and I heard the excited thump of his heart. "Do it."

I closed my eyes and breathed in, cringing when I smelled a healthy dose of desire wafting off of Caleb—that was so inappropriate right now—until I found the scent I was looking for. It came from two different directions. The strongest was near the victim's head, but a fainter scent drifted in from the forest beyond.

I turned, keeping my eyes closed, and began walking towards the source of the scent. Next to me I could hear Caleb's footfalls shadowing mine. "Will you let me know if I'm about to run into a tree?" I asked, eyes still shut.

"And ruin all the fun?"

I whacked Caleb in the shoulder.

"Ow, Dracula," he said, "how did you know where I was?"

"I followed the scent of stupid right to you."

"Low, Gabrielle," Caleb said, but I could hear the smile in his voice.

I grinned as well. I missed the easy teasing between the two of us. A wave of desire hit my nostrils, and my grin slipped. "Caleb ..."

He groaned. "It's not like I can help the way I smell. I'll just ... try staring at a tree while I follow you," he said, "... hopefully the one you run into," he added under his breath.

"Hardy-har-har," I said.

The scent recaptured my attention and I moved towards it, letting my nose guide me. The smell got stronger, and then it ended. I stopped and opened my eyes, glancing down at the object in front of me.

Nestled in the dead leaves was a glossy black business card. Caleb crouched down and picked it up.

"It's an advertisement for Thirst, a nightclub in Cluj," Caleb said. He flipped over the card and his eyes widened. "Looks like you have a murderous admirer."

"What?"

He handed the card over to me. "See for yourself."

Careful to only touch the edges of the card, I read the message: *Be here tonight at midnight. I look forward to meeting you, Gabrielle.*

I CHEWED ON the nub of my pen as I went over the case with Caleb. "So far we know that the victims died in the same manner, that more than one person has to be involved—"

"And at least one of them smells like flame broiled roses," Caleb added with a smirk.

I narrowed my eyes. "Are you mocking me?"

He raised his hands. "Those were your words, not mine."

Damn him, I *had* used those words when he'd asked about the smell on the drive back. I leaned forward in my chair, looking over the papers spread in front of us. We sat in my room, huddled around the desk next to my bed.

"Oh, by the way, the forensics team pulled a partial fingerprint," Caleb said.

My eyebrows shot up. "They did?"

"Yep," he said, reaching across the desk and taking a swig of his coffee. "I overheard that when we bagged and tagged the business card."

Ugh. The business card. I rubbed my eyes. It was proof that once again I'd managed to personally ensnare myself in a series of murders.

"Not that it matters since you'll be meeting one of the killers tonight."

I groaned. "Don't remind me." Already the Politia was making arrangements for my little murderous meet-and-greet this evening. We'd need to leave in another few hours to set up the recording devices and go over what I needed to say.

They knew I'd find the card. They wanted me to find it. Whoever "they" was.

My gaze drew down once more to the map. "Is the second murder on a ley line?" I asked. I'd assumed it was, but assuming and knowing were two very different things.

Caleb gave me a blank look.

I blinked. "Why are you staring at me like that?"

"Because you're the demonologist here."

I grimaced. "I hate it when you say things that make sense." I grabbed my bag and rifled through the papers I'd Xeroxed back at Peel Academy. Several of them were maps of known ley lines in Romania.

I pulled one of the maps out that covered the region of Bistrița-Năsăud, squinting at the smudged lines and loopy handwriting. The original map had been hand drawn, and my version was a copy of a reprint. A.k.a., the quality sucked balls. But even with the poor quality reprint I could tell that no ley lines ran through our second crime scene.

Well hell.

"This murder wasn't on a ley line," I stated, confused. I glanced up and met Caleb's eyes. "Why would the first murder occur on a ley line, but not the second?"

Caleb pinched his lower lip as he thought it over. "The location of the first murder could've been a coincidence," he said. His eyes found mine. "Or ... the location served another purpose altogether."

I furrowed my brows. "Like what?"

Caleb stared at me, his eyes troubled. "Like luring Gabrielle Fiori to Romania."

Chapter 8

I READJUSTED MY miked cleavage for the millionth time as Caleb and I stepped out of Grigori's car. Club Thirst was just a few doors down.

Grigori rolled down the window and leaned over the console. "I will be around the corner listening with the rest of the team," he said to me. "Remember what we talk-ed about."

I nodded. I'd go in, act normal until I was approached, ask the questions the Politia wanted to know, and when I was finished, I'd tuck my hair behind each ear—my cue to the undercover guards posted throughout the club to take down the murder suspect. Easy peasy.

Yeah, *right*.

Grigori paused, and I saw the moment he went from a colleague to a fatherly figure. "Don't be a hero. The second something feels wrong, you get out of there—both of you."

"Of course," I murmured.

"Do you remember the phrase you are to use if you need help?" he asked.

"'I don't think I like it here,'" I repeated from memory. It wasn't forgetting it I was concerned with. No, I was more concerned about slipping the phrase into a conversation with the murderer suspect.

"Good. You two keep an eye on each other."

"We will," Caleb said.

Satisfied with that, Grigori drove off, leaving us alone. I cracked my knuckles as we approached the entrance to Thirst. A long line stretched down the block, one we wouldn't have to wait in. But before I had time to fish my badge out of my bra, the bouncer guarding the door eyed me and then stepped aside and let us through.

"That was weird ..." I said.

Caleb shrugged and said something back to me, but the pounding music of the club swallowed his voice.

A dozen sets of eyes clung to me as I moved through the club. Self-consciously I smoothed down the tiny red dress I'd been asked to wear. The Politia wanted me to be noticed—both so that I caught the murderer's attention and so that I had many witnesses.

My gaze swept over the crowd. This late in the evening, most of the club goers were drunk, and their otherness was slipping through to the surface. Slitted pupils, a flash of scales, *fur*. Those were the monsters in the mix. The more common supernaturals—witches, seers, and such—

were less obvious, but if I looked closely, I could catch a glimpse of their manifested powers as well.

Many of the clubbers stared back at me, not bothering to look away even when I met their gaze. I had no idea who I was supposed to meet.

Gee this wasn't awkward.

"You've got to be kidding me," Caleb said, loud enough for me to hear.

I glanced over at him, but he wasn't looking at me. I followed his gaze across the room.

I only had a second to register the thrum that now overshadowed the pounding music and the collective dip in conversation before my eyes fell on the object of Caleb's focus.

Andre.

ANDRE WAS ALREADY staring at me, and ho, he did not look pleased. Yay, I'd managed to piss off my immortal boyfriend without even trying this time. That deserved some sort of prize ... other than my ass on a plate. 'Cause that's what the look he was giving me promised.

"Is it just me, or does Andre look like he's going to murder us?" Caleb asked.

"Not helping," I said, my eyes never straying from him.

The entourage of scary-looking men that surrounded him followed his gaze. Eep. They looked like they were going to eat me.

Never taking his eyes off of me, Andre pushed forward, the muscle in his jaw feathering.

"Should I shift and hold him off?" Caleb asked next to me.

I shook my head. "That will only make it worse."

"He's going to ruin the meeting."

"Maybe," I replied, the gears in my mind turning.

The crowd parted for Andre, and every step he took towards me brought his expression in sharper relief. Yep, he was definitely pissed. The current between us amplified as he neared. I could feel it vibrating in my chest and making my fingers tingle.

Out of the corner of my eye I saw Caleb's hands fist. I reached out and touched his arm. "Don't even think about it," I said. "If you start a fight in here, this whole thing is going to fall apart."

Caleb worked his jaw and reluctantly nodded, uncurling his fists and relaxing his muscles.

I felt a surge of energy run through me, and when I looked up, Andre's eyes had moved to where my hand still touched Caleb's arm. Something primal and possessive had entered into his expression. I would've rolled my eyes except this whole situation was clearly heading south, and fast.

"Grab us some drinks Caleb."

"But—"

I gave him a light shove in the direction of the bar. "Just please, do it."

Caleb reluctantly left me just before Andre closed the remaining distance between us.

Then Andre's hands were on either side of my face. "What are you doing here?" he said, his voice almost desperate.

I was expecting anger, but not this, not the intense worry written onto his features. I wrapped my hands around his wrists. "What are *you* doing here?"

"I had a break between sessions of the trial, so I came here to meet with my staff and managers." His thumb rubbed my lower lip, and his gaze dropped to my mouth.

Realization hit me like a punch to the gut. "This is your club." Of course. How had I not put that one together?

"Yes, it is." Andre took a steadying breath and gazed back up at my eyes. "Now, what are you doing here?"

My breath came faster, and I shifted my focus to the crowd around us. "They knew," I said, more to myself than to Andre, "they knew this was your club. They had to know you'd be here." But why? Why?

Andre gave me a light shake. "Gabrielle."

My eyes honed in on Andre. "There's been another murder, and the killers left a note for me asking to meet them here."

"And you came," Andre said. His voice was calm, his face placid except for that muscle in his cheek. It kept clenching and unclenching.

Uh oh.

"The Politia is here," I said quietly. "They will make sure nothing happens tonight."

"The Politia doesn't give a shit about your life," he snapped.

I flinched at his words. He said it with such vehemence.

I tried to draw away, but one of his hands dropped from my cheek and snaked around my waist. Instead of letting me go, he pulled me forward, and I stared into those deep, remorseful eyes of his.

His thumb rubbed my cheekbone. "I didn't say that to hurt you, soulmate." His expression had gone soft and a little sad. "I just cannot stand by and watch them place you in danger over and over again."

"Andre, it was my choice to join the Politia, my choice to take this case, and my choice to be here. I am the only one putting myself in danger."

He cupped my chin. "You need to leave."

Here we go again. "Andre, we've already talked abou—"

"There are vampires from the trial here."

Oh.

Hell.

"THEY'RE HERE?" I said, looking over Andre's shoulder. My fangs dropped down at the thought. All that Andre had warned me about last night replayed through my mind.

"Some of my bouncers and several of my patrons are vampires," Andre said. He glanced at the nearby exits. "Now we need to get you out of here—"

The music suddenly quieted and a voice came on over the speakers. "Evening all you lovely creatures," a woman said. The crowd stilled, and the hairs on my arms rose. The voice was melodic, seductive, ... *compelling.*

My eyes searched for the source, moving over the packed dance floor and landing on the DJ station. There.

The woman stared at me, and when my gaze met hers, her red lips widened.

The blood drained from my face. I might've just caught my first glimpse of the murderer that smelled of ash and roses, and she was the most beautiful woman I'd ever seen.

MOST SUPERNATURALS WERE easy on the eyes, but she ... she made my heart ache.

"Let's get the party started," she shouted, riling up the club. She spoke with an English accent. Not Romanian. *Foreigner.* "Get on the dance floor, and dance until you can't anymore."

Andre's hands dropped from where they'd touched me. His eyes flickered, his mouth pulled down into a frown, but he moved away from me.

"Andre!" His shoulder muscles tensed, but he didn't glance back.

Bodies brushed past me as other club patrons made their way to the dance floor. The bar and lounge emptied; everyone left what they were doing to join the dancing crowd.

The woman had her hand on the DJ's shoulder, and she whispered something in his ear. He nodded and turned back to the setup in front of him. The speakers blasted as a new song came on, and the crowd began to sway.

As far as I could tell, I was the only one who wasn't affected. There was only one thing I knew of that could cause this.

I tugged my mike towards my mouth. "Grigori, if you can hear this, then listen to me. I think I just laid eyes on one of the killers, and ..." I took a deep breath, "I think she might be a siren."

I THOUGHT I was the last siren left. I was wrong.

Pushing through the last of the people joining the dance floor, I made my way to the DJ booth. At the back of my mind I registered that I'd been immune to the glamour. I guess it didn't work on our own kind.

If this woman was one of the killers, then I had an idea how our victims walked so far in their bare feet without any signs of duress. Glamour.

The woman stepped down from the booth, and her dark eyes glittered as she watched me approach her.

As soon as I reached her, she did something wholly unexpected. Pressing a fisted hand to her breast, she knelt at my feet.

I took a step back, now unsure of myself. Out of all the things I was anticipating when I confronted the killer, this was not one of them.

She rose, her eyes moving up until they met mine. "It's an honor to meet you, consort."

I started at the name. "Don't call me that."

She smiled. "My apologies, Gabrielle."

That wasn't exactly better.

My gaze moved to the crowd. At first glance, one would think they were having a good time. But their eyes gave them away. All were empty, unseeing, marionettes strung along by a puppet master. Using glamour in this manner was against the law.

"Let them go," I said, even as the siren in me stirred.

There would be no using the safety phrase. No amount of backup would save the people in this room, and there was nothing stopping this woman from doing to the officers what she'd already done to the rest of the room—including the king of vampires.

This was really not his night. It wasn't really mine, either.

"I will, once we're finished," she said.

My eyes moved over her tan skin. It wasn't glowing—actually, I hadn't seen her skin light up at all this evening—yet the room was still under her spell. If she was a siren, how was that possible?

My eyes flicked up and our gazes locked. "What *are* you?"

SHE STEPPED UP to me, leaning in. Her mouth skimmed my cheek, making me shudder. "I am just like you," she whispered, her voice teasing a shiver out of me. She fingered my hair, and as she spoke, her lips tickled my ear. "Same seductive beauty, same powers of persuasion, same cursed lineage."

She pulled away, her eyes moving to my mouth. "But I am not a siren."

"Then what are you?" I asked.

Her gaze dropped to my cleavage. Not exactly the response I'd been looking for.

And then she reached down my dress.

I gasped, snatching her wrist, but not before I felt her yank the wires attached to the inside of my outfit. She pulled the listening device out and threw it on the floor, crushing it underneath her stiletto. "Can't have the Politia ruin all our fun." She eyed me. "You really shouldn't be working for them. They hate people like us."

"And you really shouldn't be murdering people," I snapped.

She flashed me a sinful smile and began to circle me slowly. "You have your orders, and I have mine." Her hand skimmed along my waist, and I swatted it away.

This whole conversation felt like a violation, but what chilled the blood in my veins was that some part of me, the part that called to my darker nature, reveled in it. I wanted to let this woman's murderous hands continue to touch me and her wicked lips to graze my skin. I wondered if I embraced the siren in me whether I too could wield this kind of power.

"Why are you here?" I asked. Behind her I swear I saw a shadow move, but then she spoke, drawing my attention away from the movement.

"Why, to meet you of course." She stepped back in front of me.

"And are you going to tell me your name?" I asked, perhaps a tad snarky.

She tilted her head. "Mmm, I don't think so."

I was tired of this game of cat and mouse. Specifically, I was tired of being the mouse. The siren in me screamed to be let out, and for once, I caved.

My skin glowed. "Stop killing people."

The woman looked delighted. "Finally. Took you long enough to come out and play."

She leaned forward and made a soft sound. Almost as if she couldn't help it, she brushed a kiss along my neck.

Oh hell no, this murderous ho-bag did not just steal a kiss.

I felt power swell within me the moment before I brought my foot up. I slammed my heel into her chest and kicked her. The force of my blow lifted the woman off her feet and threw her back into the wall behind her. Plaster buckled under the impact of her body as she crashed into it.

Her head lulled and she moaned. "Wasn't ... expecting *that*."

Ignoring her words, I stalked forward, both the siren and the vampire in me out for blood. I was done playing nice. She wasn't leaving here tonight unless it was in cuffs or a body bag.

Yeah, don't come between me and my winter break.

I stopped in front of her body and, grabbing her by the hair, I lifted her up. My fangs came out and my eyes dropped to her neck. I'd never bitten anyone before—hell, blood grossed me out. But right now ... right now I could smell the scent of ash and roses just beneath the surface of her skin, and my mouth watered.

"Do it," she said, watching me.

My eyes lifted to her face. She looked eager, and that gave me pause. I breathed in and then out, reining in the siren and the vampire long enough to think logically.

I wanted to munch on her. How disturbing.

I worked my jaw. "No," I finally said, conquering the urges that warred inside me. "Now tell me: who else is working with you?" I asked, shaking her head.

"Me." A woman spoke at my back. I began to turn when I felt a hand grasp my shoulder and something sharp press into my back. "Don't move unless you want to be gutted." The feminine voice spoke perfect English.

Another woman. Two female murder suspects, and both probably foreigners. So what was their M.O. for coming to Romania to kill?

"What do you want with me?" I asked. I flared my nostrils, trying to breathe in her scent, but I couldn't smell anything other than expensive perfume.

"Let my friend go, and maybe I'll tell you."

If I let the woman in front of me go, then it'd be two against one, and I had a knife digging into my back. But I was fast. I could probably outmaneuver them both if I acted now.

I jerked away from the woman behind me. But not fast enough.

I choked on air as the blade parted skin. It made a wet, fleshy sound as it was shoved through me.

A strangled cry left my lips when I looked down. The tip of the knife poked out to the right of my belly button. I literally got friggin' stabbed in the back.

"What. The hell." That's the moment that I lost it.

I screamed—more out of anger than pain—spun to face my attacker. She was a slight thing with a sweet face. Not at all what I was expecting from the person who shoved a dagger through my gut. But it didn't stop me from jumping her ass.

All that training with Andre surfaced. I threw a right

hook, then an uppercut. My movements tugged at my wound, but anger and adrenaline dulled the pain. It would hurt like hell once this was over, but right now I only spared it a passing thought.

She blocked my punches, moving faster than a normal supernatural should.

My skin flared brighter. "Stop fighting me," I said, throwing the siren behind my words.

The pipsqueak laughed at me. Laughed. "That doesn't work on me, Proserpine."

Couldn't I come across one bad guy who wasn't immune to my glamour?

I kicked out at her, but she jumped away. I frowned. She was moving faster than even Andre. What supernatural could do that?

"Remove the glamour," my attacker said to the first woman, who was now pushing herself up on shaky legs. I was so tempted to knock her back down, but I resisted the urge. After all, she *was* going to lift the glamour.

I watched her eyes flutter shut and a small smile tilt the corners of her lips.

The air shifted, and then my attacker stood in front of me. "I'll be seeing you again soon, consort," she said.

Before I could cock back my arm, she'd placed a steadying hand on my back and ripped the dagger from my body.

I screamed and fell to my knees. She'd sliced the wound open further. I clutched my midsection, rivulets of blood slipping through my fingers.

That hurt like a mother.

Chapter 9

LIKE A SWITCH being flipped the pain, anger, and adrenaline morphed into power and lust. My skin shined brighter than ever. Only now did I grasp the extent of the siren's depravity. She loved this. My hands shook at the realization. I really was cursed.

My stomach felt itchy where the wound was stitching itself back together. Blood dripped from my fingers as I pushed myself to my feet. I swayed, feeling lightheaded from the blood loss. My skin, however, throbbed in pleasure and pain.

When I glanced up, both women were gone. Escaped. Perfect.

Around me, people were leaving the dance floor, looking confused. An increasing number stared at me, mesmerized by my glowing skin.

Among the throng of people, I felt one drawing closer. The crowd parted, and Andre stood there, his eyes glittering. Even from here I could tell he was barely containing his rage. One didn't just glamour the king of vampires. Especially not in his own club.

Our gazes caught. When his eyes drifted lower, to my bloody abdomen, his expression changed. "*Gabrielle.*" The alarm in his voice did nothing but excite me further.

An instant later he was next to me, his hands roving over my body, inspecting me for injuries. I arched into his touch.

"Who did this to you?" he asked, his anger resurfacing in his voice.

Instead of answering, I ran my hands through his hair, pressing myself into him.

His nostrils flared and he tipped my chin back, and his eyes searched my face. He needn't look so concerned. I was just high on blood and lust.

My hand moved to his cheek and stroked the rough skin there, uncaring that with the touch I smeared my blood along his jawline. The siren hummed impatiently. Things weren't progressing fast enough.

Andre sucked in a breath. "Why are there lipstick marks on your neck?"

The siren swelled within me, the memory of the woman's dark nature further arousing my own. My chest heaved. I was losing control completely.

Unaware of what was going on with me, Andre leaned into my neck. "Smoke and flowers—"

Not smoke and flowers. *Ash* and *roses*.

My breath came faster and faster. The blood thrummed through my veins, headier than alcohol.

Andre stilled, and then he took a step back. Then another. "Gabrielle ..." he said cautiously, his eyes moving over my glowing skin.

I ran my hands through my hair and rolled my shoulders back. I dragged my hands down my torso, down, down ...

The entire room seemed to respond. I could feel them like a pulse that lingered outside of me, and with every beat of the strobe light, they crept closer to me. Just like the woman before me, I'd enraptured every single individual here, and I was high off of the power. I wanted them all—their blood, their bodies, their very essence.

I was gone, gone, gone.

"*Gabrielle.*" The voice cut through my lust. I turned and gazed at Andre. He wore a hungry look. Even he was under my spell.

But it was my turn to be enraptured. My soulmate. No one else stoked the fire in me like he did. I wanted to consume him; I wanted him to be a part of the inferno that was eating me up from the inside out.

"If you're going to do something stupid, at least do it to me," he grated out. His chest heaved as he spoke, like it took a terrible amount of effort to say even that.

Somewhere at the back of my mind, I knew my response to his words should've been different. Sarcastic. Instead my entire body throbbed for him, the press of my fangs against my gums almost painful. My humanity was a distant thing.

I closed the distance between the two of us and wrapped my arms around his neck. I rubbed my body against his, and I heard him make a guttural noise, somewhere between a growl and a groan. It made my skin shine even brighter than before.

He closed his eyes. "I'm sorry," he said, even as his arms closed around me.

"I'm not," the siren sang. "Now open your eyes and do to me what you've wanted to do since we met."

That was all the encouragement I needed to give him. His eyes went molten; a look of longing flared deep within them. I caught a brief flash of fang and then he leaned down and kissed me.

Our mouths moved against each other urgently. His tongue parted my lips and stroked the inside of my mouth. I moaned against him and clutched him tighter. More. I wanted this and so much more.

His hands moved against my skin, pulling me closer, caressing exposed skin. I ran my own fingers over the thin fabric of his shirt, feeling the hard muscle beneath. Distantly I realized that I was getting my blood all over us.

Andre nipped at the tender flesh of my lower lip. I felt a prick of pain and I moaned as he drew a small bit of blood from it.

The crowd pressed in on us still, so Andre lifted me into his arms and carried me to the back of the club and up a flight of stairs. Our lips stayed locked the entire time. I moved against him suggestively, my body demanding that this go further.

Andre kicked open a door and led me into another one

of his VIP rooms before slamming the door shut again. He set me down on a couch and draped himself over me.

His movements were jerky as he caressed me. There was something about them that made me pause. My shimmering skin dimmed. It only seemed to make his movements more halting.

Finally I pulled back, my earlier rush starting to ebb.

"Thank God," Andre gasped, leaning his forehead against mine.

"What?" I panted, the last of the glow leaving my skin.

His arms tightened around me. "I was worried that the first time we'd sleep together it was going to be under your compulsion."

"Under my ... ?" I felt my nausea rise, and I covered my mouth. "I was forcing you ..." I couldn't finish the sentence. The idea that I had just now tried—very aggressively—to get in Andre's pants was embarrassing enough. Add to that, that I'd used glamour on him—I'd taken away his power of choice. Had we slept together, it wouldn't have been consensual.

Andre's brow furrowed. "No," he said, shaking me gently. "I know what you're thinking. And it's just not true. You commanded me to do to you everything I'd wanted to do since we first met. You ordered me to have full control of the situation." Andre's nostrils flared and a tremor moved through his body. The crease between his brows deepened. "Do you know how incredibly stupid that was?"

I glanced away, my jaw working. He was adding insult to injury.

He gently cupped my chin and turned my face so that I

had to look at him. "Don't *ever* give me that kind of power, Gabrielle. There are so many, many things that I'd—" His voice cut off and he shook his head. When he looked at me again, his face was pained. "I don't want your first time to be in some sleazy club while neither of us is fully in control of ourselves."

I swallowed and rubbed the palms of my hands against my eyes. When I pulled them away, I realized that smeared, sticky blood still coated them. Suddenly, my personal problems were only one of several extremely screwed up things that had happened this evening.

Beyond the room I heard a distant door bang open and the music stop. Shouts bubbled up from downstairs and I groaned.

Just when the evening couldn't get worse, help showed up like a late period.

Yippee.

I STARTED TO push myself off the couch when Andre placed a hand on my shoulder and gently pushed me back down.

"What are you doing?" I asked.

He shifted his body lower, so that the wide expanse of his torso pressed between my legs. I blushed, which, considering what we were about to do five seconds ago, was ridiculous.

"Checking your injury," he murmured. He pulled back the sliced edges of my dress, and his fingers deftly moved over my skin. "The wound is almost completely healed," he said, his breath fanning out against my stomach. He glanced up. "What happened?"

"I got shanked."

His lips twitched. "I can see that."

I filled him in on everything that had happened today, from the second murder to the events that took place downstairs while he'd been glamoured.

When I was finished, he pressed a kiss to my stomach. "I will find the people who did this to you," he whispered against my skin, "and when I do, I will kill them. Slowly."

A small shiver ran through my body at the menace in his voice.

"You're going to have to get in line."

Languidly he pushed his torso up until his face hovered over mine, and he slid a hand behind my head. "My bloodthirsty queen," he said affectionately, smiling down at me, "I should've known my soulmate wouldn't be some simpering damsel in distress."

Queen. My heart skipped at the name. Then his words sunk in, reminding me of something I hadn't mentioned. "I wanted to drink her blood," I whispered. I bit my lip.

Andre stilled above me. "That's ... only natural, given your nature," he said. "But that does mean that we'll need to feed together, and soon."

Feed on human blood. I grimaced. "How romantic," I said, my voice breaking. It was really beginning to happen—my gradual transformation into a vampire. It would eventually end with my death.

It was all too much.

"Come here," Andre said. He scooped me up and pressed me against his chest. Only then did I realize I was trembling.

"It's all going to be okay," he whispered into my hair.

Rather than calming me, his words caused my shoulders to shake and my trembling to increase. I leaned my head against his chest and let out a shuddering breath.

"Shhh," he murmured, running a hand over my hair. "I've got you. It's going to be okay." I nodded against him.

We stayed like that for a while, Andre talking soothingly to me, sometimes in English, sometimes in Romanian, sometimes in Spanish. And it worked. My breathing gradually evened out and my shaking subsided.

Eventually he pressed his lips against my temple. "We need to go down," he said. "I can hear the officers asking about you."

I nodded and extricated myself from his embrace. Almost immediately my body ached from his absence. As Andre stood, I eyed him. My blood had stained his button down and the skin of his forearms, where the sleeves had been rolled back.

"I got my blood all over you," I stated.

He grinned, and it was pure male smugness. "I don't exactly mind."

When I shot him a confused look, he explained. "This is what vampires would consider evidence of a good lay."

My eyes widened and my mouth parted. Suddenly the room felt too small and too hot. Andre's grin got a little slyer when he noticed how flustered I'd become.

I shook my head to clear it of my current thoughts. "What about the other vampires?" I'd sort of blown my cover at this point.

The smile dropped from Andre's face and his voice took on a steely edge. "I will worry about them."

Andre slung an arm protectively over my shoulders and moved his other to rest on my stomach where I'd recently been stabbed. We left the room like that and headed downstairs.

When we reached the main area of the club, the crowd was back to normal, meaning that they weren't mindlessly dancing or trying to get near me.

I chewed on the inside of my cheek as guilt gnawed at me. I'd been no better than that woman; I'd glamoured the room right after she'd let them go. Because of the circumstances, I probably wouldn't get charged for the unsanctioned use of it, but the memory of how I'd acted still made me feel unclean.

Caleb was the first to spot me. He pushed his way past a group of officers and enveloped me in a hug, knocking away Andre's hands. "Jesus, Gabrielle, I thought they took you." He must not have seen Andre whisk me away after the two women left.

Caleb stepped back and only then did he register the blood that drenched my dress and smeared across my skin. "Holy shit! What happened?"

I sighed. This was going to be a long night.

Chapter 10

IT TOOK ME two hours to finally make it back to the inn. By that time Andre had returned to his trial, and every fiber of my tired, achy body missed his presence. It seemed stupid to stay away from him when we were both in the same city. Especially now that other vampires knew I was here.

I suppressed a shudder at the thought. Getting sucked into the coven's archaic justice system was the last thing I wanted at the moment.

I muttered goodnight to Caleb in the hallway outside my room before stumbling inside. As soon as I closed the door behind me, I made a beeline for my bed. I collapsed onto it, clutching my pillow to me. I think I moaned a little.

"Oh I see how it is—the bed gets a moan, but you ignore your BBF."

I shrieked at the voice and flipped onto my back, pillow clutched to my chest. At the sound, Oliver who stood in the middle of the room, screamed as well.

He clutched his heart, gasping. "Oh my God, Saber-tooth, don't *do* that to me," he said. "You scream like a banshee."

"I—I don't do that?" I stuttered. "How about you don't do that!" *Oliver is in my room.* Oliver, who I'd left back on the Isle of Man.

The door to my room banged open and a shirtless Caleb rushed in. "Gabrielle, are you ... ?" His voice died away when he saw Oliver.

Oliver turned and stared, awestruck, at Caleb's muscles. "Oh my," he murmured. "This image is *definitely* going into the spank bank."

I groaned. So. Not. What. I. Needed. "Oliver, stop eye-raping the beejezus out of my partner."

"But he's so tasty-looking," Oliver said.

"I'm the vampire. Not you."

"Please tell me you've had a nibble," Oliver said.

I saw Caleb's hands twitch, and I'd bet my savings that he wanted to cover himself. Welcome to my world.

"Oliver, what are you doing here?" Caleb asked, stepping into the room.

Oliver gave him a look like it should be obvious. "Visiting Gabrielle. Duh."

I rubbed my eyes. "I must be dreaming," I said, sitting up. "There's no way you're really here."

"Nope, you're definitely not dreaming."

"This is some horrible nightmare," I insisted.

Oliver sashayed over to me and pinched my arm. Hard.

"Ow!" I yelped, swatting his hand away.

"See?" he said, "Not dreaming." His eyes strayed back to Caleb, who now leaned against the wall, looking sleepy and amused. Oliver tilted his head. "Then again ..." He took a step forward, a nefarious little smile on his face.

Caleb's eyes widened and he held up his hands. "Whoa, whoa, whoa. Don't even think of trying anything, fairy."

Oliver sighed. "Damn, this isn't a dream."

"Seriously Oliver, what are you doing here?" I asked. I'd been so close to sleep. So, so close.

He raised his hands in the air, baring himself like an offering. "Ta-dah," he said. "I'm your Christmas present."

This wasn't happening. All that is holy, please tell me this wasn't happening.

I pinched the bridge of my nose. "How, exactly, did you get here?"

Oliver waved a hand dismissively. "Ley lines."

Ley lines. Of course. He probably trampled right through our crime scene. Fairies.

Oliver's eyes moved over my blood-spattered body, and then he whistled. "Geez Sabertooth, did you munch on someone?" He gasped as another thought came to him. "You dirty slut!" he squealed. "You lost your V-card, didn't you? I did *not* peg you for the S and M type, but then again, you are—"

"She got stabbed, Oliver." Caleb's voice sounded tired and surprisingly defensive.

Oliver's expression morphed into one of shock. "Oh ... *dear*." His surprise only lasted a moment, and then he moved into action.

He came over to my side of the bed. "You haven't even been able to clean up yet, have you?" he clucked. "C'mon sweet thing, let's get you a shower." He picked up my hand and gave it a tug.

I moaned and resisted. At this point, I was willing to pass out in bloody clothes.

"You sound like a zombie. Actually, you kind of look like one too ..." Oliver turned to Caleb. "Are you sure she just got stabbed?"

"Meanie," I mumbled.

Caleb folded his arms, and his eyes flicked to me. "Want me to kick him out? Just give me the word, and I will."

"Hey!" Oliver said.

Painfully I pushed myself upright. "No, that's alright," I said to Caleb, "though I do appreciate the thought."

Oliver huffed, but he was wise enough not to say anything for once.

Pulling my shoes off, I stumbled over to the bathroom, ignoring the men in my room.

It didn't last long. "Are you sure you're going to be alright?" Caleb asked, leaning in the doorway.

I bent down and turned on the shower. "I'll be fine."

"What are we supposed to do with him?" he asked.

I rubbed my forehead. "I have no idea."

THE BUZZING OF my phone's alarm woke me. I wanted to cry. It was morning already? The alarm had to be wrong; I swear I'd just closed my eyes.

When I reached over and to turn it off, I felt a warm body brush against my back, and a hand squeezed my breast.

What. The. Hell?

I made a strangled noise, and the hand squeezed tighter.

"Oliver!" I yelped, my face turning all sorts of red. Not cool. This was so *not cool*.

"Huh?" I heard the rustle of fabric as his head lifted from the pillow. "Oh—ah, I'm ... er, touching your boob—*ew*."

"Could you remove it, please?" I asked, my voice strained.

Why me? I shook my fist at the ceiling.

"What are you doing?" he murmured, removing his hand and eyeing my fist. He shook his head and lay back down. "You're such a big weirdo." His body shifted, and I felt something press into my back.

I couldn't help it, I shrieked. "Ohmygod, ohmygod, ohmygod! Morning wood! And it touched me! Ohmygod. *You don't even like women.*" I said this last part accusingly.

Oliver squealed as well. "Geez Sabertooth, stop screaming. It's freaking me out."

"It's freaking you out? It's freaking you out!" I was officially losing it. "Well I'll tell you what's freaking *me* out. My gay friend has a—"

Oliver rolled his eyes. "It's not like I was getting turned on by you, harpy woman. Get over yourself."

"You were copping a feel in your sleep!"

Oliver opened his mouth, then closed it and paused,

a horrified expression gradually passing over his face. "I was." He sucked in a breath and glared at his hand accusingly. "But I don't like boobs ..." he whispered to himself.

A knock on the door interrupted us. I scrambled out of the bed and opened it, eager to put as much distance between me and that incident as possible.

Caleb stood on the other side, already dressed for the day. Morning people. "Is everything okay?" he asked. He took me in then eyed the room beyond me. "I heard screaming."

"That would be the banshee you're referring to," Oliver yelled from the bed.

I cleared my throat. "Everything's fine. Just finished getting my morning's friendly frisk from Oliver." I yelled this last part over my shoulder.

"Want one?" Oliver called back to Caleb.

Caleb pressed his lips together in an attempt to keep from laughing. "Tempting, but I think I'll pass."

"Your loss," Oliver replied, his voice muffled as he turned over.

"Still haven't figured out what to do with him?" Caleb asked almost sympathetically.

"I can hear you!" Oliver shouted. A second later I heard him throw off the covers. He padded over to us, clad in only in royal purple boxers with yellow fleur de lises all over them. "And I have many uses."

Caleb's eyebrows shot up. "You two slept together like that?"

"I didn't think I'd get groped!" I said.

"It was an accident," Oliver said, exasperated. His eyes

flicked to Caleb. "But it will probably happen again—maybe I should switch rooms," he said, eyeing my partner.

"Or get your own, moocher," I said.

Caleb pulled out his phone to check the time. "Grigori's going to be here in twenty minutes, so ..." *So you might want to get your asses moving.* He was too polite to say that, but his meaning was clear.

"Yeah, yeah." I rubbed my face, now remembering why I had to get up at the buttcrack of dawn. I had to give my statement. *Again.*

Just one more awesome event to add to my sucktastic winter vacation.

Boo.

I SLURPED DOWN my third cup of coffee in one of the Politia's conference rooms.

"So do you know what type of supernaturals either of them were?" Grigori asked. Another officer sat next to him, but Grigori was responsible for taking my official statement.

I rested my hands palms up on the table and stared at them. "No, I have no idea what they were."

Frustration and embarrassment welled up in me. I was too young and too inexperienced to be an expert on this case. At least, that's what I told myself to feel better. A small part of me wasn't buying it. I really wanted to prove myself wrong, and I hadn't been able to yet.

"But when you spoke into the mike last night," Grigori continued, "you told us you thought one of those women might be a siren."

I nodded, playing with my coffee's plastic lid. "At the time I thought she was. She glamoured the crowd last night. I thought only sirens had that ability, so I assumed that's what she was. But her skin didn't light up when she used it. And she smelled funny, like ash and roses." Not that I knew what I smelled like. Maybe I smelled like roasted flowers.

"Also," I added, "she told me she wasn't a siren."

Grigori scribbled something down on a notepad he had with him before continuing.

"And the other women," he said, "did she have any special traits or abilities?"

My hands fisted. "Like me, she was immune to glamour, and she moved faster than any supernatural being I know of." I stared at my nails, my mind far away. "Both women referred to me as 'consort,' and she also called me some name …" I trailed off as I tried to remember it. "It started with a 'P'." I frowned at the memory. The women were clearly fans of the man in the suit.

It went like that for another hour as Grigori squeezed out every detail of the evening. As we were wrapping up, he asked me one final question. "Why do you think they wanted to talk to you?"

I thought of the first woman's interest in me and her strange reverence. I shook my head. "I have no idea."

WHILE OLIVER WAS out shopping and playing tourist in Cluj, Caleb and I spent the afternoon piecing together what we knew. So far, we had two random murder locations, two elusive murder suspects, and only the most obscure motive.

"At least we know now why our victims showed no signs of resistance other than the wounds on their feet," Caleb said.

I pushed down the bile at the thought. They'd been glamoured into compliance, into offering over their lives.

"Do you think that these victim's could've given their blood willingly if they'd been asked to under glamour?" The question burned on its way out of my lips.

Caleb hesitated. "Maybe," he finally said. He glanced down at his notes. "You said that one of the suspects mentioned she was following orders. If that's true, who do you think is giving them?" Caleb asked, tapping a pen against the table.

"I don't know," I said. But I did—or at least I had an idea. The ritualistic manner in which each victim was killed, the way the siren wannabe bowed to me, the names I'd been referred to.

"You're not saying the obvious," Caleb stated. When I glanced at him he held my gaze. "Gabrielle, the devil has to be behind this."

After a moment of silence, I gave him a sharp nod, conceding to his words. "I've sort of been in denial."

"I can tell." Caleb stared at me for a beat longer. He seemed to decide on something before he spoke again. "And I know you can tell that I've been distant for a while now."

Oh boy, we were going to have this conversation.

"It's just that you were with the devil for an evening, Gabrielle, and you're a vampire. I've been conditioned to see those things as threats to the supernatural community."

I shifted in my seat. "Can we just go back to talking—"

"Good and evil are real things in our world, and genetically, you're predisposed for evil."

"Gee, thanks Caleb."

He shrugged, biting down on the edge of his pen. Then his open features darkened. "On the night of Samhain— the devil had you for God knows how long. I can't imagine all you went through. How you must have suffered."

An image of Leanne's empty eyes surfaced. I pushed it away. "Caleb, I really don't want to talk about this." I hadn't, not since I'd given my official statement. Only Andre and the officers recording my statement knew.

Caleb leaned forward and captured my hand in his own. "I need you to know why I've acted the way I have."

I glanced down at the way his hand folded around mine. The gesture was relatively innocent, but his scent betrayed his feelings.

I nodded for him to go on, pretending that I couldn't smell his desire.

"I worried that when you came back, you might've ... changed. And I was worried that, as your partner, I'd have to report it to the Politia."

I froze. "You would've done that?"

He hesitated. "Yes," he finally confessed, "I would've."

My chest hurt. Of course I understood, but it was painful to think that he'd give up that quickly on me.

"And how about now?" I asked. "You've kept your distance since that night, Caleb. Do you still worry that I might turn evil?"

Caleb shook his head. "I'm not worried about you—haven't been for a long time. But I am worried *for* you. The Fates themselves don't seem to have full control of your destiny, and the devil wants you—something I've never even heard of before."

Neither had I. But now that I had met him, I knew he did covet material things, including a woman of flesh and blood.

Caleb squeezed my hand and looked away. "I am scared for you, Gabrielle because I don't think the devil will stop coming after you."

He wouldn't. Not until he owned my soul.

Chapter 11

EVEN AFTER CALEB left, I'd stayed at my desk, doggedly following the leads that we had. Two women, one that smelled like ash and roses, another who moved faster than a vampire.

I was aimlessly flipping through the notes I'd copied back at the library, when I heard a soft whisper.

"*Consort ...*"

I shivered and glanced out my window. Darkness had just descended, and the snowstorm that had everyone so worried was now in full swing. A curtain of snow obscured the tree line outside the inn, and even with my night vision, I could only make out the stark contrast of the white snow against the dark night.

"*Gabrielle ...*"

I dropped the papers on the table and stood up. "Caleb? Oliver?" I felt ridiculous calling out their names since both were probably in the dining room grabbing dinner.

When no one responded, I snatched up my coat and paused. What, exactly, did I think I was doing?

"*Death ...*"

I cocked my head. The voice came from outside. It shouldn't have; sound shouldn't carry that way in a snowstorm. I glanced out my window once more. Deep within the tree line, a shadow flickered.

Something was out there.

I slid my coat on and left my room. Perhaps it was the woman from the club, come to finish whatever it was she started. Or perhaps it was someone or something else. Since I'd arrived, it seemed as though I'd been hearing and seeing things. Now was as good a time as any to look into it.

I strode down the hall and through the lobby, noticing that Caleb and Oliver were in fact eating dinner in the dining room when I passed it. I don't know if either noticed me, but no one tried to stop me when I crossed the lobby and opened the front door.

As soon as I stepped outside, the storm assaulted me. I pulled my flimsy jacket closer as the wind tugged at my hair and snow got ensnared within it.

What are you doing, Gabrielle? Planning on hunting down phantom voices?

The thought had barely crossed my mind when it spoke again. "*... awaits you.*" The voice slithered over my skin.

After a long moment where I stood on the stoop of the inn like an idiot, the voice spoke again. "*Come to me.*"

I wasn't an idiot. I knew that I should turn on my heel and forget what I'd heard, or at least grab someone.

But I was more curious than I was sensible.

I took one step, then another, heading for the tree line. It was the same place I'd seen the shadow move.

I'm just going to check. That's all. I moved out of the light of the inn, and my vampiric eyesight took over.

I entered the wooded area and closed my eyes, relying on my sense of smell and sound to guide me. When I sensed nothing, I spoke. "Are you going to show yourself?"

"*You ... should ... not ... live,*" the voice hissed.

I took a step back. Okay, I *was* an idiot.

"Who are you?" I asked, edging my way back out of the forest.

"*Messenger. Deliverer.*"

My eyes darted around the darkened woods. There was no one here. No scent, no pulse, no steady breathing. Only this voice.

"*You ... are ... his.*"

I could hear the beat of my heart between my ears, the sound growing louder and louder. All my senses crackled, searching the darkness for this being, and my muscles tensed, as though readying for attack.

"*Gabrielle.*" Andre's voice cut through the night, and the noise inside my head silenced. He was at my side in a second, brushing my hair back. "What are you doing out here?"

I blinked at him, as if waking from a daze. Concern pulled his brows together. I touched the side of his face, where the moon illuminated his high cheekbones. I shook my head. "I thought I heard something."

Andre's eyes moved between mine, and then his gaze flicked to the forest around us. He wrapped an arm protectively around my shoulders. "Let's get you out of here."

It was only as we neared the tree line that the voice spoke one final time. "*You ... will ... die ... soon.*"

ON THE WALK back to the inn, Andre brooded but stayed silent. I knew he had a million things he wanted to say, and I could feel the tension pulling his muscles taut.

A small smile tugged at my lips. I wondered how long he'd last before he unleashed his thoughts. The front door of the inn? The lobby? I might be this man's soulmate, but he was still as headstrong as all get out. Self-restraint was a new concept for him, one that he'd only begun to practice since he met me.

He made it to my room. "What was that, Gabrielle?" He shoved a hand through his hair as the door clicked shut. The angry, smoldering look he gave me skyrocketed the tension in the room.

I leaned back against the door. "I heard a voice."

Andre's eyebrows rose. "A voice," he repeated.

I rolled my lips in on each other. "Yep."

"And you followed it." I could hear the skepticism lacing his voice. "After everything that's happened to you, you followed this voice."

I gave him an obstinate look. "I can't just live in fear."

He folded his arms. "Of course not. You must go greet threats with open arms."

Be mature, Gabrielle, be mature. "Screw you, Andre."

Okay, I was still working on the whole maturity thing.

I went to push past him, but he caught my arm and reeled me in. "That was not a very nice thing to say," he said, his voice low and menacing. His eyes glinted. At the moment Andre was a hundred percent predator. "I am not asking you to live in fear; I'm asking you to be smart about these things."

His nostrils flared and he lifted his chin as he scented the air. His pupils dilated. "What is that smell?"

"What smell?"

Andre let me go, only to walk further into the room ... towards the rumpled bed. I'd had one of those "Do Not Disturb" signs outside my room, so the maid hadn't come in.

Andre fisted the sheets and brought them to his face.

Ah. Oh. He could smell Oliver's scent mixed with mine.

Rage crackled off of it the second he lowered his hand. "What. Is. This?"

I did probably the worst thing I could in that moment. I laughed. But I mean, seriously? Oliver and me?

"You think this is funny?" He practically growled the words.

I tipped my head back and forth, weighing his words. "Kinda?"

Oliver chose that exact moment to come barging into the room. "Lover bunny!" he shouted as he skipped inside.

Next to me, Andre went rigid.

"You've been ignoring me all day, and I want to have fun with you ..." Oliver's words died on his lips when he saw us.

He stopped in his tracks. "I didn't know you two were in here getting jiggy with it." Oliver looked like he was going to say more. I shook my head and drew my hand across my neck.

Confused, Oliver glanced at Andre, who still clutched the rumpled sheet in his hand and was flashing the fairy a look that promised retribution.

Understanding dawned on Oliver's face. He backed away. Smart fairy. "I'll just leave you—"

"Have you been sleeping with my soulmate?" Andre cut in, his voice low.

"Errr, not like that. Although she does have nice boobs," he said thoughtfully. After a pause he added, "Only pair I've ever fondled and enjoyed."

I rubbed my forehead. "Oliver just ..."

I saw Andre's muscles tense to attack Oliver, so I did something Andre himself had taught me to do: I tackled him. We tumbled onto my bed, wrestling to get the upper hand.

"Stop. Being. Possessive," I ground out.

Andre rolled on top of me. "You push me too far, soulmate." Well damn, he didn't even sound winded.

Oliver made a small noise, and then I heard the sound of his retreating footfalls. My door opened and closed, and I breathed a sigh of relief. At least Oliver had the sense to get out of the warpath of my raging boyfriend.

Andre didn't make any attempt to go after him. Instead

he stared down at me, his eyes dark pools. "Soulmate, how could you?" Betrayal laced his voice.

I raised my brows. "Did you really think I did anything with Oliver? *Oliver?*" I asked.

"You're a siren," Andre replied. "Anyone—man or woman, gay or straight—can be attracted to you."

Well, I could've used that piece of knowledge before this morning's grope session.

"So you assumed that I'd cheat on you?" I said. "Me, your soulmate."

I could see some of the anger drain from Andre's features. Beneath it was something vulnerable. Dare I think it? Was Andre ... unsure of himself? That was new.

I hooked a leg around his hips and flipped us, readjusting my body so that I straddled his torso and pinned his arms. "You are insane if you think that anything happened," I said, then backtracked. "Well, okay, Oliver *did* grope me," Andre stiffened beneath me, "but on accident while we were asleep." I rushed the rest out.

"On *accident?*" Andre looked murderous. He began to push me aside, his focus on the door.

I tightened my grip. "Chill, Andre, it's not a big deal."

His expression begged to differ. "I will not *chill.*"

I wiggled my hips and bent over him. I smiled slowly as his attention refocused itself on me.

"Having you beneath me is kind of ... hot," I said, gazing down at him.

His eyes smoldered. "You think you have me trapped?"

"Last I checked, I'm the one pinning you down."

His trapped hands curled around mine. That ... wasn't

supposed to happen. "You've gotten good at grappling," he said, "but you still have a ways to go, young grasshopper."

My eyes lit up. "Hey, that was a pop culture reference *and* a joke! I'm officially impressed." Playful Andre was a rare treat.

Faster than I could react, Andre hooked a leg around me. I let out a small squeak when he flipped us. Within seconds I'd gone from holding him down to being pinned beneath him.

"Your words are insulting," he said, his hair tickling my cheeks as he bent over me, "but I forgive you." He nuzzled my neck. His lips brushed over it, trailing kisses down to the hollow of my throat.

I tilted my head back and closed my eyes, reveling in sensation of his mouth on my skin. He hesitated against me, and I felt the air in the room change from playful to serious.

His mouth hovered over the base of my throat for what felt like an eternity. "I love you," he whispered against my skin.

I didn't move. Had I heard him right? 'Cause it sounded like …

Andre drew his head back and stared me in the eyes. "I love you, Gabrielle."

Chapter 12

My GAZE LOCKED with his.

He let go of my hands and caressed my cheek. "I have for a very long time—"

"I love you too." The words just slipped out, as though my mouth had consulted my heart, not my head.

He pulled back just long enough for me to see his astonishment.

"What, you though this was a one-way thing?" I asked jokingly. But I was far from joking. Adrenaline swamped my system.

Instead of responding, he dipped his head down and pressed his lips to mine. The connection between us throbbed, and my skin pulsed. This kiss was more intimate, more raw, than our others. I could've sworn I felt him tremble as he held me, but perhaps that was my imagination. I knew that my heart was trying to leap from my body.

His hands wound themselves into my hair as he deepened the kiss. My lips parted and he brushed his tongue against mine. I let my hands trail over the sculpted muscles of his arms, wishing not for the first time that I could feel the press of his bare skin against mine.

With a final press of his lips, the kiss ended. "I've never had this," he whispered against my lips. "Relationships, yes, but never, never this." He cupped my face like I was some precious thing.

I reached up and traced his lips with a finger, wonder at him—at *us*—filling me. "Neither have I." We both smiled at that, Andre's lips rubbing against my finger.

Tentatively his thumb touched the soft skin beneath my eyes. "You haven't been sleeping well, have you?"

There was no use lying to him. "No, not really."

"Are you still having dreams of *him?*"

I licked my lips. "Sometimes."

Andre made a noise low in his throat. "Sneaky little bastard," he muttered.

It took everything I had to keep a straight face at his words.

He exhaled and gathered me close. "Tonight I get the night off from the trial, so I can be with you the entire night—if you'd like that."

I couldn't stop the wide grin that broke across my face. "Naw, that sounds *awful.*"

Andre squinted. "Is that sarcasm?"

I rolled my eyes, and he let out a bark of laughter and

squeezed me tighter. "You are such a strange creature. I think that's what I love best about you." He gazed at me tenderly.

"You better watch yourself, punk," I said, even though happy laughter bubbled inside my chest.

"*Punk?*"

I couldn't tell whether Andre's expression was more amused or insulted.

"I didn't stutter, did I?"

And then we were rolling and laughing. "Someone needs to wash that mouth of yours out," Andre said, pinning my arms again.

"Don't act like you don't like it."

He stole a kiss. "Damn my wicked soul, but I do. I absolutely do."

"Can you help me?" I asked Andre several hours later. We were still laying together on the bed, but we'd spent most of the time chatting and laughing. For being bossy, and protective, and old school, Andre was actually pretty freaking fun to be around. His looks didn't hurt either.

"Always, Gabrielle," he said, entwining our hands. "You never have to ask for something like that."

His words warmed me to my core. I pushed off the bed and padded over to the desk in the room. "I know you're busy, but I've been placed as an expert on this case, and I don't really know what I'm doing." It hurt a little to say those words, especially to Andre, who badly wanted me to quit.

Andre followed me over and scanned the papers. He flipped through them, and then picked up the files I had on our two victims. He pulled out a photo of the victims and compared them. For a long time he studied them.

"This looks like an old ritual they used to do hundreds of years ago."

My breath froze in my lungs. This was too good to be true. "What was the ritual?"

Andre's brows drew together. He placed the photographs back on the table and rubbed his jaw, still staring at them. "Three mortal wounds inflicted on the victim simultaneously. This," he tapped the photos with his index finger, "this is a threefold death."

MY EYEBROWS SHOT up. Andre had managed to piece together in less than a minute what we hadn't been able to in days.

I came to his side. "Threefold death?" I repeated.

He nodded to the photo. "Here you have asphyxiation, an incomplete beheading, and partial impalement.

"Why haven't we ever heard about threefold death?"

Andre handed me the photo. "Well, it's an old ritual—and an obscure one, at that."

"Ritual," I repeated, unease tightening my muscles.

"Triple death represented the killing of the three parts of man—the body, the soul, and the spirit. It was a symbolic way of completely eradicating a person's existence. Usually it was reserved for people of importance—specifically, *unpopular* people of importance, if I remember correctly. It was the ultimate punishment for those who'd done bad things or pissed the wrong person off."

"That sounds like a line from *The Mummy*," I said.

Andre gave me a funny look. Guess he'd never seen the movie. "In certain areas of the world, it was considered the highest dishonor you could do to a person."

"But these victims are angelic, so why do this to them?" I asked.

He frowned. "I have no idea."

We both stared at the photos. "So whoever is doing this has religious motives?" I asked. We'd fallen back to the investigative team we were all those months ago.

"Probably."

I thought back to last night's encounter. "One of the women at the club smelled like ash and roses. Have you ever come across a scent like that before?" Perhaps learning what she was would help us figure out her and her partner's motives.

His lips thinned. "I vaguely recognize it, but I have no idea what being it belongs to."

I scrubbed my face. These were all dead ends. We had so many clues—I even met the freaking killers—but we couldn't pin down anything.

"Andre, even if we were able to prove that woman's guilt, how do you detain someone like that—someone you can't control?" Someone like *me*.

Our gazes locked. "You don't want me to answer this," Andre said softly.

"Tell me."

He worked his jaw. "How do you capture someone who

can wield absolute power over you? You don't," he said. "You kill them."

The next morning I met Caleb and Oliver in the inn's dining room.

"Oh look who it is," Oliver said as I sat down, "Miss I-Sexile-and-Ignore-My-Friends Fiori."

"Do you seriously want to go there?" I said. I'd woken up on the wrong side of the bed—a.k.a., without Andre— and I wasn't taking it well.

"Oh, I'm already there." Oliver snapped his fingers and rolled his head, and he did it all with a straight face. This little fairy was serious.

"Listen Pixie Sticks, you can't just barge into Romania while I'm working and expect me to entertain you."

"Oh, so that's what you were doing last night? Working? I didn't realize Andre paid you for sex."

"Whoa," Caleb said, raising his hands. Guess he'd never seen me and fairy boy duke it out.

I snorted. "That's real good coming from you," I said to Oliver.

"What's that supposed to mean?"

"No," Caleb interrupted us. "It's too freaking early for this."

Oliver ignored Caleb and fixed me a glare. "Better watch yourself, harpy, or you're going to find yourself hexed."

I snarled back at him. "Do your worst, Sparkles. You'd be improving my luck."

Caleb's chair screeched as he stood up, and then his

hands slapped over my mouth and Oliver's.

Oliver and I blinked at each other as Caleb closed his eyes and sighed. "Finally some peace and quiet." His eyelids snapped open. "You two are friends," he said to us, "so please try to act like it. Also, I'm way too fucking young to be the mothering type, so this is the last time I'll be nice about it. Next time my hands are getting involved."

Oliver's eyebrows shot up and he cocked his head, looking thoughtful at the idea of Caleb getting his hands involved. Caleb noticed.

"Damnit Oliver," Caleb said, "I can read you like a book, and right now it is disturbing as hell."

Oliver just winked at him, and I started to laugh behind Caleb's hand. Oliver's twinkling eyes flicked to me and he extended his pinkie. I reached out and hooked mine with his.

Seeing that we were playing nice, Caleb dropped his hands and shook his head. "You two are so weird." That was the second time someone had said that to me within the last week.

"What do you expect?" Oliver said. "We're BBFs—best bitches forever and ever."

"Hug it out?" I asked him.

"Oh my God, yes times a million, bosom buddy."

So we hugged in the middle of the dining room as random hotel guests looked on.

I squeezed him. "Oliver, you can still sleep in my room," I said. He'd refused to enter it last night after the little scuffle with Andre, instead spending the night in Caleb's room.

"Nuh uh. No way," he said, still hugging me. "I'm staying with Caleb from here on out."

My eyes moved to Caleb, who shook his head furiously back and forth.

I rolled my eyes at the both of them. "It's going to be fine, Oliver," I said, patting him on the back. "Don't let Andre intimidate you."

Oliver stepped out of the hug and cocked his hip, raising his eyebrows skeptically. "Easy for you to say. If he gets angry at you, he'll what—spank you for being naughty? Me, however, he'll drain dry."

"He wouldn't; you're my friend."

"Um, clearly you didn't see the psychotic look in his eyes," Oliver said. "Nope, I'm staying far away from your room."

"Fine, then as my Christmas gift to you, I'll get you your own room."

Oliver's face lit up. "Really? You'd do that?"

I smiled. "Duh." It wasn't like I couldn't afford it.

Oliver clapped his hands together joyfully. "Can we get rooms that connect?" he asked. "Best bitches forever *need* rooms that connect."

Chapter 13

NOT LONG AFTER I'd gotten Oliver his own room—thankfully not one that connected to mine—my phone buzzed.

"Hello?" I answered, leaning back in my room's chair. This desk was quickly becoming a second home.

"Gabrielle, it's Grigori."

"Hey," I said, letting the chair fall back on all four legs, "what are the plans for today?"

"We got a call in last night that two women fitting the description of our suspects were loading a van outside of a warehouse here in Cluj."

I sat up straighter. A lead. A shiver rushed down my spine. Some part of me had assumed that the voice that beckoned to me last night was the woman. But if she had an alibi ...

"When a couple of officers checked it out, they found

packing supplies large enough to hold an altar. We have inspectors there at the moment," he continued, "but I wanted to bring you and Sergeant Jennings over to see if anything stands out."

"We'll be ready to go as soon as you can come," I said.

"Then I'll be there in fifteen minutes."

"Great. By the way," I said, "I think I have information on the murders." I hadn't had time to look into Andre's theory, but it was the only lead we had.

"Go on."

So I told him about the threefold murder theory.

"You could be on to something," he said. I could hear the excitement in his voice. "I'll pass the information along. See you soon."

"Bye."

I clicked off the phone and packed up some of the things I'd need for today. We were one step closer to catching those women.

"The Politia doesn't pay me enough for this shit," Caleb yelled over the howling wind as we stepped out of Grigori's car and into the blizzard. I was surprised that we'd managed to drive at all, given the weather conditions.

We trudged over to the roped off warehouse, keeping our chins tucked in and our arms held close to our bodies. I'd grown up in warm Los Angeles, so I'd never experienced a snowstorm, and I was woefully underprepared. Woefully.

Once we were inside, I shivered and rubbed my arms.

"I think I have snow down my shirt and up my nose," I said to Caleb.

"I'm not even going to comment about where I have snow," he said.

Grigori led us through the room and down a short hallway lined with offices. Crime scene tape cordoned the rooms off, but from what I could see, all were empty. Whoever used this place had either removed all traces of their business here, or they'd only used a small portion of the space.

At the end of the hallway, someone had propped open double doors that led into a large open room. When I caught my first glimpse inside, I was ... unimpressed. Some crates lined the walls as well as what looked like several wooden two-by-fours. But other than that, the place was stripped bare.

Reluctantly I walked further into the room. My eyes gravitated to a series of smudged markings on the ground. I pushed past some of the officers standing near them and crouched.

I knew enough about the supernatural world to know what the rubbed out chalk had been used for. "A summoning circle," I said softly.

Some of the markings crisscrossed through the middle of the circle. The original lines were too destroyed to recreate the original drawing, but it didn't take much imagination to hazard a guess.

A pentagram.

"Have any idea why our suspects might cast a circle?" Grigori asked.

I thought back to Samhain. During that period of time, I'd seen a circle closed twice, once to communicate with the dead—which ended in a possession—and the other time to seal me inside a ley line with the devil. Needless to say, I wasn't a fan of summoning circles.

I pushed myself back up, and faced Grigori. "They wanted to either keep something out, or keep something in."

Something like a demon. Or the devil.

OLIVER JUMPED UP from the lobby's couch, where he'd been trolling the Internet. "How could you leave me trapped in this shithole?"

"Shhh," I hissed, shooting a glance at the innkeeper who was on the phone at the moment. "Can you not be rude for five seconds?"

Even after Caleb and I had been dropped back off at the hotel that evening, I couldn't stop thinking about our newest lead. A warehouse empty save for a few crates and a smudged out summoning circle.

What dark rites had it been used for? Contacting the dead? Or something darker? And why? The plot was thickening.

"I wanted to go shopping today," Oliver said, "but *no,* Romania decided to throw a hissy and strand my ass here. And you were gone. Where have you been? And why can't I come along?"

I folded my arms over chest. "Want a little cheese with that whine?"

Oliver narrowed his eyes at me. "Do you know how much time I've had on my hands?" He didn't wait for me to answer. "Enough to paint my nails and detail each one." He lifted his hands, and sure enough on each finger was a different Christmas design. One had a Christmas tree, another a snowman, and another a Santa hat.

"Hey," I said, grabbing his hand, "you're actually pretty good at that."

Oliver snatched his hand away. "Of course I am." He sniffed. "That's what happens when you have several hours on your hands. "Oh, also, I looked at your notes," he said, checking out his nails, "and I'm pretty sure one of your murder suspects is a cambion."

I STARED AT Oliver while his words sunk in. Why was I surprised? He'd figured out that demons were killing people during the Samhain murders, he just hadn't thought to share it. Fairies.

"A cambion," I repeated.

"Mmm-hmmm," he said, turning his attention back to his computer.

I leaned over the couch and snatched his computer from him.

"Hey—"

I began walking down the hall to my room, knowing he'd follow now that I had his laptop. It was leverage for his help. That, and what I was about to say.

I threw him a glance over my shoulder. "I promise to go shopping with you if you tell me everything you know about cambions."

"During this trip?" Oliver asked hopefully, peeking over the couch.

"Once the investigation is over, you can pick the date." Why did I feel like I was signing my soul away by agreeing to this?

Oliver weighed this information. "I'll only agree to it if you actually buy clothes," he said.

"Fine."

"And I get to pick them out."

"Oliver ..." This was going from bad to worse.

"And you have to wear them."

I ground my teeth together. "You know," I said, "I bet your bargains would give the devil a run for his money."

Oliver folded his arms and stared me down. "Damn straight they would."

I shifted my weight, throwing a longing glance at the door to my room. At this point, I'd do just about anything to solve this investigation and get back to the Isle of Man. "Fine, I agree to your hellish demands. Now, will you help me?"

"I suppose," Oliver said, acting like he was all put out when I knew better. He was a big ham when it came to attention. "Just know that I'm doing this for you, not the lame-ass institution you work for."

Did everyone and their mother hate the Politia?

"Awesome," I said, barely containing a massive eye roll. "Let me just grab Caleb." I trotted over to Caleb's room and knocked on his door. When it opened, I nearly dropped Oliver's computer.

It was the middle of the day and yet Andre stood in front of me.

Chapter 14

"What the h-hell?" I stuttered.

Andre glanced down at himself. "I'm pretty convincing, aren't I?" he said.

More like terrifying beyond belief. It was Andre's body, Andre's voice, but it wasn't Andre's soul that resided beneath his skin.

I socked Caleb in the arm. "Knock it off. I cannot even express just how creepy that is."

Caleb laughed, as though this were all one big joke.

"I'm serious," I said softly. I was picking up Andre's quiet menace.

Caleb-as-Andre grinned. It was such a Caleb mannerism, his mouth lifting more on one side than the other, that it made Andre look like a crude parody of himself. "Sorry," he said, his tone suggesting he felt otherwise.

Andre's skin rippled and in his place stood Oliver. "This better?"

Behind me I heard Oliver yelp. "Oh my God, *ew*, stop that!" he said, throwing a hand over his eyes. His fingers split apart wide enough for him to peer between them. "Do I really look like that?" he asked me.

"No—this is the hot version of you," I said sarcastically.

He swatted my arm and dropped his hand from his face, inching closer to Caleb. Caleb watched him, wearing a satisfied smirk. I peered at Caleb-as-Oliver. I'd seen him shapeshift before—often in fact—but he'd rarely impersonated people.

"People are harder to mimic," Caleb said with Oliver's voice, as if reading my mind.

Oliver crept closer and, using his index finger, poked Caleb-as-Oliver.

"Hey," Caleb-as-Oliver said, rubbing the flesh Oliver poked. Oliver began to circle him. Once he'd made a full circle, he nodded to himself. "Damn, I look *good*."

Caleb-as-Oliver focused his gaze on me, his eyes mischievous. "Want to see what you look like?"

My response was immediate. "No—"

Even as I spoke Oliver's skin rippled into something paler, more delicate. The clothes Caleb had been wearing hung loose on him now, and all of Oliver's masculine edges dissolved into soft, feminine curves.

I stared into my own face. My lips were too red, my cheekbones too high, hair too dark, and my skin too pale.

Even more disturbing was that Caleb lay beneath that skin. My skin.

I glanced away. Looking at my double was not the same as looking in the mirror. No, it was way worse.

"Don't I look pretty?" Caleb asked jokingly, toying with a lock of my hair. Except it wasn't Caleb's voice that spoke. It was my own.

I cringed at the voice. Like everything else, it was too much. Too feminine, too melodic. "Stop it," I said, refusing to look at him—her—me.

"Geez, Gabrielle," Caleb said in my voice, "we all know you're hideous, but you don't have to look away like that."

"You're not funny, Caleb," I said, keeping my gaze averted. "Please, stop."

"Really?" he said in my voice. "Do you seriously not want to look at yourself?"

I shook my head.

I could feel his gaze boring into me but eventually he reverted back to himself. "Well that was—"

I threw my fist forward and socked him in the face, making sure to hold back most of my strength. Even still, the force of my blow knocked him on his ass.

"Bitch went down," Oliver threw in, helpful as always.

I stood over a moaning Caleb while he held his nose.

"Don't ever fucking pull that again without our permission," I said.

Caleb's words came out muffled. "You didn't have to punch me."

"That wasn't a punch," Oliver said, "that was her knocking the idiot out of you." Oliver turned to me. "I don't think it worked, either."

I tilted my head. "I could always try again."

Oliver pursed his lips in thought, as Caleb got to his feet. "Hasn't anyone told you to use your words?" Caleb said.

I raised my eyebrows, amused. "This is coming the guy who threatened to get his hands involved the next time Oliver and I got into an argument."

"For the record," Oliver said, "I'm still interested in this hand business."

Caleb muttered something not so nice under his breath as he brushed himself off. "There will be no hand business," he said.

Oliver's lips drew down in a pout.

"So," Caleb said, looking back and forth at us expectantly. "What is it that you two wanted to discuss oh-so-badly?"

"Unholy creatures," I said.

Caleb's face scrunched up. "What?"

Oliver leaned into me. "Nope," Oliver whispered, "you definitely did not knock the idiot out of him."

"So, what exactly is a cambion?" Caleb asked once we filled him in.

I flipped through my notes to answer that exact question. I know I scanned a page about this supernatural being back at Peel Academy. Now I just had to find it. Which was proving difficult.

"They are the offspring of a human and an incubus," Oliver said.

My head snapped up, my eyes round as saucers. "You

mean ... ?"

"Yep," Oliver said with a grin, "your little bedmates a couple months ago wanted to make lots of little cambions with you."

"I think I just barfed in my mouth." No really, I just might've.

Caleb looked back and forth between the two of us. "Incubi were visiting you?" he asked, alarmed.

Oliver waved him off. "Yep, they were trying to get in Gabrielle's nasty ol' granny panties."

"Oli-ver," I said, throwing a pen at him. Caleb looked disturbingly interested.

"Ow," Oliver said, rubbing his arm where the pen hit him, "you big skank-a-saurus. That hurt."

"Aww, did the wittle fairy get a wittle boo-boo?" I responded.

"Does the *wittle* siren want me to open a *wittle* can of whoop-ass? 'Cause I will," Oliver replied.

Caleb groaned, as our conversation devolved. "Not this again."

My eyes thinned as I studied Oliver. "How do you know so much about cambions?"

"Pillow talk." Oliver slapped a hand over his mouth as soon as the words were out.

My mouth dropped open.

"I don't think I want to be here," Caleb said.

"Did you ... ?" I blinked. "With an ... ?" No, he wouldn't, not with an incubus ...

Oliver's cheeks pinkened. "It's nothing." He laughed nervously.

Guilty, guilty, guilty.

"Oh my God, *Oliver!*" I said. "Those things want to steal your soul."

"Good thing he doesn't have one," Caleb muttered under his breath.

Oliver glared at him. "They are very misunderstood creatures."

I shook my head. "Forget I asked. Just ..." I shook my head again and shuddered.

"So, what sort of beings are cambions?" Caleb asked, steering the conversation back on track.

"They have the same powers as sirens, but they're different beings," Oliver said. "They can use glamour to get what they want."

"And what is it that they want?" Caleb asked.

Oliver shrugged, checking out his nails. "Beats the hell out of me. Probably the same things as everyone else— money, sex, power."

"But not love?" Caleb asked.

Oliver's eyes flicked up. He peered at Caleb through his lashes, a sardonic smile on his face. "Love? Now that would go against everything the Politia believes about dark creatures, wouldn't it?"

Caleb held his stare. "I don't agree with every belief the Politia holds."

"Hmm," was all Oliver said.

"The real question, we need to answer is this," I said. "Why would a cambion wish to kill rather than seduce?"

AFTER CALEB AND Oliver left, I grabbed the papers on dark creatures I'd Xeroxed back at Peel Academy and began flipping through them. My fingers paused when I reached the page on cambions.

Cambions, or Black Death Beings—named so after the song "Ring Around the Rosie" because they are said to smell like flowers and ash—are the children of incubi and humans.

Exceedingly rare, cambions are nonetheless dangerous creatures. Like their cousins, the sirens, cambions can use glamour to ensnare victims. However, like their parents and unlike sirens, cambions feed off of sexual acts to gain power.

Next to the writing was a woodcut image of an overtly sexual female, a rose in her hand and a snake curled at her feet.

Had there been any lingering doubt about the woman's identity, this had dissolved it.

We now knew the identity of one of our suspected killers, but what of the second one? The woman who stabbed me, the one who moved faster than a vampire—what was she?

And why would either of them kill? And why angels? I twisted Andre's ring round and around my finger, trying to divine the answer, but nothing came to me.

A shadow outside my window moved, catching my attention. I glanced up at the stormy scene outside and jolted in my seat when the shadow coalesced.

The devil had come to visit.

Chapter 15

I STOOD UP abruptly, the chair I sat in tipping over in my haste. I'd seen him plenty in my dreams, but the last time he'd appeared in the real world was on Samhain.

Evening, Gabrielle. His voice slithered along my skin. I forced my hands to stay at my sides though I desperately wanted to rub my arms.

Outside the snowstorm had become a full on blizzard, and in the midst of it the devil stood, his hands in the pockets of his dark gray suit, his hair perfectly coiffed. He would've looked magnificent if he wasn't so goddamned scary.

But can't the frightening also be magnificent? he asked, and I could hear the teasing note of his voice. That's how close the devil and I had gotten—he teased me now.

That and he read my mind.

I was so screwed.

"Get out of my head," I said, watching him. I noticed the snow pass right through him. *He's not really here. He's not really here*, I chanted to myself.

Oh, I can promise you that I am here, he said. *Would you like me to prove it?*

"No," I said too quickly.

He laughed, and the sound raised all the hairs along my arms. *You are delightful when you're frightened.*

"What do you want?" I asked.

To warn you.

I raised my eyebrows. "Since when do you care about my wellbeing?"

A slow smile spread across the devil's face. *Don't ask questions you don't want the answer to.*

I felt lightheaded from breathing too quickly. I put a hand to the windowsill to steady myself, and only then did I feel the tremors that ran up my arm.

I'd run if I were you.

"Why?" I asked. Any command given by the devil was one I should ignore, but morbid curiosity won out.

The word was barely out of my mouth when a car plowed into the parking lot. The devil grinned at me, and his image blew away just as the car drove straight through him.

I didn't do anything immediately, not until I saw the driver-side door open and a huge man step out of the car. A glint of fang caught my eye. That was all I needed to see.

The coven had learned of my existence, and now they'd come for me.

I turned from the window, letting my hair curtain over my face in case the vampire caught sight of me. Then I began moving. I slipped out of my room. The halls were quiet; most of the guests had already headed off to bed.

Behind me I heard the front door open. Now I began to run, throwing glances over my shoulder. At the end of the hall was a back door. I threw it open just as I heard a shout behind me.

Crap.

I sprinted out into the blizzard. Only once the fierce, icy wind hit me did I realize my critical mistake: I was much more vulnerable out here. Without a coat I couldn't last long, and the snowstorm obscured both my hearing and my vision.

Newly fallen snow crunched under my boots—thank God I'd had shoes on—as I ran. Even as I sprinted away from the inn I knew that it was only a matter of time before someone caught up to me—my footprints in the snow guaranteed that. If I wanted to shake these vampires, I was going to have to use my glamour.

The snow around me brightened as the inn's back door opened. I threw a glance over my shoulder and saw the vampire who'd exited his car moments before now gaze over the landscape. His eyes moved across the dark terrain until they landed on me. And then he smiled.

That was all the encouragement I needed to figure out a contingency plan. Andre, I needed to talk to Andre. I slipped my hands into my pockets and exhaled when I felt the bulge of my cellphone. Pulling it out, I speed dialed him.

He answered on the first ring. "Soul—"

"Vampire," I gasped out as I ran, "one's here, at the hotel. I don't know what he—"

A dark body slammed into me, and my phone went flying out of my hand. All at once my fear channeled itself into action. I rolled as I fell, landing on top of my assailant, my side pressed into his chest.

"Gabrielle!" I could hear Andre's tinny voice shout from my cellphone.

I yanked back my arm as far as I could and elbowed him in the nose. Something crunched, and he howled in pain. Just as I went to push myself to my feet, his arms latched around me, locking me to him and pinning my arms down at my sides.

I wiggled and my attacker grunted. I couldn't get my arms free, and if I couldn't get my arms free, I couldn't hold my own.

My skin began to shimmer and the siren surfaced. "Let me go," I said, my voice lilting.

Immediately my assailant's grip relaxed, and I pushed away from him. He got up, confused but still determined to take me.

"Don't touch me," I said. "Get back in your car and leave me. Forget this ever happened."

He turned his back to me, and with jerky movements he walked towards his car.

I sauntered over to my phone, calming my breathing, before I picked up my phone. I wiped the snow off on my shirt and put it to my ear. "The situation has been dealt with," I said, going for a light, casual tone. I didn't really pull it off.

"Gabrielle, are you okay?" Panic laced Andre's voice. I leaned against a tree, my body weak now that the adrenaline had left my system.

"I think so," I said, placing a hand to my heart as if the action could slow my pulse down. At the back of my mind one thought screamed for attention: why did the devil warn me? What interests did he have in my safety? Or had he known he'd provoke that entire situation by telling me?

Andre's voice cut through my thoughts. "Did he hurt you? Because if he did, trial be damned, I will rip him apart one limb at a time," he growled.

Yikes. For the millionth time I was grateful that I was Andre's soulmate and not someone else. Because he was a scary-ass dude when he wanted to be.

"Andre, I'm fi—"

For a split second a sharp pain flared at the back of my head, and I pitched forward.

And then the world went dark.

SOMEONE JOSTLED ME awake. I blinked my eyes open slowly as I was yanked out of a car. I stumbled as a wave of vertigo hit me and fell to the ground. The cold chill of snow bit into my cheek, and I went to cry out when I realized I couldn't.

Someone had duct taped my mouth shut. Bastards.

"Get up," a feminine voice ordered me.

I turned my head to look at who was speaking, but my eyes wouldn't focus.

"I think you hit her too hard, Vicca," a masculine voice said. The cold bite of his voice let me know that he didn't particularly care for my wellbeing; he was just stating a fact.

I made a noise at the back of my throat and rolled to my back. As soon as I did so, I regretted it. All of my weight pressed on my hands and arms, which had been bound behind me. I tugged against the restraints, but at the moment I was too weak to break through them, and my captors had done a thorough job of tying me up.

"I'm not a fucking errand boy," Vicca said. "If the other Elders wanted her to be treated gently, then they should've sent someone else to do this."

I shakily pushed myself to my feet, and then started to list to the left. What had they done to me?

A hand wrapped around my upper arm, and Vicca came into my line of sight. She was beautiful the way queens were—heavy lids, high eyebrows, a gracefully sloped nose, and understated lips that were, at the moment, curled into a snarl. Like my very presence upset her.

She yanked my arm roughly and dragged me forward with her. "You're being forcefully detained for repeatedly ignoring court summons," she informed me as she pulled me towards a paved stairway. The man who had chased after me now shadowed my other side. "And this evening you'll be expected to give your testimony for the events that occurred on the night of our king's birthday gala."

Oh man, so *this* was the coven's justice system? Andre really wasn't kidding about their cruelty.

I began to shiver in my damp clothes as we approached

a gothic style building. I felt energy thrum along my skin, and I drew in a relieved breath. Andre was somewhere nearby.

The skin at the back of my head prickled as my head injury stitched itself back together. Now that I flared my nostrils I could smell the tangy scent of blood caught in my tangled hair.

Almost as if he read my thoughts, the male vampire leaned towards me and breathed in my scent. His eyes fluttered and a smile tugged at the corners of his lips, as though the smell of it was ecstasy.

Okay, vampires were officially sickos. Andre and me excepted, of course.

The vampire's eyelids lifted and his smile widened, revealing his fangs. "You're lucky you're Andre's plaything," he said, "or else we'd be sipping that delicious blood of yours," he said.

I recoiled from him, my shoulder brushing against Vicca's side. Without letting me go, she shoved me away from her and straight into Psycho Vamp.

His ran a rough hand down my face, and I had to bite the inside of my cheek to keep it together. "I can smell the siren in your blood. Did you know it calls to us? Begs us to come closer?"

Ew, ew, ew.

"You bite her, and even I won't be able to save you from Andre," Vicca warned him.

He glowered at her. "I know that. I wasn't going to."

Vicca looked unconvinced, which made me really, really nervous.

It's going to be okay, I chanted to myself, mostly so that my pulse stayed calm. These beings could literally smell fear, and I didn't doubt they'd exploit that weakness if they could.

The male vampire drew away from me to open the door for Vicca, and she dragged me in after her. Just as the three of us stepped inside, Vicca's body went rigid. Behind me, my other captor stiffened.

I was the last to see what had startled the two vampires I was with, but I was now coherent enough to recognize the pulse of energy. Once my gaze met his, I smiled beneath the duct tape.

Waiting for us, arms crossed, was Andre.

Chapter 16

ANDRE DROPPED HIS arms and stalked towards us, all sinuous, rolling movement. The muscle in his cheek clenched
and unclenched.

Under normal circumstances Andre would've been at
my side in an instant, but this Andre ... he was calculating.
Guarded. None of his subjects knew we were soulmates,
and if these old, hardened vampires were to be conned,
Andre had to act entitled but not enamored.

Andre came to a stop in front of the three of us, and
his eyes flicked between my two captors. "You both better
have amazing explanations for why you kidnapped a fel-
low vampire, tied her up, and ..." His nostrils flared, and I
saw his entire body tense. He smelled my blood.

Andre's jaw worked, and for a moment I wasn't sure
whether our little charade was up—because I swear he

looked murderous. But he didn't lose control.

He calmly glanced between Vicca and the other vampire. "You drew blood," he stated, his voice pitched low.

My muscles tensed at his tone. Andre was one wrong comment away from snapping.

"She glamoured me," the male vampire said.

"I know what she did Fredrick; I was on the phone with her."

"Then you know—"

"*That it's against the law?*" The lines on Andre's face deepened with his anger. Oh Freddy had just poked a sleeping beast, and now it was awake.

Fredrick nodded uncertainly. Faster than a human eye could follow, Andre slammed the vampire against the wall and held him there by his throat. "Don't you fucking tell me what is against the law. *I am the law.*"

Fredrick choked out a nonsensical reply.

"What's that?" Andre asked, squeezing his throat so hard that his windpipe must be collapsing.

My breath caught at Andre's brutality. He was so good to me that I forgot that he was also a ruthless leader.

"Did I hear you mention the Politia?" he asked. Andre squeezed Fredrick's neck until the vampire nodded.

"Then you should know that the only reason you are not dead is because your *prisoner* prevented the Politia from dissolving our truce, you ungrateful fool."

When Andre's grip loosened, I assumed he was done. I assumed wrong.

So did Fredrick.

As soon as relief flooded Fredrick's features, Andre

threw him clear across the room. I cringed at the sound his body made—the meaty slap of skin when it met resistance, the sickening crack of splitting skin and breaking bones, the smell—the horrible smell—of blood. Stolen blood.

Vicca's hold on my arm slackened, though she didn't run. Either she didn't fear Andre's wrath, or she knew she couldn't escape it. I snuck a glance at her. Other than a small smile, her expression was unreadable.

Andre moved to where Fredrick lay crumpled. "And as for glamour, it is sanctioned when used in self-defense. Trust me when I say that I know it was in self-defense. I know the sound of fear when I hear it. But perhaps I am wrong. You could always remind me."

Andre pulled his foot back, and I cried out at the same time Fredrick whimpered. Well, I tried to anyway. My voice came out sounding more like a dying mummy.

Andre hesitated, glancing over his shoulder at me. Something in his eyes flashed. Guilt? Remorse? Whatever it was, it passed by too quickly, and then he was the vicious vampire king once more.

His leg, still poised to strike Fredrick, lowered as his gaze passed from me to Vicca. "Let her go," he commanded Vicca. The warmth I was so used to seeing in Andre's eyes had seeped away, leaving them cold and unfeeling. He was in control of himself once more, but at the cost of his emotions.

I tried not to shudder at the sight of him playing the undead, inhumane overlord. It was a horrible reminder that my soulmate was not a good person. At least, not always.

I felt Vicca's grip tighten and her nails bite into my skin—like she was considering defying him for a moment—but then she pulled her hand away.

"Why do you care about her so much?" she asked accusingly.

Andre looked down his nose at her, and his gaze bore into hers. "I do not owe you an explanation," he said, "and I will not be asked to defend myself." His voice took on a lethal edge. "You, however, owe me an explanation, smuggling Gabrielle here like a common thief," he growled.

For the first time since I'd laid eyes on her, Vicca lost her superiority. She looked chastised and, judging by the flash of her eyes, vulnerable.

He stepped away from where Fredrick lay moaning and approached her. "Vicca, Vicca, Vicca," he said, making her name sound like a reprimand. For the moment I was totally forgotten, though I got the sense that Andre was perfectly attuned to my presence. "What is an Elder like you doing fetching a witness?"

An Elder? That was the second time I'd heard that word this evening. I scoured my brain for its meaning, and then I remembered. The term referred to the vampires Andre himself had sired. My eyes shot to Vicca once more, and a hot, foreign emotion coursed through me. Jealousy.

I PUSHED THE petty emotion down, though it wasn't one to be easily ignored. Who cared if my soulmate screwed this chick an eon ago, and then changed her so that she could be his special friend forever and ever?

I felt my fangs drop and the siren pulse angrily just beneath my skin. Okay, I was a liar on top of everything else. I wanted to rip this woman to shreds. And then Andre, because I was an equal opportunist like that.

Andre's eyes flicked to mine, and I belatedly realized that he could smell the change in my mood. I wish I could telepathically send him my immense displeasure.

"She's not just *a* witness," Vicca hissed, oblivious to my primal urge to wipe her from the face of the earth. "She is the only living witness to what happened. One who has avoided our summons for months. We need her testimony before we can sentence you."

My attention snapped to what Vicca was saying. Testimony? Sentencing? This was bad. What I'd seen the night of Andre's birthday ... it wouldn't help his case. Not only had Andre gone psycho, he'd killed in my name. Me, the girl who was destined to lead some awful vampire genocide. I'd end up dead, and who knew what horrible fate would befall Andre.

"She was unconscious when it happened," Andre lied, and I breathed a sigh of relief. I now had my cover story.

Andre walked over to me, his eyes softening. My own probably held a strange cocktail of panic, anger, and fear. "Now," he said, "I am going to remove Gabrielle's bindings and take her in myself. You'd do well to leave this room before I decide to punish you the same way I did Fredrick."

She didn't need more encouragement. In an instant she was gone.

"You too," Andre said, his gaze never leaving mine.

I could hear joints popping and an agonized groan as Fredrick pushed himself up.

"We will be in the courtroom in a few minutes," Andre said. "Warn the rest of the coven that if anyone so much as considers checking in on us, they will regret it. I am not in a good mood."

Fredrick made some meek noise and bowed—bowed—to Andre's back before scurrying out of the room.

Once we were alone, Andre ripped the duct tape from my lips.

"*Fuck,*" I gasped out from the pain. I glared at Andre. "Did you have to rip it off so—"

He silenced me with a kiss. Only now that we were alone did he finally drop the façade. I felt the way his hands trembled as they caressed my cheeks. His lips brushed against mine in an apology.

He broke off the kiss and leaned his head against mine. "I am so sorry. So, so sorry." He swept the hair off my face and held my jaw in his hands before his gaze drifted to my bound arms. One second he stared at them, and in the next he was ripping them off.

As soon as the tape was removed, Andre came back around to face me. "We don't have much time. This is what you need to know: When I entered Bishopcourt the night of my birthday gala, you were fleeing Theodore, who was trying to kill you."

I nodded. That was so far the truth. "Why was he trying to kill me?" I asked, keeping my voice hushed in case any vampires were trying to eavesdrop.

"He thought you were unnatural—an abomination."

I swallowed. Hearing Andre say those words hurt, even though I knew it was just the cover story.

Sensing my mood, Andre tipped my chin up and gave me a lingering kiss. When he spoke again, he was all business. "Theodore raised the gun, I tackled you, and when you went down you cracked your head against the stairs, which knocked you out until I picked you up."

"So I remember nothing of what you did to Theodore or your motives," I said.

"Correct. Stick to that story, or else," Andre said, his expression dark.

"Or else what?"

"Or else they'll try to make you an accessory to murder. If that happens, you'll be convicted and sentenced to the highest punishment."

Death. But not just death. That was not only what waited for me. Damnation and an unholy reunion with the devil. My breath stilled even as my heart galloped.

Andre placed a hand on my chest, as though that action might slow down my racing heart. "I never wanted this to happen," he said hoarsely.

I forced myself to breathe and pushed down my terror. "I'll stick to the story."

"Good," he said, "because I don't think I could survive the alternative."

Our gazes met, held, and then like magnets we came together, our bodies flush. Our lips met and our breath mingled. Only here, wrapped in Andre's arms did I feel like all was right in the world. It was a beautiful illusion, but I wrapped the fantasy around me and reveled in it.

An image of Vicca entered my mind, and the illusion shattered. I pushed Andre away roughly. "You and Vicca ... ?"

Andre's brows pulled together. "What is it, Gabrielle?"

But I couldn't finish my train of thought because even though I was jealous and hurt, I was embarrassed that I felt this way at all.

I saw the moment Andre put it together. His eyebrows shot up and his eyes widened. "Are you ... *jealous* of her?" Andre's lips twitched as he spoke the last word, and when I narrowed my eyes at him, his mouth drew up into an amused smile.

"You're *happy*?" I asked, disbelief coating my words.

He gave a small bark of laughter and ran a hand through his hair. "It's about time I'm not the only one in this relationship to get jealous."

Fair point, but this was different. "Andre, you *turned* her," I tried to explain. "Clearly that relationship was meaningful enough to want her by your side forever." Those words shredded my throat coming out.

He stepped in closer. "You're right," he admitted. It felt like a knife to my chest. "A long time ago I met a beguiling woman named Vicca, and I fell in love."

I swallowed down the thick knot at the back of my throat.

Andre's face got a faraway look to it. "At least I thought I had," he said. "Lust, attraction, romance—all are heady drugs, but like all drugs, they wear off." His gaze refocused on me. "And when they inevitably did, I realized that I didn't love her—not true love, the kind that makes you the best version of yourself."

Andre glanced at the door. Our private moment was almost over, and not even the king of the vampires could stall his trial much longer.

"I'd never felt true love," he said, looking back at me. "Not until you. In seven hundred years, I'd never gazed at someone and felt this bone-deep ache the way I do when I look at you. Like the other half of my bruised soul lies beneath your skin. And it's more than everything I'd ever hoped for. It's finding my humanity. It's living for the first time. It's ... redemption." He drew the words out, and they lingered in the air between us.

The tips of his fingers grazed my cheek, and I glanced at the ground, bashful now that he'd reassured me of his love.

"It's always been you Gabrielle, even before you existed. And long after our bodies have turned to dust it will still be you. It will always, *always* be you."

Chapter 17

A TENTATIVE KNOCK interrupted us, and so caught up in the moment, I jolted at the sound. Andre sighed and took my hand. "Our time's up. Are you ready for this?"

No, not at all, but it wasn't like I had any other good options. I'd already decided to stay in Romania and risk this exact situation. As the saying went, I'd made my bed, and now I was going to have to sleep in it.

I took a deep breath. "Let's get this over with."

Together we crossed the entrance hall, and Andre pulled open one of the two solid oak doors and ushered me in.

I didn't know what I was expecting on the other side, but it was something along the lines of a lot of crimson and black furniture, corsets, candelabras, and maybe even some spider webs. So the gilded murals and finely pressed business suits threw me. It was almost disappointing.

At least the vampires were real. They were all unnaturally still as we entered, making it appear as though someone pressed pause on time.

I saw some of their nostrils flare as they breathed my scent in. What were they scenting? My emotions, or how just how human I was?

I gazed around the room. It was set up like the courtrooms I'd seen on TV, except instead of a single judge, there was a row of them.

"The Elders," Andre whispered into my ear.

Sure enough, Vicca sat up there, her expression stoic, though I could've sworn she had an evil glint to her eyes.

Up until several months ago, Theodore would've been among them, and roughly a decade ago so would have my father. It was a strange and sobering thought.

A vampire stepped up to us. "Miss Fiori," he said, giving me a slight bow, "the Elders have generously rearranged today's schedule so that you can give your testimony as the first order of business."

Generously. I wanted to snort at that. My guess was that the schedule had been rearranged so that they could snatch me, get my testimony, and return me before Andre was made aware of the situation. And if they had, then my testimony would've been inconsistent with Andre's. We'd have both been screwed.

"I was kidnapped, and now you want me to testify?" I raised my eyebrows and gazed at the sea of vampires. Their expressions remained passive.

"As a member of this coven, it is your duty to testify

before our court, something you've managed to evade up until now." As if he couldn't help himself, the vampire snuck a sly glance at Andre. I guess there was no mistaking exactly who was responsible for my absence in court. Funny how I, and not Andre, was still getting punished for it.

"I am here on an official investigation for the Politia," I said. "My primary allegiance during this time is to them."

Now *that* statement got a reaction. The sound of hisses echoed throughout the courtroom.

"Blasphemy," someone whispered. That was cute, coming from a vampire.

Another whispered, "Why does he let her get away with this heresy?"

Someone responded, "He won't. He never does."

One of the Elders spoke up. "Enough stalling. Gabrielle Fiori, daughter of the late Santiago Fiori, tonight you will answer the court's questions. Once you do so, you will be allowed to leave and return to your *investigation*." His voice dripped with disdain.

The Elder's eyes moved to Andre. "Sire, I trust you will not stand in the way of these proceedings though this young vampire means something to you?"

Andre stared at the Elder for a long moment before inclining his head. "You have my word."

Well hell, I was in for a long night.

"PLEASE FOLLOW ME to the stand," said the vampire standing next to me.

I glanced at Andre, who stared at the vampire until he

fidgeted, before inclining his head. Andre may be the defendant in this trial, but there was no mistaking that he was still in charge.

He released my hand, and I followed the vampire up to the stand, a strange sort of disbelief settling over me. This was really happening. I'd been kidnapped and now, rather than reporting the incident, I was testifying. Vampires had a majorly screwed up justice system.

At my back I could feel Andre's comforting presence. It was the one silver lining of the whole situation.

As I sat down and faced the pale, expressionless audience, I made a promise to myself: I would not screw this up.

"Why would Theodore want to kill you?"

I stared down at my twisted hands. "He thought I was unnatural."

"And why would he think that?"

I'd already explained this to the other lawyer—don't even get me started on the strangeness of vampiric lawyers—but now the other side was cross-examining me, looking for holes in my story.

I drew my gaze up and gave the male vampire a sharp look. "I don't know." I bit back a longer response. The less they could get out of me, the likelier I was to pull this off.

"Surely you have an idea?" he prodded.

"Objection," the other lawyer said.

"Overruled," one of the bored Elders said.

In the courtroom beyond him, Andre controlled his expression, but every once in a while I glimpsed the muscle in his cheek feathering.

My attention returned to the lawyer. "You've been a vampire longer than I have, you tell me."

That didn't sit well with him. His eyes thinned, but he moved on.

"So walk us through what happened during that period of time you were alone in Theodore's presence."

I did, explaining how he divulged his attempts in the past to kill me, and how he tried again that evening but was thwarted when I used glamour on him. While I spoke, I stole a glance at the Elders. Several of them were scenting the air, and I realized they were gaging how anxious I was when I spoke. They wanted to smell whether I told the truth.

"And what happened once you escaped?" the vampire asked once I finished.

"I ran out of the room and down the stairs, and that's when I saw Andre. Behind me Theodore had pulled out a gun and aimed it at me. When he saw the gun, Andre tackled me. I slammed my head against the staircase, and the impact knocked me out."

The lawyer's nostrils flared, and I inwardly cursed. He could smell *something*. I didn't dare look at the Elders for fear that they too would scent the lie.

The lawyer took a step closer, an excited spark to his eyes, and I almost jumped at the movement. I was spooking myself, but it didn't matter. I could feel my cheeks heating up, and I knew that if no one had noticed before that I was lying, now they would.

"The reports filed never mentioned you having a head injury," the lawyer stated.

I opened my mouth and paused. Panic rose within me. Andre and I hadn't gone over this. *I don't know the answer. I don't know the answer.*

I took a steadying breath and collected myself once more. I'd always heard that what made a lie believable was staying as close to the truth as possible. "They wouldn't have since it had already healed."

"And how fast would you say the injury took to heal?"

I shrugged. "I have no idea. I was a bit distracted that evening."

"Strange that you were unconscious precisely during the time that Andre killed Theodore—what was that, several minutes? Yet your injury healed so quickly once you woke that it went undocumented—"

Andre's lawyer jumped to his feet. "Objection! The prosecution is insinuating that the witness is making false claims."

"Sustained," and Elder said.

The lawyer still had an excited spark to his eyes, like a shark scenting blood. Or a vampire. He continued to question me for what felt like an eternity but was probably only another twenty or thirty minutes.

I adamantly stuck to the story that Andre had fed me. Thank goodness for that too, since I'd seen some of the audience's eyes flicker with anger and morbid fascination. I had the distinct impression that they wouldn't mind me dead, vampire or not. But through it all was the lingering worry that the Elders and the prosecution had literally sniffed out the lies in my story.

Eventually my testimony came to a close, and the trial was adjourned for the rest of the evening due to the bad weather conditions. Imagine that—they had just enough time to get my testimony, but nothing else.

Sneaky didn't even begin to cover it.

I was led from the stand to where Andre waited for me. The skin around his eyes was tight with tension. He draped an arm around my waist and placed a kiss along my temple. A few eyebrows went up, and I had to suppress a smile. I guess they were surprised that the big bad vampire king would show affection to his little pet.

But the gesture was more than just some casual PDA. Andre was warning his subjects to tread lightly when it came to me since I was a current favorite.

"Gabrielle Fiori," a voice rang out above the commotion. I turned and met Vicca's gaze. Her eyes dropped to where Andre's arm draped around my waist, "stay close for the remainder of the trial. We don't want to have to detain you again if we need to call you in for further questioning."

"Further questioning?" I thought this was it.

Her gaze drifted up from Andre's arm to me, and the smile she flashed was predatory. "Don't think your role in this is over."

I DIDN'T LET my guard down until Andre and I sat safely in his car, and the courtroom was far behind us.

"I think they know," I finally whispered, my voice cracking.

His hands tightened on the wheel. "They can't prove anything based on the way you smell," Andre said, staring at the road.

"So you smelled it?"

His mouth thinned, and he gave me a jerky nod.

"That's what I thought," I said softly, glancing at the storm raging outside. I raised my eyebrows. "Should we be driving in this weather?"

"No, but I wasn't going to leave you there at the mercy of the coven."

I swiveled my head and studied his profile. "Thank you."

He clenched his jaw. "You should not be thanking me. They kidnapped you, and I couldn't do a damn thing about it."

The corners of my mouth drew downwards. "Kidnapping doesn't seem so harsh compared to some of the violence the coven's used to." The memory of Andre squeezing Freddy's throat played out in my mind.

Andre looked over at me, and he squinted his eyes. "I'm not a good person," he said, reading between the lines. "None of us vampires really are."

"You're good to me." Even I recognized that was a bit of a booby prize. I mean, I was his soulmate. It'd be strange if he *didn't* treat me well.

Andre turned to look at me, his features warming, and he gave me a small smile. "You are the light of my existence."

Ironic that he was finding his humanity at the same

time I was losing mine. Or maybe it wasn't ironic at all.

We road in silence after that, until the car came to a halt in front of a beautiful but unfamiliar building.

"Where are we?" I asked.

Andre turned off the ignition and turned to face me. "My home."

My brows drew together. "Your home?" I repeated, confused. I didn't know whether I should feel annoyance that he hadn't told me we were making a pit stop or excitement to see what was probably Andre's oldest and dearest home.

I rubbed my eyes. "Andre I want to see your place, but I have to get back."

"You misunderstand," he said, reaching out and tucking a lock of hair behind my ear. "I'm asking you to stay here."

I drew back and searched his features. "You're not asking me anything," I stated. This wasn't a request. This was a coup.

His expression turned protective. "Please, Gabrielle, go along with this. I can't have my coven snatching you again while I'm unaware."

"Andre—"

"You have to trust me that I know my people."

"How about instead of trust, you keep me informed?" I asked.

He palmed the side of my face. "You're a teenager Gabrielle, and you are the love of my life. I want you to be safe, happy, carefree. I want to keep the darkness that surrounds us both at bay as much as possible. You deserve that."

Damn him. When he put it like that, it was hard to feel indignant. And boy did I want to feel indignant.

"But Andre, I have a case to solve, and my friends—"

"Arrangements have already been made."

I opened my mouth and closed it. "*What?*" I finally said.

"Someone will be bringing your things and your friends as soon as the storm lets up."

I pushed my hands through my hair. What he said made sense, so why did this bother me so much?

Because you're being treated like a precious flower. A delicate, fragile flower that's easily crushed.

"No," said, making up my mind.

Andre's eyes flashed. "Gabrielle ..."

"Take me back to the inn."

Andre's eyes slitted. "No."

"Yes," I said, staring him down.

"Arguing is not going to change my mind."

I knew it wasn't, and I didn't want to waste the effort on arguing when I had glamour.

My skin began to glow, and I opened my mouth. "Andre, take me—"

Before I could finish the order, Andre leaned across the consul, tipped my chin back, and kissed me roughly.

The siren practically squealed with pleasure. Damn her. I moaned against Andre's lips as my skin flared. Encouraged, he cradled the back of my head and deepened the kiss. I felt his tongue brush against mine, and warmth spread throughout my stomach.

He broke away and, lust drunk, I didn't realize he'd left

the car until he was opening my door and pulling me out. I touched my tender lips, dazed. But just as the siren in me began to ebb away, Andre removed my hand from my mouth and resumed the kiss.

He picked me up and, lost in him, I wrapped my legs around his waist as he carried me. I threaded my fingers through his hair and drew away long enough to drink in his beauty.

Dark, expressive eyes stared back at me, and right now they looked ... remorseful. Using my thumb I touched the skin at the corner of one of his eyes. "Why do you look so sad?" I asked. My voice no longer sounded like my own. The rich melody that came out of my mouth was pitched both lower and higher. It had layers to it; it made words music.

He swallowed. "Don't concern yourself, soulmate," he said, his words laced with regret.

My eyes moved between his. "But I want to." I ran my tongue over my fangs. I hadn't noticed them drop down, but now that I did, my gaze dropped to his neck. No pulse stirred, but I knew blood lay beneath, and that excited me.

He sighed. "I cannot win. I do not know how," he said.

I kissed his cheek. "Win what?" I asked. The siren shrank away some as worry replaced lust.

"A battle involving you and fate," Andre said, moving us down a hall.

I frowned. He wasn't usually so cryptic.

Andre brushed his palm against my temple. "Instead I help fate along and push you away."

My brows pinched down. This talk was killing my lusty

buzz. Making a small noise, I pressed my lips to Andre's and moved against him. I smiled against his mouth as I felt his grip tighten and his body tense. And then we were lost in the kiss once more. At the back of my mind I knew I was forgetting something important.

He pressed me against the wall, and I practically purred with pleasure.

Andre broke off the kiss and bowed his head. "I can't do this." He sounded defeated.

Why were we talking again?

I ran a hand through his hair, and he turned his cheek into it, kissing my palm. "Damnit," he whispered, "I really can't do this."

Reluctantly he extricated himself from my embrace. I wanted to cry out. "Why—?" I began.

He pressed a chaste kiss to my lips. "I'm ... sorry. For not listening to you earlier."

I cocked my head as he took my hand and led me through the house—his house. "What are you talking about?"

"I order people around for a living," he said. "Getting my way has become a habit."

I blinked a few times, that niggling thought finally coming to me. "Did you just ... manipulate me into staying with you?"

"I tried."

Hurt and betrayal bubbled up. "How could you?"

He gave me a pained look. "I couldn't. Not in the end."

And he didn't. I'd give him that. But now I was pissed that I'd been played so easily. "Take me back," I whispered.

Andre's jaw worked, but he nodded.

As we got in the car and began the drive back, a thousand thoughts swirled through me. First I pieced together Andre's plan—distract me and get me inside his house. Anger and betrayal flared hot within me at this, but as my mind drifted, less welcome thoughts entered.

Like the fact that I'd been about to use glamour to force Andre to take me back to the inn. Technically I'd been just as willing to manipulate him as he had been me. Only he'd stopped himself. I doubted that I would've. And I doubted I would've felt remorseful afterwards. Did that make me the worse of the two of us?

Feeling the car slide through the snow, I wondered just how stupid my decision to return to the inn had been. We could only see a few feet in front of us and the car was losing traction often enough to set me on edge. Would Andre be able to make it back okay?

While I thought about it, why *was* it important to stay at the inn if I might get kidnapped again by my coven? Before this evening, I would've jumped at the chance to stay over at Andre's place.

"This was a mistake," I whispered.

Andre glanced over at me. "What's a mistake?"

This. Being out here on the road. I'd been hurt, so I'd made a stupid, rash decision. One I already regretted. I sucked in a breath to say exactly this, but I never got a chance.

It happened in an instant. Movement outside caught my eye. To the left of the car a shadow deeper than the darkness flashed, coming straight for us. My throat seized up and my eyes widened as I tried to process what I was seeing. The shadow looked at me—looked at me and smiled. Impossible, but true.

"What the—?" Andre's words cut off as the thing slammed into the car.

My hair whipped across my face and my head snapped back at the impact. Andre threw his arm out to brace me. The sickening sound of crunching metal cut through the silent night and the car spun.

The darkness blurred as the car skated over the slick road. Next to me, Andre unbuckled the seatbelt and vaulted over the consul. I felt the brush of his legs and torso as he covered my body with his own.

The wall of a nearby building rose up outside my window; the car was headed straight towards it.

Our eyes met. I'd like to say that all sorts of sweet, unspoken things passed between us in that moment, but I'd be lying. I only had time to process that we were both about to be in a lot of pain before metal met stone.

The force of the collision threw my body into Andre's, and his into the wall. The screech of more crumpling metal played in the background like a gruesome soundtrack.

My head slipped past Andre's shoulder and rammed against something solid. I barely heard the sickening crack of it before the world blacked out.

Chapter 18

I FOUND MYSELF staring at a fireplace, a strange sense of déjà vu settling over me. In the distance I heard a roar, followed by an agonized scream.

Then silence.

I rotated around, and as I did so, the room's details came into focus. The portraits, the map made of human skin, the chair with the same disturbing carpet.

The unholy chill.

I was back inside the castle of the damned. I dragged a hand to my mouth and staggered back as a familiar form stepped into the doorway.

"Hello consort."

I SHRIEKED BEFORE I could help it, and the devil frowned. "As much as your reactions amuse me, they annoy me more," he said, entering the room.

I scrambled behind a velvet couch sprinkled with blood splatter. Already I was beginning to feel the choking sensation of evil. It twisted around my insides, seizing me up. "Am I dead?" I asked, white-knuckling the back of the couch.

A corner of his lips turned up. "More or less."

I let out a strangled sound and felt myself deflate. "You did this, didn't you?" I accused.

He arched an eyebrow and perched on the edge of the soiled chair. "No, I'm afraid I can't claim this victory—though it was a paltry effort on the part of Argipifex. He will be punished accordingly."

Paltry effort? I was in the devil's clutches at the moment.

"Now," his eyes raked over my body, "come to me. I wish to show you the rest of the house."

My eyes darted to the entrance of the room. Beyond it lay the front door. I didn't want to move further into the house. I wanted *out*.

Noticing what had drawn my attention, the devil pushed away from the chair and took a menacing step forward. "If you want to be difficult, I so can I."

I pushed down my terror and drew on my courage. "Better be careful—I bite."

Something hot and desirous flashed through his eyes. "Yes, I look forward to seeing those fangs up close."

Ewww. Not the reaction I wanted.

I shifted my weight. "Stay away from me if you don't want to end up impaled again."

The mask the devil wore dropped away, and rage contorted his features. Oh boy, I'd hit a nerve. "Do not speak of that night if you wish to avoid my wrath."

How could I have ever thought him handsome? Cruelty drew itself into every facet of his face.

The devil fixed his features. "Tell me little bird, do I please you now?" he asked. He emphasized his question with a charming smile.

"Stop reading my thoughts."

"The good boy look always did make the ladies' break." He smoothed his hair down. "Not that it matters," he said. "You can think me an ugly thing, and it will not change your fate. But—"

I blinked and he stood before me. Panic seized up my muscles. My body quaked in his presence.

He picked up my hand and pushed back the sleeve, exposing the pale skin of my forearm. Everywhere his hand touched, I felt something intangible wither away.

"—knowing you desire me will make you more delicious to devour," he finished.

My trembling increased, and the room turned pink as tears gathered. One slipped out and trailed down the side of my face. Damnit, I was *not* meek.

I steeled myself and yanked my hand away. "I will never agree to your demands. I didn't the last time you asked, and I won't now."

He grabbed my jaw and squeezed it. "You will once every last thing you care about has been stripped away from you. Everyone and everything save for me."

"What makes you think I care about you?"

He smiled at me, the soft light of the fire making his teeth look sharp and his grin vicious. "You know so very little about yourself."

I tried to step away from his grasp, but he wouldn't let go of his hold on me.

"Let go," I said. The command came out more like a whimper.

"You cannot escape this. You cannot escape me. You're mine, Gabrielle. Mine."

"Why?" I whispered. It was the same question I'd asked during Samhain. Why had the devil taken an unusual interest in me.

The smell of brimstone rose, and fire seemed to dance at the back of his eyes. I thought he was going to hurt me, but instead he pulled my face closer to his, close enough that I could tell he didn't have pores—and why would he? He wasn't human.

"Fate, consort," he said. "You are fated to be mine."

I GASPED, SUCKING in frigid air.

"*Gabrielle.*" Panic laced Andre's normally steady voice. I felt his feather-light touch against my cheek. The trail of his fingertips was too soft; he touched me as though I were breakable. Or already broken.

My eyes fluttered open, and I found myself cradled in Andre's arms. His dark eyes stared back down at me, wide with fear and worry. Blood smeared his face and soaked his shirt. I breathed in the metallic tang of it. It was everywhere.

He let out a shaky breath. A bloody tear snaked down his eye, and he used his shoulder to wipe it away. Still carefully clutching me, he bent down, placing an ear against my chest.

"Andre?" I reached out and touched his face, disoriented.

He drew his head away from my chest, his expression slightly less panicked.

"I'm here. We were in an accident, and you were badly injured." Again, the feather-light touch, this time to push away a stray strand of hair. I noticed how his hand shook. The gesture reminded me that my own body had shook moments before ...

The devil. Fate. Hell.

Oh boy, I was screwed.

I SQUIRMED IN Andre's arms, ignoring the searing pain as I jostled my injuries.

Andre's grip tightened. "Try not to move. You're still badly hurt."

My eyes darted about, my breathing coming in quick, misty bursts.

"It's okay Gabrielle, you're okay." Andre's voice pulled my attention back to him.

"I'm not, Andre." I began to tremble all over again. "I'm not."

"What has you so spooked, soulmate?"

"He took me," I said, my eyes darting over Andre's face.

"Who?"

"The devil."

Andre froze. "You mean while you were unconscious?"

"Yes."

"Has he ever done that before?"

"Never." Not while I'd been unconscious. The devil was growing bolder and my own situation more dire.

A muscle ticked in Andre's jaw, and his muscles tensed beneath me. "It's getting worse."

"I know." I pushed myself up, swatting Andre's arms away when he tried to stop me. "Ugh, I feel like hell," I mumbled, rubbing my eyes with my palms. I only managed to smear blood and grit around. "And considering that I've practically visited the place, that's saying something."

"We spun out, and you cracked your head open," he said. "I was so scared that ..." He trailed off, unwilling to finish that thought.

My eyes lifted and I took in the crumpled remains of the car. It looked like a third of the car had been lopped off. The third I'd been sitting in.

My gaze snapped back to Andre, who was also covered in blood. "Are you okay?" I asked. My eyes scoured over him. His skin was paler than it should be. "How much blood did you lose?"

"Don't concern yourself with me."

"You're not the only one who's allowed to go into panic mode," I said, running my hands over his arms.

"I do not panic," he said, affronted.

Ignoring him, I trailed my hands over his back. It was soaked. I'm sure if I looked, it'd be crimson colored.

I cursed. "Andre—"

"The wounds have already healed," he said, gently removing my hand from his back. "We need to get moving if we don't want to explain to the mortal police how we survived that crash uninjured."

My gaze moved up. It seemed we'd already attracted plenty of attention. Lights had turned on in some of the nearby buildings, and faces peered down at us. No one, however, had decided to weather the storm. Judging by the very faint sound of sirens, even the ambulances were having a hard time of it.

"What about the car?"

Andre smiled. "The car won't nark on us either."

I rolled my eyes. "Andre ..."

His lips wavered, then spread into a cheeky grin. "I'll take care of it. Right now, let me worry about you."

Andre stood up and helped me to my feet. I teetered, feeling off balance. Next to me Andre swore and scooped me up, pinning me against his chest.

"I can walk," I insisted.

"I know you can, soulmate."

I didn't press the issue any more than that, mostly because I still felt like a piñata that had been beaten within an inch of its life. Andre whispered soothingly to me in Romanian.

I rubbed my head. "That's the second time tonight I got hit in the head. I think I've killed off all of my brain cells."

The murmuring stopped, and I felt Andre's soft lips brush against my temple. Then it began up again. "It seems there's a growing list of dead men walking."

Andre glanced beyond me into the darkness, his eyes searching. I could see the menace drawn across his features. Andre was a string pulled too taut. He would snap soon, and it wouldn't be pretty for whoever or whatever came in his way. "I will find out who did this, and I will relish their agonized screams."

"You're not going to find him," I said, locking my jaw to keep my teeth from chattering.

"*Him?*"

"Or it—I don't know the Underworld's gender rules. The thing that attacked us was a demon. Argipifex," I said.

"How do you know the demon's name?" Andre asked, his boots crunching in the snow.

"The devil told me."

"The devil told you," he repeated.

I pushed my lips together and nodded.

Andre worked his jaw, but managed to push down his emotions. "Did he hurt you?" Andre asked, his eyes glinting. He looked unreal, my vengeful, raven-haired king, ready to do battle with hell itself on this snowy night.

I reached up and dusted the snow off of his hair. It was just an excuse to touch him. "No," I said.

Relief flowed into Andre's features. "Good," he said, caressing my cheek. "Now, tuck your face and hands into my chest, soulmate."

"Um, why?" I asked, my teeth beginning to chatter.

"Because I'm taking you back to my place on foot, and you'll get severely wind burned if you don't protect your exposed skin."

Ah. I was getting a supernatural piggyback ride. Sort of. In another situation this might've been kind of awesome. But right now, injured and in a blizzard, it sucked big time.

I turned my head and hands in. Andre rearranged his grip to protect me from the wind as much as possible.

"Ready?" he breathed.

I nodded against him.

He tightened his hold and took off. The force of his speed plastered me against him, and the wind howled in my ear. Going this fast, the cold felt like a knife, cutting through my thin layer of clothes and slicing my skin.

Luckily I was a supernatural. I didn't think a human could endure this without permanent damage. But I would. At least I hoped so. If not I was definitely haunting Argipifex's ass. That little bastard would pay for killing me in the most miserable way possible.

Soon the cold numbed the bite from my skin. My eyes began to close when Andre slowed down. He shifted his grip, and I heard the click of a door opening and felt a delicious blast of heat.

"Stoke the fire and start up a hot bath," Andre called out to his staff as he walked us in, slamming the door shut behind him.

I caught elusive glimpses of my soulmate's house as he carried me through it for a second time, but like last time, I was too distracted to pay much attention to my surroundings.

"I'm sorry," I murmured. My words slurred since I couldn't feel my lips.

"Sorry about what?" Andre asked as he carried me up a flight of stairs.

"Insisting you drive me back."

Andre glanced down at me, frowning at my mouth. "Soulmate, I am the one who's sorry. I never should've put you in that position."

We entered what must've been the master suite. Andre's quarters. As the heat began to thaw my skin, I noticed that Andre seemed a bit shaky, his strength not quite so inhuman.

"Andre, put me down," I said gently, even though my legs were so numb I'd probably trip over them trying to walk.

He gazed down at me, worry creasing his features. "I will, my life, just give me a moment."

We moved through his bedroom, and I heard the sound of running water. As soon as we entered his bathroom, the pounding sound of it surrounded me. Like a shadow, Andre's staff ghosted out of the room, closing the door behind them.

Andre walked us right into an enormous Jacuzzi tub, the kind that could easily fit several people.

Andre's brow furrowed. "This is not necessarily going to feel good."

That was all the warning I got before Andre knelt, submerging my body into the water.

I hissed between my teeth as the extreme temperature change stung my skin. The warm water swirled around us, turning a murky scarlet as blood and dirt mixed with it.

I shook out my arms and legs, and the burning sensation worsened. It took a lot of self-control on my part not to string together a pretty line of curse words.

The sentiment must've shown in my expression, since Andre gazed at me pityingly. "I hate to tell you this, soulmate, but this is only mildly warm water."

"How c-can you t-tell?" I chattered, even as warmth seeped into me.

Andre nodded to the faucet handles. Water still poured out of the faucet. "The way they're angled."

Even as he said this, he bent over and cranked one of the faucets. I yelped when, a second later, scalding hot water brushed the skin of my leg.

I narrowed my eyes at him. "That was just mean."

His mouth twitched. "I told you I wasn't a good guy." He said this even as he removed one of my boots, and then the other. He shrugged off his coat, and I gasped as he bent down to continue his work.

His head snapped up, his gaze locking on mine. "Is your ankle injured?" he asked, assuming I'd made the noise out of pain.

"Your back ..." I said, horrified. I reached out to touch the crimson stain that covered most of his back. It was so much bigger than I'd assumed when I felt it back at the site of our accident. How much blood had he lost?

Andre's eyebrows rose in understanding, and in the next instant he ripped the shirt off and tossed it over his shoulder. The skin beneath his shirt was smooth. Whatever wound was once there had already healed over.

Silver lining of the evening: shirtless Andre made an appearance. I could die a happy siren-beast.

Andre peeled away one of my socks and began to rub my feet, snapping my attention away from his sculpted torso. I tried to pull my foot away, but he held it hostage.

"No," he said, and I heard a growl in his voice, "you are not going to be difficult about this."

"Bossy much?"

"I'm a king," he said. "It comes with the territory."

After he finished rubbing one foot, he moved on to the other.

"Andre," I started again, "you lost a lot of blood."

A reluctant smile tugged at his lips. "I'm going to be fine, soulmate." His face darkened up when his eyes moved back to me. "You, on the other hand, are still quite mortal," he said, "and even though you make blue skin lovely, it's not a good look for you."

He got a splash for that.

"How come blood doesn't seem to bother you?" I asked when he placed my foot back into the water. We were in a pool of it, yet he acted just as disinterested in it as I felt.

"I'm over seven hundred years old," he said. "I've had plenty of time to learn how to manage my needs." He picked up one of my hands and massaged warmth back into it.

"Plus," he said, his gaze moving up to meet mine, "true, crazed bloodlust only happened to junkies, and those vampires were weeded out long ago."

"Oh." Another pop culture myth debunked.

My skin tingled where Andre's deft fingers touched it, my first indication that I was getting better. He placed my hand back into the water and reached over to grasp my hips.

I sucked in air at his touch. I could be frozen over, a step away from death, and yet his touch still brought me back to life.

Andre's eyes moved to mine, and I felt the soft stroke of his thumbs against my skin. He threw a leg over my own, so that my torso was imprisoned between his thighs. With a sly grin he picked up my other hand and began rubbing blood back into it while I shamelessly ogled him.

My gaze traveled up Andre's sculpted chest, which was much too tan considering that he lived in darkness. My eyes scoured over the chiseled bands of muscle that roped around his arms.

Andre paused in his work. He gazed down at my hand, his nostrils flaring, and I felt his body tense.

"What?" I asked. That one word came out breathless and flustered.

Molten eyes met mine. "Your scent ..." Almost as if he couldn't help himself he leaned in, his lips skimming my throat. That live wire between us flared, electrifying my skin.

I turned my head so that my own mouth dipped near his hairline. I breathed in Andre's spicy scent and blinked when I realized it was his pheromones. They must be pouring off of him. The scent had my skin glowing pale, golden light.

Andre drew back, and I saw barely contained lust behind his eyes. He closed them and took in a shaky breath. "It is so damn hard to keep my hands off of you, even now, when you're recovering from injuries."

His words sent a bolt of heat through me. A few more lusty looks and some sexy talk from him would have me sweating soon.

I lounged back, leaning my head against the rim of the tub. "Then don't." Despite my glowing skin, that wasn't the siren speaking. Just as the devil might be growing bolder with me, so was I getting bolder with Andre.

The lust Andre had tried so hard to push away swamped his features once more. His eyes glittered. "Don't tempt me," he said.

"What if I want to?" I asked, not backing down. Oh yeah, I was definitely feeling better.

In the past Andre had kept himself tightly controlled. But now, he didn't look like the master of his emotions. "You need heat and sugar," he said, "you're low on blood."

"I need *you.*"

I saw how my words evaporated the last of his self-control. Hunger took over his features, and his gaze fell to my lips. He reached a hand up and ran his thumb over my lower lip, mesmerized by my mouth. Still he paused, like he just remembered that he was indulging in something he shouldn't.

So I pressed a kiss to the thumb that rested against my lips.

That spicy smell of his amplified, and a subtle tremor moved through him. He closed his eyes. When he opened them, a possessive ferocity shined within them.

"We shouldn't be doing this. Not when you're still recovering," he said.

I flashed him a slow, sultry smile, my skin beginning to

illuminate. Who knew I could so easily fall into the role of femme fatal?

Seeing my smile, Andre cursed under his breath and ran his hands through his hair. Almost as if he couldn't help himself, he glanced back at my lips and stared. And stared.

His hands dropped to his sides, and he leaned in achingly slow, drawing out the moment so that when his lips touched mine, the touch was sweeter than honey. A kind of desperation took over as our mouths moved against each other.

He coaxed my lips open with his own, and then the taste of him invaded my senses. My fangs nicked our tongues, and the sweet tang of blood joined the mix.

Andre groaned at the taste, and I felt my skin ripple approvingly. We were creatures of blood and darkness, and at the moment I fearlessly embraced this.

His hands skimmed my shoulders, sliding under the damp coat I wore. Without breaking off the kiss, he tugged it off of me.

I smiled against his lips, and he made a noise at the back of his throat. "You undo me, soulmate," he murmured.

His hands dropped to my waist, and he pushed my shirt up. He drew away to pull it over my head. I heard the distant smack as it hit the bathroom floor.

Wind whistled through Andre's teeth as he sucked in air, his gaze riveted to my chest. I glanced down and saw I wore one of the lacey bras Oliver gave me.

"*Jesus Christo*," Andre muttered running a hand over his mouth, his gaze transfixed.

The last of Andre's resistance crumbled right there. His lips were on me once more, but this time, the slow burning sensuality was replaced by an insistent, carnal craving that demanded more, more, *more*. For once, me, the demanding siren inside of me, and Andre were all on the same page.

Hurriedly we shucked off the last of our clothes, save my lingerie and Andre's boxer briefs. Those required some admiration.

Andre chuckled at whatever expression I wore. "The best is yet to come, soulmate." He wrapped a hand around my thigh and another around my back, and stood, lifting me with him.

His words jackhammered my pulse.

I latched onto him, reveling at the feel of our bare skin pressed together. "Where, exactly, are you taking me?" I whispered against him, pressing a kiss to his neck.

"To my bed."

Chapter 19

His bed? Brilliant light flared along my skin; I might as well have sent up a smoke signal informing all interested parties that I was turned on. It would've been less obvious. "So the doctor thinks I'm healed enough for physical activity?" I asked.

"What makes you think we'll be doing anything other than tending to your injuries?" Andre said.

My eyebrows shot up, and I drew back enough to see his face.

Laughter danced in his eyes. "I have every intention of giving you a thorough physical examination."

My lips twitched, and then I laughed. A melodic echo laced my laughter. It was eerie as hell.

One sizzling look from him, and my laughter died away, replaced by throbbing need.

Luxurious warmth licked along my back as Andre entered his room, and we drew closer to a fireplace.

Andre rounded a large four-poster bed not so different from the one at Bishopcourt. He laid me down on it, rearing back long enough to gaze yearningly at my body. I watched the flickering firelight dance over him. Right now he looked like a creature of the night. A very, very sexy one.

His eyes traveled to my face, and when they did, affection mingled with lust, the emotion moving across his face and shining in his eyes. "What good deed did I possibly do to deserve you?"

"Good deed?" I asked skeptically. "You think a good deed brought you me? I'm probably punishment for all the bad you've done. You got cursed with me."

A smile curled the edges of his lips. "You're probably right—you are awfully surly," he admitted. I swatted his arm and he grinned. As he stared at me, it melted away. "But I will be thanking fate till the end of my days for bringing me such a wonderful curse."

At the mention of fate, I felt a chill rise from within me that had nothing to do with the storm outside. The devil had also mentioned fate this evening. *Don't think about it.*

Ever so slowly, Andre draped his body over mine so that I felt each point of contact as skin met skin.

I gazed up at the face of my soulmate, the king of the vampires. Loose tendrils of his hair hung down, and I laughed as water droplets slid down them and hit my skin.

He looked at me reverently, heat entering his gaze as we stared at each other. "Be mine forever, Gabrielle."

"I already am," I breathed.

HIS WEIGHT SETTLED heavily against me, and I stroked a thumb from the nape of his neck down the length of his back.

Andre showered kisses down my face and moved against me. Despite the remaining clothes, I felt the movement *everywhere*. I threw my head back, closing my eyes.

"All that is holy," I said, breathless, "you obviously know what you're doing." Sometime during Andre's 700 years of life, he'd learned exactly how to undo a woman.

Andre nuzzled my neck and brushed a kiss along it. "I'm glad I can give you this." Again he moved against me, and again I felt my body's sensual reaction everywhere.

In my other ear, I felt the breath of another mouth. *No, consort.*

I stilled.

Andre drew back, his brow creased. "Are we moving too fast?"

I shook my head furiously. "No," I said—practically pleaded. But inside I was beginning to freak out. Had the devil just interrupted us?

Andre eyed me cautiously. "Perhaps we should slow down ..." he said. I could feel him retreating.

Screw this. I wrapped a hand around the back of Andre's neck and pulled him to me. There was nothing sweet about the kiss I gave him; it was demanding, lustful. I moved against him as his tongue swept through my mouth. He groaned and gave in, his hands running down the length of me.

Consort, stop. The devil's voice tickled the skin of my ear, and I stiffened, breaking off the kiss.

Above me Andre paused. "Gabrielle ... ?"

Our eyes met, and I swallowed. He caressed the side of my face. "What is it?"

You are mine and mine alone.

I flinched at the voice.

"Gabrielle," Andre said more insistently.

I winced as I spoke. "It's the devil. He's demanding that we stop."

Andre cursed. "He does not get a say in the matter."

Oh yes I do. You are mine, consort. Not his.

"I am no one's," I said out loud.

Anger and confusion replaced lust on Andre's face. "The bastard's still talking to you, isn't he?"

I really wanted to punch the devil in the face. Instead I rubbed my ear. "Yeah, he is."

"What's he saying?"

"Essentially, that you can't have sex with me."

Andre's features went carefully neutral, which meant he was getting well and truly pissed. "And why is that?"

I couldn't look at him when I spoke. "I think he wants to save me for himself." My skin crawled and my stomach rolled at the thought. I couldn't bear his touch, so I definitely couldn't imagine doing *that* with him. The devil wanting a bride, that was the thing nightmares were created of.

"He doesn't get to have you," Andre said vehemently.

Ah, yes, this delicious subject. I swallowed. "Andre,

there's something I haven't told you," I stared at the crimson comforter.

"What is it?" Andre asked, his voice lethally calm—this was when Andre was his most dangerous.

I closed my eyes and replayed the end of my visit with the devil. Those parting words, the sureness in the devil's voice.

"Gabrielle?"

My eyes opened, and I focused on Andre's dark gaze. "The devil told me that he and I were fated to be together."

Andre thinned his eyes, gave me a sly, disbelieving look, then tipped his head back and laughed. I wondered how many people had died to that terrible sound, because there was no humor in it. But there was plenty of wickedness. "Is he mad?" Andre asked.

"Most definitely." When it came to the devil, that was a given.

"*We* are soulmates," he said.

"Yes." I knew that for certain.

"He is known as a trickster for a reason," he said. "He lies."

I watched the firelight flicker across Andre's face. "That, or fate doubled dipped."

Chapter 20

THE NEXT MORNING I stared out the window of Andre's study, watching the way the wind whipped small flakes of snow against the mansion.

Fated to two men. Clearly the Fates couldn't agree on what was to become of me. At the moment, I despised all of them; they made it seem as though my sole destiny was to be with some dude.

Fate aside, companionship couldn't be the only reason that the devil wanted me, could it? But then again, why else? I had some interesting abilities, but nothing the devil could gain from, right?

When I ruminated on this topic, Andre's words always echoed back: *power.* This was all a power play. I just couldn't yet see how I'd give the devil more power.

I stretched and grabbed the laptop Andre had loaned

me. Well, technically he'd given it to me, but I didn't exactly need another computer.

Still, I made good use of it, emailing Grigori, Oliver, Caleb, and the head Politia about where I was and the events that took place last night.

An email sent from Grigori's phone came back right away, asking me whether I was okay and informing me that due to the bad weather conditions and the upcoming holiday, all Politia officers had received the next two days off.

Holiday? I checked the computer's calendar. "I'll be damned." It was Christmas Eve. Somehow, between everything that had occurred since my birthday, I'd forgotten.

I turned my attention back to the email and typed up a message to Grigori letting him know I was alright and how to get ahold of me now that my phone was probably lying under a foot of fresh snow.

Once I sent the message, I leaned back, feeling useless. I grabbed a pastry from a nearby platter, my fifth one this morning and probably my twelfth since last night. After the devil crashed our little party and majorly ruined the mood, Andre had gone back to tending to me.

I downloaded a video chat app onto the computer and decided to give my mother a call. The line connected, and my mom's smiling face showed up across the screen. My eyes pricked at the sight of her.

"Merry Christmas Eve, sweet daughter of mine," she said.

With effort, I pulled myself together. "Merry Christmas Eve, mama," I said.

In the background I could hear carols playing over the radio, and a pang of homesickness hit me. I should've been there with her. But she couldn't afford a plane ticket for me, and I couldn't just buy one with my own money. Not unless I wanted to tell my mother just how I came to be a millionaire dozens of times over.

"Did you get my package?" she asked, interrupting my thoughts.

"Er, no," I said guiltily. I probably would've if I'd been on the Isle of Man. But I wasn't, and she couldn't know that her teenage daughter was staying in a new country. "But I've heard that international shipping to the Isle of Man is a nightmare." Inwardly I cringed at the lie.

"Aw," her face fell, "Well, maybe it will arrive today. I'd really hoped you'd get to open it on Christmas."

We chatted for a long time after that, catching up on good books, TV shows, and what we'd done since we last talked. It was pleasure and pain, talking to her, since I missed her so dang much. And guilt always seeped in when I had to lie or omit the truth.

Just like right now.

"Where are you?" she asked.

"Peel Academy's library," I said, not missing a beat.

"Wow. Some library," she said, noticing the gilded molding and the marble side table next to me. "They let you eat and talk in there?"

Whoops. "Ah, *no*, but the place is abandoned during the holidays."

"Oh, well honey, I hope you're not spending all your time in there when you could be celebrating with your friends." She looked genuinely concerned. If only she knew the truth. She'd go ballistic.

She smiled over the screen. "In case I don't talk to you tomorrow, Merry Christmas," she said, "I love you."

"Love you too. Merry Christmas."

THUACK.

The knife made a solid sound as it embedded itself into the target. I'd discovered Andre's training room late in the afternoon, and I'd lingered ever since.

I spun a knife in my hand. I'd forgotten how good it felt to exert control over something—even a simple weapon. It was almost cathartic after the last few days I'd had. Not to mention feeling my muscles catch and release with exertion. There was some basic satisfaction to being capable of defending myself.

Power tickled over my skin as I stared at the target—someone else's power. Andre was waking up, and that meant that I might be able to train with him. The thought had the corners of my mouth curling up. Between Andre and me there was enough pent up sexual tension to make for some *very* interesting grappling.

I threw the knife in my hand, watching it tumble hilt-over-blade, before sinking into the target with a satisfying thump.

Another bull's eye. I stepped back a few yards and glanced down at the belt I wore. Three knives were still strapped into the sheaths that circled my waist.

Two months ago, when Andre began to train me, I

balked at the idea of training with swords and knives—
medieval weapons. But now, I understood. In a fight, a
knife, a sword, a battle-axe, arrows, throwing stars—all
these weapons and more could be retrieved and reused,
unlike modern weaponry. A spent bullet could never be
procured again in the heat of battle.

Not that this stopped supernatural beings—Andre included—from using guns. All and all, they were still quite
effective.

But the other equally important reason Andre trained
me with swords and knives was that these weapons required muscle control, good form, dynamism, and—
when one was engaged in combat—improvisation.

Thuack, thuack, thuack. I threw the rest of the knives in
quick succession, a pleased smile dancing along my lips
when they hit the target exactly where I had intended.

"Remind me never to piss you off."

I started at the voice. I swiveled around to see Andre
standing in the doorway, arms folded.

"You're getting even better," he commented, dropping
his arms and sauntering into the room. "Though I still
would've gotten the drop on you."

"It's good to see you too," I said, turning back to my
target to retrieve my knives. As I did so, my face heated.
Even with our hard-to-ignore connection, Andre *was* still
able to sneak up on me.

"Is my soulmate embarrassed?" Andre's voice was
amused.

Damn vampires and their sense of smell. When I
reached the target, I began yanking the blades out. "You

shouldn't go provoking women who play with knives," I said, sliding one into a sheath while reaching for another.

The air shifted, and then Andre's lips brushed against my ear. "Maybe I like my women dangerous."

I smiled. Tonight there *would* be some naughty combat. In one fluid motion, I spun, aiming the edge of the blade I held for Andre's throat.

He caught my forearm, predicting the move, and bent my wrist back until pain forced me to drop the knife. Even as I did so, I brought my leg up and kicked him in the chest.

Or at least I tried to.

He let go of my arm in time to catch my leg, and then he twisted it. I only had an instant to lift my other leg. Had I waited a second later, Andre would've snapped the bone.

And he probably would've done it, too.

When we first began training, I assumed Andre wouldn't hurt me. I assumed wrong.

The first injury was a dislocated shoulder. And it took me a week to forgive him. During that time, Andre still dragged my ass to training, still threatened bodily injury when we faced off, but boy was he remorseful. I wouldn't talk to him, wouldn't smile at him. Never had I heard someone apologize so much as he did that week.

Lesson learned: I might be able to bring a man to his knees faster by kicking his legs in, but nothing felled a man quite like a woman's wrath.

My entire body twisted in the air, and I landed hard on the ground. But already I'd pulled my boot back and kicked Andre in the face as his body followed mine to the floor.

Andre bellowed as bone crunched, and for a split-second his grip on my leg loosened. It was as good an opening as I was going to get. I slammed my boot against him again, eliciting another roar from Andre, and then I wrenched my foot from his grasp.

I tensed my muscles, ready to lung at Andre and go for a kill shot again, but before I had the chance, he sprang forward, knocking me back into the ground. Even injured, he was a force to be reckoned with.

And *this* was precisely why Andre risked injuring me: pain honed us. Physically it made us better, quicker, more resilient, and it forced us to think and strategize through agony.

And it might be the only way I'd survive the devil.

With one hand Andre captured my wrists, and with his other hand he snatched one of the knives from my belt.

He pressed the edge of the blade against my neck, just as I had originally intended to do to him. "Never allow your enemy—"

"Yeah, yeah, yeah," I said, feeling the knife slice into the skin of my neck as I spoke. "If I get pinned to the ground, I'll be deader than you are."

Andre frowned at that, and then his eyes caught sight of the blood at my neck. He grimaced and threw the knife aside before leaning down and placing a kiss to the wound. "I'm sorry for this, soulmate," he murmured against my skin, just like he did every time he hurt me while we fought.

"It's okay," I said, mostly because I knew how badly Andre did feel about my injuries. He was raised in a time where women were treated like breakable objects. Hurting me went against some of his most deep-seated beliefs. But even those beliefs could be overridden by fear for my future wellbeing. "I'm, ah, sorry about your nose," I added. "Sorta. Okay, I'm not, but only because that's like the seventh time I've ever gotten a hit on you."

"Oh?" Andre said. "You're not sorry?" he murmured as his lips skimmed up my neck and jawline, heading straight for the pay dirt that was my mouth. Ah, naughty grappling. My favorite.

"Nope," I said, being obstinate.

His mouth halted. "Well in that case ..."

He drew his lips away from my skin, and I groaned. The bastard was going to hold out on me until I caved. "Okay, fine," I conceded, "I'm super sorry. Are you pleased now?"

Andre's mouth returned to my skin, and I felt him smile against it. "Very much so."

His lips had just alighted upon mine when his phone rang. He groaned against me. "I'm not done with you," he whispered into my mouth, and then he pulled away to sit on his haunches.

"Yes?" he said brusquely into the phone he'd procured from his pocket.

"*Sir,*" said the voice on the other end of the line, "*I looked into last night's attack, just like you asked.*"

I pushed myself up onto my forearms, and Andre's eyes met mine. He knew I could hear the conversation.

"And?" he asked.

"*It seems your theory is right that a demon attacked.*"

His theory. Ha!

"*Only it's so much worse,*" the man said.

"How so?" Andre's grip had tightened on the phone.

"*In demonic circles there's a bounty out on Gabrielle's head. It's rumored that the devil himself placed it.*"

My eyes widened. Had that been why I'd seen so many shadows since I'd arrived? Were they all demons who were after me?

"And what, precisely, is the bounty for?" Andre said, his low pitched low.

I heard the man on the other end of the line exhale before he spoke again. "*Whoever can successfully deliver the girl to the devil has been promised title and power by the Unholy One.*"

It didn't take a rocket scientist to deduce that whoever was going to *deliver* me wasn't planning on dropping me off at the devil's doorstep. Nope. My butt was going to get shanked.

"We need to stop this," Andre said, menace lacing his words.

A pause. Then, "*Sir, I'm not sure we can.*"

Chapter 21

"Merry freaking Christmas to me," I muttered the next morning as I padded into Andre's study with a cup of coffee and a book. Other teenagers got clothes and electronics for Christmas. I got my name on a hit list.

All last night, Andre had been on the phone with his contacts, bribing and threatening anyone and everyone he could to get my name off that list.

Problem was, there was no actual list. From what I understood, the hit was nothing more than a whisper in the night, passed from one shady being to another. Try as Andre might, he couldn't remove a threat that had no origin and no traceable trajectory.

I took a deep breath. Time to lose myself in a good story and forget about the hot mess that was my life.

Just as I plopped down on a couch in Andre's study and

cracked open my book, the front door was thrown open and I swear to God I heard what sounded like yodeling.

I closed my eyes. There was Oliver, doing who the hell knew what.

A minute later he entered the study, escorted by one of Andre's servants.

"Great Mother of Earth and Heaven and All Things Delicious, there you are!" Oliver said. "We were so worried!"

He crossed the room and swept me up into a huge hug. Behind him Caleb entered the room.

"Caleb," I said, shocked. "What are you guys doing here?"

"Andre sent a car over to bring us over," Caleb said stiffly, as though admitting to this made him uncomfortable.

"But the roads—"

"They were clear enough this morning to pick us up. Merry Christmas, by the way."

Next to me Oliver pried my book from my hands and tossed it over his shoulder. "Merry Christmas!" he said.

"Hey—I was reading that," I said, glaring at Oliver.

"Yeah, and now you're not because the fun has arrived."

I narrowed my eyes at him.

"So," Caleb said, interrupting us, "what exactly happened two nights ago, Gabrielle?" He sat down in a nearby wingback chair.

I gave him a strained smile. "It's a long story."

I SPENT THE next twenty minutes rehashing last two nights'

events, beginning with the kidnapping, and ending with the demonic hit list. I decided to omit the part about the devil talking to me while I was getting down with Andre. That had *uncomfortable* written all over it.

"The devil told you that you were fated to be his?" Caleb asked. He looked a little ill.

I winced and nodded.

"And he meant fate as in, 'there was a prophecy, and I'm owed my due,' or was he speaking in more general terms?"

I tipped my head back and forth, weighing his words. The devil was an arrogant, slippery being, but from everything I'd learned last night … "I think he meant the prophetic kind of fate," I said.

Caleb's throat worked, but he nodded. He stood up and rubbed his forehead. When he drew his hand away, realization flashed over his features. "Holy shit," he said, staring off in the distance.

"What?" I asked anxiously.

His eyes met mine. "I have a theory."

"A theory about what?" I asked.

"About you, the murders, the devil. But shit, it's not good, Gabrielle."

Oliver glanced at me, his eyebrows raised.

"What is it?" I asked Caleb.

His eyes were distracted. "Let me get my suitcase …" He trailed off as he left the room, his paces quick.

"Luggage?" I asked, turning to Oliver.

Oliver shrugged. "Andre invited us to stay here for the remainder of the investigation."

208

"And you both agreed to it?" I asked, disbelieving him.

"Hey, I like Andre, even if he does scare the shit out of me. Plus, he loves you and you love him."

D'awww.

"Also, I wanted to get out of that piece of crap inn," Oliver added. He'd had the perfect response, and then he had to go and butcher it.

"What about Caleb?" I asked. "There's no way he'd agree to stay here."

"Well he did."

I thinned my eyes. "And how did you manage that?"

Oliver sniffed, smoothing down his shirt. "I promised him you'd go on a date with him."

"*Oliver!*"

Said fairy buffed his nails against his shirt. "What?" he asked innocently. "It's his fault he's a sucker."

I let my forehead fall into my hands. "I'm starting to think our classicist textbook was right—fairies are evil little creatures."

"Says the girl with fangs."

Touché.

Oliver threw a sly glance over his shoulder, to where Caleb retreated. "So," he said, turning back to me, "now that Caleb's gone, care to tell me the rest of what happened over the last two nights?"

"And what makes you think that there's more to it?"

"Please, honey. It's me you're talking to. I know an edited story when I hear one."

My eyes flicked to the doorway.

"He won't be back for a while. Now spill."

And so I did, receiving a squeal from Oliver every time I mentioned a juicy detail.

Once I'd finished relating it to him, Oliver's eyes were wide. "You mean to tell me that Andre was finally DTF, and the devil cock blocked you?"

I let out a sad laugh and pushed a hand through my hair. "Pretty much."

"Damn, sweets, that blows loads."

I gave him a dark look at his little innuendo.

"Or not." He cleared his throat. "Anyway," he continued, "I never would've pegged the devil as a possessive bastard when it came to his woman."

"*I am not his woman.*"

Oliver patted my knee like I was cute. "I say you screw them both."

"Oliver!"

"What?" he said, trying to look innocent. "Fate gave you two men; girl you should *own that shit.*"

"Hello, Oliver, one of those men just happens to be *the devil.*"

Oliver cocked his head thoughtfully. "You know that whole evil incarnate business might be really hot—he's probably a god in the sack."

Ew ew ew! "For the sake of our friendship, I'm going to pretend I didn't hear that."

"Fine," Oliver said testily, "enjoy virgin-hood. I hear you guys make great sacrifices."

I was about to respond when the sound of footsteps drew my attention to the doorway.

A moment later Caleb entered the room, a manila folder tucked under his arm. He dropped it on a nearby coffee table, and Oliver and I got up to take a closer look.

Caleb crouched in front of the file and opened it up. Inside were a series of photographs from the second crime scene. He flipped through them, his expression determined. Expectant. And suddenly I didn't think his theory was any theory at all. A nervous thrill shot through me at what he might've discovered.

From the stack he pulled out a series of photos that focused on the wooden altar.

I gave him a questioning look, but he didn't see it.

"There," he said, pointing to the image. It was a close up of one of the scenes carved onto the altar. Depicted on it was an image of a man carrying a woman away.

"What about it?" I asked.

Instead of answering me, he flipped to another photo of the altar and tapped on a bit of detailing between the carved images. "That's a pomegranate."

"It is?" I said. Huh, it looked more like a peach to me, but then again, I wasn't exactly a botanist.

"So what?" Oliver said. He'd become our unofficial partner. Typical.

"The pomegranate has an important meaning in Greek mythology," Caleb explained. "It symbolizes the story of Hades and Persephone."

It took me a moment to recall the story. Persephone was the daughter of Demeter, the goddess of the harvest, and she was unfortunate enough to catch the attention of Hades, the god of the Underworld.

The myth went something like this: One day when

Persephone was frolicking in a field—or whatever it was innocent Greek girls did back in the day—Hades kidnapped her and took her to the Underworld to be his captive bride.

Meanwhile, topside, Persephone's mother was grieving the loss of her daughter, and in her sorrow, she was causing all the earth's crops to die. The gods took notice and tried to retrieve Persephone from Hades before the land fell into a perpetual winter. Only by that time, Persephone had eaten a couple pomegranate seeds—food of the dead—and the sustenance bound her to the Underworld. Because of this, it was no longer a simple matter of retrieval.

But to prevent the total destruction of the world, something needed to happen. So a bargain was struck: Persephone would live with her mother for a part of the year, and she'd live in the Underworld with Hades for the other part of the year.

And everybody lived happily freaking ever.

I focused on the detailed carvings again. "Holy shit," I murmured. Looking at the pictures with the myth in mind, they fit.

I allowed myself a moment of surprise and excitement—Caleb had figured out what the altar's images were depicting. "Do you think other investigators have figured this out?" I asked.

"Probably. We won't know for sure until we exchange notes. But Gabrielle," Caleb's eyes met mine. "That's not all."

A wave of unease passed through me at the worry in

his eyes.

"The woman at the club," he said, "you told me that the first thing she did when you met her was kneel."

"Uh huh," I said, not sure where this was going.

"That's kind of strange, isn't it?"

I shrugged. "I don't know what's normal for a killer. She called me consort. I can only assume that she worshipped ... the devil." I furrowed my brows even as I said this. A Satanist that performed pagan rituals over an altar depicting Hades and Persephone? The religions seemed mutually exclusive.

Rather than dampening Caleb's enthusiasm my words seemed to stoke it. "The other woman who was there called you something unusual too, didn't she?" he said. "Something that started with a 'P'?"

I stared at him for a moment trying to connect the dots. When I did, the blood drained from my face. I thought back to the club, to my interaction with the petite woman who'd stabbed me. "She didn't call me Persephone, though," I whispered.

Caleb's determined expression didn't change. "She goes by several names," he said, "And at least one other starts with a 'P'."

"Which one?" I barely breathed as I watched Caleb.

He looked at me pityingly. "Her Roman one—Proserpine."

"Did our suspect call you that, Gabrielle?" Caleb probed.

As soon as he'd mentioned the name, I'd remembered.

Like a puzzle piece it fit with the rest of the memory.

"Sweets?" Oliver asked gently. I blinked and looked at him, then at Caleb.

"She did." A thoughtful silence descended as we all took this in. These killers thought I was this Persephone, the daughter of the goddess of the harvest.

Harvest. My eyes snapped to Caleb. "I need to grab something," I said, rising from my seat. Uncomfortable silence descended as I reached into my book back. If I looked up, I was sure I'd find Caleb and Oliver giving each other uneasy looks. They probably thought I'd lost it. Who knew, maybe I had.

I flipped through my bag until I pulled out what I was looking for. I laid the cream-colored slip of paper down on the coffee table. On it were five lines written in loopy handwriting. Caleb and Oliver craned their necks to read it along with me.

> *Daughter of wheat and grain,*
> *Betrothed to soil and stain,*
> *Your lifeblood drips,*
> *The scales tip,*
> *But will it be in vain?*

Shit.

That first line—it only took a little imagination to realize that Cecilia was describing Persephone. I rubbed my forehead. It was one thing for two killers to call me Proserpine, and another for a Fate to.

"But why? Why would anyone assume I was Persephone?" I said out loud. "We're not the same," I said. My mother may have had the looks of a goddess, but she wasn't one. She lived as a mortal and died just like one. "I mean, I'm dying, for crying out loud. Wasn't Persephone all about life and fertility?" I asked, looking between Oliver and Caleb.

"Well, the devil isn't quite the lord of death, either now," Caleb said. "He's simply the lord of the Underworld, the lord of the damned."

"There's still the fact that the myth preceded me by thousands of years. That marriage between Hades and Persephone happened a long time ago—if it ever happened at all."

"Hmmm," Oliver had that I-know-something-really-important-but-I-don't-much-care tone of voice.

"What?" I asked.

Oliver shrugged and picked a nonexistent piece of lint off of his shirt. "What if the myth isn't really a myth? What if it's a prophecy?"

The thought made me pause. Another prophecy? But I already had one—and it was disturbing enough as is. Instead I said, "But the details are all wrong." I mean, *all the details.*

"The details may not be what's true. *You* may be what's true," Caleb said.

My eyes flicked to him. "So you also think the myth of Hades and Persephone might be a prophecy."

He hesitated. "Maybe—it makes sense."

I sat back on my heels and pondered that, my stomach plummeting. The devil was undoubtedly after me, and on

Samhain Cecilia had called him Pluto, the Roman name for the god Hades. Could the man in the suit be both the devil and Hades?

"This shit may not be science," Caleb added, "but that doesn't mean you should ignore it."

I looked between Caleb and Oliver. "So you think that I'm the devil's Persephone, his consort, and what, these killers are running around, offing people in the devil's name?" I tried to sound skeptical, but I didn't pull it off. The devil liked to collect his due in flesh and souls.

"Yes, but not in just his name," Caleb said. "They're killing in your name, too."

RIGHT ABOUT NOW the breakfast I'd eaten earlier wasn't sitting so well in my stomach. I put the back of my hand to my mouth.

It was one thing to think that the murders were to appease the devil. It was another to consider that people were being killed to appease *me*.

Oh God, if I was responsible for those deaths, how could I ration that my soul was worth the cost of those lives lost?

"Well, I'd say that all in all this is turning out to be a crappy Christmas," Oliver said, interrupting my dark thoughts. He stood up. "I think this calls for a quest to find alcohol. Anyone want a drink?"

"Hell yes," Caleb said.

When Oliver looked at me I said, "Don't bother bringing me a glass. I'll take the bottle straight."

Oliver whistled. "We got a sailor in the room."

Instead of responding, I covered my face with my hands, my shoulders beginning to shake. I was about to lose it.

I heard Oliver pause, then crouch down next to me. He gave me a tight squeeze and kissed my temple. "I'll be right back with enough spirits to raise yours and make you forget," Oliver said, pushing himself back to his feet. A minute later I could hear his footfalls get fainter as he moved away from the study.

Caleb and I sat quietly for several moments—together but apart—and then I heard him get up. He dropped down next to me and slung an arm over my shoulder.

"Hey," he said, shaking me, "it's going to be okay."

"No it's not." I dropped my hands and took in a shaky breath of air.

The devil was coming for me again, and innocent lives were being lost because of it. And if the myth of Hades and Persephone was prophetic, then I should cast away my hope now. Because in that myth, Hades kidnapped Persephone and took her away to his kingdom to be his wife, his queen. He tricked her.

And it worked.

Chapter 22

BY THE TIME the sun was setting, Oliver, Caleb, and I had made good use of Andre's liquor. We'd been playing pool for what seemed like hours in Andre's game room. Who knew the king of vampires enjoyed these types of pastimes? Never would've guessed it.

I tipped back my drink, enjoying the way the spicy liquid burned going down. I quickly figured out that dark rum was my favorite liquor. And like I'd promised earlier, I was swigging it straight from the bottle. My worries were now fuzzy things.

"Hey, Jack Sparrow," Caleb called, "it's your turn."

I eyed him as I took another gulp, then brought the bottle from my lips. Using the back of my hand, I wiped my mouth. "Sure thing," I said, capping the bottle.

I tossed the drink onto a nearby couch and staggered

over. I lurched to the right and grabbed the edge of the pool table for balance. Both boys were staring at me.

"What?" I asked a little too loudly. "Scared you're going to lose this round? Should be." I drew the words out. My skin flared and then settled. It'd been doing that now that the alcohol flowed through my system. And each time it did so, Caleb's eyes flickered with interest.

As soon as my skin went back to normal, Caleb was shaking his head. "Shit, Gabrielle, I'm cutting you off. I can't handle this glamour." He walked over to the couch I'd thrown the bottle on, and grabbed the rum.

"Look who's talking, chameeeeeleon," I sang, my voice hitting several notes at once. For the last few hours Caleb's features had flickered and changed as the alcohol coursed through him.

Caleb placed the bottle on a high shelf. I snorted at that and leaned back against the pool table. "I can just glamour you into getting that for me."

"Do that, and I'll report your ass," he said, coming back to the game.

That shut me up.

"Fine. No more booze—for now." I reached over to take the cue stick from Oliver's glittering hand. I tugged, but he wouldn't let it go. I guess he still hadn't completely forgiven me for calling his iridescent wings "cute."

"Majestic, sexy-as-hell, exquisite—those are all appropriate descriptions," he had said. "Not *cute*. Puppies are cute. I. Am. Not. Cute."

Now he said, "I'm not giving this to you until you ask nicely."

Geez these boys were grouchy.

I tightened my grip on the stick. "Oh Beautiful One with the sparkly, erotic wings, please may I have the damn cue stick?"

Begrudgingly Oliver let it go. *Very* begrudgingly. "I almost feel bad for Andre right now," he said. "He's got his hands full with you."

I lifted my hand into the air and gave him the bird. As I did so, the air seemed to shift. I felt the ripple of awakened power along my skin. I sucked in a breath and straightened. Andre had woken up.

I PANICKED, TURNING to Oliver. "He's awake."

"Who's awake?"

"The monster under the bed—who do you think?"

"Andre?" Oliver rolled his eyes. "So?"

"So," I sputtered, "I'm drunk on his expensive liquor, and I'm supposed to fill him in on Caleb's theory."

"Bitch please—*Caleb's* theory? I was the one who told you about the myth being a prophecy."

"Not the point."

"Then what is the point?" Oliver asked, pursing his lips.

I scrubbed my face. I could feel my mood slipping through my fingers, turning dark and despairing. I didn't know if the alcohol had caused it, or if it had actually been holding it at bay all this time.

"I don't want to tell him," I whispered into my hands. And what would I say? That we might be soulmates, but I was destined to be the devil's wife? My head began to pound at the thought.

I dropped my hands, and a bloody tear snaked down my cheek. I could feel Caleb's curious eyes on it.

"Sweets," Oliver said gently, his annoyance with me forgotten, "you're going to have to."

"What has Gabrielle so worked up?" Caleb asked coming over to us.

"I think the king of the vampires is awake," Oliver said.

Caleb took a step closer to us. "How can she possibly know that?" he asked, eyeing me.

"It's sunset," Oliver said smoothly. He turned so that Caleb couldn't see his face and winked at me. I gave him a small, tight-lipped smile in return.

I could feel the connection between Andre and me getting stronger, which meant he was getting closer.

"Oliver ..." I didn't know what I was asking for at this point. Maybe just someone to soothe my fear.

He squeezed my hands. "Sorry love, but you're going to have to tell Andre."

"Tell me what?"

My eyes fell on the door to the game room, where Andre stood, taking in the scene. In one of his hands was a small gift-wrapped box.

"What's going on?" he asked, sauntering in. His voice sent pleasant skitters up my arms, but fear sliced through me. This was going to ruin his Christmas, and I'd already made a hot mess of his birthday.

I was a holiday wrecker.

Andre's assessing eyes passed over me. "Gabrielle, your heart is beating much too quickly." He took several steps towards me, looking scary as all get out. His nostrils flared. "And the room stinks of booze—*you* smell of booze." His eyes hardened when they met mine. "I will ask one more time: what is going on?"

"Time to scram," Oliver whispered to Caleb, grabbing his arm. Caleb hesitated, looking between Andre and me.

I too began to edge away from Andre.

"You are not going anywhere, Gabrielle," Andre said, "so don't even consider it."

Yikes.

Very slowly Andre turned to stare at Caleb, who had taken a step closer to us. "I will need to ask you to leave us," Andre said. "I would like to speak to my subject alone."

Caleb's jaw tensed and the two stared each other down. I wanted to roll my eyes at the display. After a tense few seconds, Caleb jerked his head in acquiescence and backed away from us. Oliver, I noticed, had already bolted from the room. Smart fairy.

"No tricks, Caleb," Andre called out after him. "If I sense you lingering, I will not be pleased." That was a euphemism if I ever heard one.

Caleb gave a wave of acknowledgement and left the room. The door clicked shut behind him, and then Andre and I were alone.

For a beat Andre stared at the door, and then, painfully slow, he turned his attention to me.

Ho, was he scary when he wanted to be. Like right now. I was sobering up real quick.

He stalked forward and I backed up until I bumped

222

into the pool table. Andre didn't stop until his chest brushed mine.

Once he reached me, he set the small gift on the edge of the table. Then he ran his knuckles down my cheek. "Why does my soulmate fear me right now?"

My throat worked, but I didn't respond.

He tilted my face left and right, assessing me. "I can smell the alcohol in your blood, and I've never seen you drunk. I'm guessing it's not Christmas that has you worked up?"

I closed my eyes and shook my head. Oliver was right; I had to tell Andre. "Caleb discovered something about the murders," I admitted.

Andre took my hands and held them between his own. "This is a good thing, is it not?"

"No," I choked out. A bloody tear dripped down my cheeks, and then another.

Andre's brows furrowed, and his hands left my own to cup my jaw. Frowning, he wiped away my tears with his thumbs. "Please don't cry," he said, his voice gravelly. "I can't stand the sight."

That only made me cry harder. After a moment, Andre pulled me into his arms, holding me tightly to him. He kissed the top of my head and stroked my hair, murmuring gentle words to me in Spanish. It would've been incredibly sexy if I weren't such a wreck right now.

I hadn't fallen apart when I was kidnapped, nor when we got into an accident. I'd held it together when I'd visited the devil and again when he dropped in on Andre and I. I'd even stayed strong throughout the day, thanks to the alcohol.

I'd bottled up my emotions for too long, and now they were spilling out all over the place.

When I finally got myself under control, I stepped away from him. The arms that had encircled my back now dropped to my waist.

"Are you ready to tell me what has you so worked up?" Andre asked.

I stared at his chest. "Yes." Then I took a deep breath and told him.

THE MUSCLE IN Andre's jaw ticked. And ticked again as I waited for him to rally against Caleb's—and Oliver's—theory. I even wished for that frightening laugh of his, just to hear his absolute disbelief.

But he hadn't said anything. Only stared at me with agony in his eyes.

"You think the theory might be valid?"

He watched me for moment before responding. "It could be."

I looked away. "But I'm *your* soulmate."

"Yes, you are. Nothing changes that," he said, his arms tightening around me. "And I will die before I give you up to him."

"But if it's a prophecy ... then it will come to pass."

"It was also prophesied that you'd become my queen and exterminate our people, and that hasn't yet come to pass."

A darker thought entered my mind. "Or perhaps you

do die for me, Andre, you and every other vampire. Perhaps the devil still gets me anyway. Perhaps both prophecies come true."

Andre stepped closer to me. "You can choose to be bound by those prophecies, Gabrielle, but I won't."

His words angered me. "And what am I supposed to do, ignore them?"

"Belief—not fate—rules the world," he said. "Believe in us, believe in free will."

His words reminded me of what Leanne had told me two months ago: *You've outwitted fate over and over again.*

My eyes moved up to Andre's. Perhaps I really was his curse. The soulmate he could never quite have. I guess it really did come down to what you believed in at the end of the day.

And me, well, I believed in happy endings.

"Okay." I nodded to him as the thought seeded itself in my mind. "I can do that. I can believe in us."

WE STAYED IN the game room just long enough for the alcohol to work itself out of my system. Eventually Andre led me out.

"Even if the devil is behind the murders," he said, opening the door and holding it open for me, "he did not kill those victims, Gabrielle. People of flesh and blood did this. They are who you need to worry about because they, and not the devil, are the ones doing the killing."

I chewed on the inside of my cheek. Capture the killers, avoid the devil.

"Can I see the files again?" Andre asked.

"Sure." I led us back to the study, where my book bag containing the files lay. Oliver and Caleb were already inside, Oliver texting like mad on his phone, and Caleb pacing the room.

As soon as we entered, Caleb froze, his eyes scouring me as though he feared Andre had hurt me. I rolled my eyes. "Dramatic much?"

"I was worried," he said.

Behind me Andre went rigid, and I heard the low growl he made. "Worried about what, shifter?" Andre said, his words even.

I crouched in front of my bag. "Caleb—don't answer that. It's a loaded question. Andre, please don't eat my friend."

Andre sighed, his anger morphing into exasperation. "I don't know how many times we must go over this, Gabrielle, but I don't eat people."

I stifled my smile and grabbed the file folders from my bag. "Here they are," I said, standing up and handing them to Andre.

"What's going on?" Caleb asked.

"Andre's helping us on the case."

Caleb scowled at that, but said nothing.

I turned my attention back to Andre. He opened the topmost file and picked up one of the photos from the second crime scene. From what I could tell, it looked to be a close-up of the altar.

Andre made a small noise.

"What?" I asked.

"These aren't just images of Hades and Persephone," he said, shaking his head. His eyes scoured the photo. "These are images of the Eleusinian Mysteries."

"WHAT ARE THE Eleusinian Mysteries?" Caleb asked.

Andre glanced up from the photos. "They were initiation ceremonies for the cult of Persephone and Demeter. These were secret religious rites that reenacted the abduction of Persephone."

All three men looked at me.

I took a step back. "What?"

"Nothing ... *Persephone*," Oliver said.

I slitted my eyes at him. "Don't call me that."

"Then what should I call you—Denial?"

"How about Gabrielle?"

Oliver buffed his nails on his shirt. "Well that's just no fun."

"The cult is still around," Andre said, "though I believe it's now called the Eleusinian Order. And if I had to place money on it, I'd guess that's who's behind the murders."

Caleb cut in. "So if this cult believes that Gabrielle is Persephone, then we a big problem. Their goddess is still among the living."

Oliver's eyes cut to me, and he raised his eyebrows. "Me thinks I know how this story ends."

I did too. If this murderous cult believed I was their Persephone, then they might take it upon themselves to unify me with my Hades.

They might take it upon themselves to kill me.

"So if the devil is behind these murders, then why two? And why in different cities?" I asked Caleb over breakfast the next morning.

By then the storm had died down enough for travel, and we were up early to find out whether today we'd get back to work or be sent home. We'd already contacted Grigori and let him know about our findings, so our "expertise" would hopefully no longer be needed, and we could get the hell out of here.

I didn't have much time left in Romania, regardless; I knew that I couldn't hold my protective boyfriend off for much longer. Last night Andre seemed ready to drag me kicking and screaming onto his jet and fly my ass out of the country. The only reason he hadn't done so probably had something to do with the fact that his pilot had Christmas off.

"Well, we know it's not ley lines," Caleb said, "and if the devil is behind this, then some meaningful pattern will eventually show up."

Hopefully this detail wouldn't matter now that we'd essentially proved a cult was behind the murders. The Politia could just round up everyone in the cult and smack charges on them all.

Something told me it wouldn't be quite that easy.

My phone went off. As soon as I saw Grigori's name flash on the screen, I snatched it up. "Morning, Grigori," I said, eyeing Caleb. He'd stopped spreading butter on his toast to hear our conversation.

"Morning. Are you and Caleb ready to get back to work today?"

My shoulders slumped. Not going home after all. "Of course. What's today's plan?"

"While the storm passed through Cluj, our murderers struck again—twice."

My mouth parted in surprise. "Two more murders?"

"In two cities dozens of miles apart from one another—and from us. Seems our killers were busy over the holidays."

I rubbed my brow.

"The department is investigating your leads," Grigori continued. "In the meantime, we'd like to take you and Caleb to the crime scene in Alba Iulia to see if it fits your theory."

I closed my eyes and pinched the bridge of my nose. "Great. We'll be ready to go in thirty minutes. We're at Andre's place." I rattled off the address and hung up shortly thereafter.

Another day, another murder scene. I sighed inwardly. The sooner Caleb and I did this, the sooner we'd get to go home.

THE SNOWSTORM HAD let up, but the visibility was still awful. I stared out at the bleak scenery from the front seat of Grigori's sedan, my mind far away. The car ride was quiet for miles, with the exception of Caleb's quiet snores.

Through the snowy haze, I watched Alba Iulia materialize. It was difficult to catch clear glimpses of the city as we drove through it, but from what I could tell, it had the same regal, Old World European beauty that Cluj had.

The buildings began to thin out, looking a bit more decrepit, and I realized that we'd almost passed the city by. Eventually even those remaining buildings gave way to just a scattering of homes littering each side of the road.

When fifteen minutes had gone by, and we hadn't shown signs of stopping I stretched my limbs. "Do you know how much further we have?" I asked Grigori.

"We should be there soon if the road continues to be as clear as it has been," he said.

I yawned, then blinked my eyes rapidly. Between dreams of the devil and the murder investigation, I hadn't gotten much sleep since I'd been in Romania. Now it was starting to show.

I grabbed the coffee Grigori had snagged me from the station and took a deep gulp, then another, wincing when the bitter black coffee hit my tongue.

I frowned. *Black like my soul.*

I kept the coffee in my lap as I stared out the window. The gentle rock of the car seemed to lull me, and my eyes drooped.

You've got to be kidding me.

I brought the coffee to my lips and drank deeply once more before setting the cup aside. If that didn't wake me up, then nothing could.

But even as I thought the words, my limbs and eyelids began to feel heavy. I fought to stay awake, but really, what was the harm? Grigori would wake me up when we arrived.

With that final thought, I closed my eyes and drifted off.

Chapter 23

WHEN ANDRE ROSE, it was with a smile. *How my enemies would laugh at me, to see me now,* he thought. For one like him, humanity came with a price. So did love.

They were weaknesses to exploit. He knew that because he'd so often exploited those weaknesses in others.

Before he met her.

Now his wrath was a charade he had to keep up, his viciousness a cloak that hid something soft beneath it.

He moved through the windowless chamber of the guest room he'd stayed in, wondering when he'd let Gabrielle see him sleep. She'd learned and accepted so much, but there was still so much of their world she hadn't seen, hadn't experienced.

And damn him, but he wanted to shield her from it for as long as possible.

At the thought of her, he stilled.

Where was their connection? He should've felt her energy pulling at him, beckoning him to find her. Now it was dim, nearly nonexistent.

True and terrible fear coursed through him. Where was she?

Not in the house.

He began moving at once, prowling his halls like an animal. His servants stayed out of his way. They knew to remain scarce when he was like this.

Andre glanced out the window. The snow was still coming down, not as heavy as it had been during the last couple days, but enough to deter one from going outside or venturing onto the road.

Had she gone back to the inn? He ignored his twinge of hurt at the thought. *I am the king of vampires; slights are met with anger,* not *sadness.*

Instead he made his way to his room, running a hand through his hair. He saw the rumpled sheets of his bed where she'd slept, ignoring the pang of lust that came with the image of her wrapped up in them. His woman in his sheets.

His eyes fell on Gabrielle's luggage.

She hadn't gone back to the inn.

That realization should have brought relief, but instead fear and anger clawed away at him. She hadn't gone back, yet she wasn't in his house.

Andre pulled his cell out of his pocket and dialed her phone. The call went straight to voicemail.

Bloody hell.

A courageous servant came up to him. "Sir, your guests—"

"Get a car ready," Andre said, unzipping her luggage, and praying that Gabrielle left those files behind.

"But sir, the snow—"

"Damn you, I said *get a car ready!*" he bellowed.

He didn't know where he was going yet, but he had an idea.

I WOKE TO a deathly chill and the smell of brimstone and decay. My eyes were covered and a cloth had been forced between my teeth.

My shoulders throbbed from where they were wrenched behind my back, and my wrists were raw where they'd been tied together.

Someone had kidnapped me and tied me up. A wave of frustration passed through me. Damn vampires couldn't do this the easy way.

But as I sorted through my most recent memories, dread replaced frustration. It couldn't have been a vampire that had taken me. It had been broad daylight when I was last awake. Caleb, Grigori, and I had been heading to one of the most recent crime scenes. We'd never arrived.

I remembered passing through Alba Iulia, curious as to why we hadn't stopped when the murder supposedly took place there. I'd assumed that it had occurred just outside the city.

I strained to remember what had happened after that. I'd been tired, so I'd downed my coffee, which only seemed to make me sleepier. There'd been an unnatural heaviness to my limbs.

I swore, the sound muffled by the cloth in my mouth.

The coffee had been laced with a sedative. I'd been drugged.

ANDRE DUG THROUGH Gabrielle's clothes, searching for those damn files. Instead he came across lacey lingerie. His nostrils flared at the sight. Still, he snarled and threw the bag aside when he didn't find what he was looking for.

He grabbed the next bag, her laptop case. He almost shuddered out his relief when he saw the familiar manila folders sticking out.

The coven, and not the Eleusinian Order, could be behind this. He dialed Vicca.

"Hello Andre," she purred.

"Has the court decided to detain Gabrielle again?" Andre asked as he made his way down the hall.

"Last I heard, she was under your roof. You know as well as I do that no one would try to kidnap her if she was staying in the royal quarters under your watch." Vicca paused, and when she spoke again, her tone dripped with interest. "Has the little siren vanished under—?"

Andre ended the call before she could finish. Vampires weren't behind this. He'd figured as much.

Like a madman he stalked to his office, throwing the folders down on his desk. If the Eleusinian Order was after Gabrielle, then he was going to have to figure out where the killers would take her. If it wasn't too late.

It couldn't be.

He opened the files and began thumbing through them. Stashed in one of them was a map of Romania. On it the crime scenes had been circled.

My brilliant queen. He grabbed the phone and dialed the Politia's offices in Cluj. "This is Andre de Leon, and I need to speak to Ivan Serban," Andre said in Romanian.

As usual his name elicited no questions. With a click, the line was transferred, and after two rings Ivan picked up. "This is Chief Constable Ivan Serban."

"Evening Ivan, this is Andre. One of my subjects, Gabrielle Fiori, is in Cluj working on one of your cases."

"Yes, I'm aware of this. What is it you want?" the chief constable said.

"She was supposed to meet me this evening, but she never showed."

"What makes you think this concerns the Politia? This sounds like coven business."

"You misunderstand," Andre said, anger sapping his voice of inflection. "I have reason to believe that she left my mansion when the sun rose with one of your men—Inspector Grigori Vasile." The inspector's name had rolled off Andre's tongue from memory. Gabrielle might think her business with the Politia was hers alone, but Andre had made a point to make it his as well. "She has not come back since the sun has set, which means that her safety falls under your jurisdiction."

When his words were met with silence, Andre went on. "I will lay it out for you, Ivan: I am not only her king, I am also the person standing in as her sire. And I'm dating her. So you could say that I have a lot of vested interested in her."

The supernatural community didn't know much about vampires, but they did know they were territorial creatures with a penchant for violence.

"I will go to great lengths to protect her," Andre continued, "and if harmed, I will go to great lengths to avenge her. So do me a favor and place a few calls. Find out what happened to her, and I'll make it worth your while."

Ivan cleared his throat. "Call me back in ten minutes, and I will give you whatever information I can find." Ivan's tone was gruff when he spoke, as though he had control of the situation. As though he hadn't simultaneously just been threatened and bribed within the same breath.

As though he hadn't just been bought.

"Make it five." Andre glanced down at Gabrielle's map. "Oh, and while you're at it, give me the names of the cities where the two most recent murders took place."

Someone had taken his soulmate. *His.* And now they would pay.

THE REALIZATION THAT I'd been drugged followed quickly with an even grimmer one. *Grigori must've done it.*

The betrayal left a bad taste at the back of my mouth. Literally—that coffee was awful.

My thoughts turned to Caleb. He'd been asleep while we were traveling. Had he been drugged too?

I scented the air, searching for his familiar smell, but it was absent. Oh God, where was he?

Pull it together, Gabrielle. You can't help him until you help yourself.

I wrestled with the bindings around my wrists. Someone had tied them together with rope, lots and lots of it. I tugged, trying to break the bonds, but I was weak from being drugged. Even my blindfold seemed to be immovable, no matter how many times I rubbed my shoulder against it, trying to pry it free.

I gave up trying to loosen my bindings for a moment, relaxing my body against the soft mattress I'd been laid out on. I was on someone's bed. Tied up. That meant that one, someone probably had carnal deeds on the mind, and two, only my cursed luck would land me into a situation where this wasn't kinky. Just twisted as hell.

Soft, fluttery material brushed against my legs when I readjusted myself on the mattress. I froze at the sensation. It felt distinctly different from the wool sweater and jeans I'd been wearing.

Had someone dressed me?

Across the room a door opened, and I pushed myself upright and onto my knees.

"Proserpine," a female voice said, "we meet again."

ANDRE ADDED THE locations of the last two crime scenes to the map Gabrielle had started.

He knew what he was looking for, already knew what he was going to see. Still, he let out an oath at the sight of those four dots arcing across the map.

Not a ley line, but still a pattern of sorts. An incomplete

one.

What did four crime scenes dozens of miles apart have in common with one another? Nothing, unless he penciled in a fifth dot as he did now.

He drew lines between them, joining each of the dots until a star formed. A pentagram.

Andre was the one who had reassured Gabrielle all those months ago that pentagrams weren't evil signs. Not unless they pointed down as this one did.

Symbolism. Unholy symbolism.

The other Satanic versions usually had the Beast's face inside, the tips of his horns represented the two topmost points of the pentagram. On the map those points were the cities of Cluj-Napoca and Bistrița-Năsăud, where the first two murders had taken place.

Beneath what would've been the devil's chin rested the fifth point of the star, the dot that Andre had added in.

Andre leaned on his knuckles against the desk and stared at it. A crime hadn't occurred there yet, but if he did nothing, then tonight one would. And his soulmate would be the last victim.

THE WOMAN'S FOOTFALLS crept closer to where I crouched on the bed. I recognized her voice from the club; she'd been the second attacker that night in Cluj, the petite one who'd shanked me.

Ho-bag.

I tracked the woman's movements with the senses I still had. She came right up to me, and I stiffened. Her hand brushed the back of my head and I flailed against her.

"Stupid girl," she hissed, "I'm removing the cloth from your mouth, so that we can talk."

I stilled at her words. If she took off the gag, then I'd be able to glamour her.

She untied the material and the bed dipped as she sat down next to me.

Fear made my skin flare up quickly; the siren in me was especially receptive to dark emotions. "Untie the rest of me," I beckoned in that eerie voice.

And she laughed.

"Proserpine, that does not work on me. Do you not remember our first meeting at the club?"

I hadn't thought of it, but of course. Why would she allow a siren to speak if she could fall under my influence?

I worked my jaw, my mouth sore. "Are you going to take off the rest of the bindings?" I asked when she leaned away from me.

"You only need your mouth to talk."

I ground my teeth together. "Fine, then if you want to chat, don't call me Proserpine."

"Why not?"

"It's not my name."

"It would've been," she said, "had my sister not pressed your parents to change it to something else."

"Your sister?" I asked, and then I cursed at myself. Stop chatting with the enemy.

"Yes. She and I don't exactly see eye-to-eye."

"And she knew my parents?" I couldn't help myself, curiosity pushed me to ask the question. That and the slim hope that I might be able to talk my way out of this mess.

"She knows you," the woman answered.

I breathed in her scent, but I smelled nothing. "You are not human, are you?"

"No," she said.

"Then what are you?"

"I'm a fate."

Chapter 24

ANDRE STARED AT the map as he held the phone to his ear.

"Andre?" Ivan said when he answered the phone.

"What do you have for me?" Andre asked. No formalities. He didn't have time for them.

"Grigori took the day off."

Andre ran a hand through his hair. "He took her." Grigori might've also taken the shapeshifter—perhaps even the fairy. Andre hadn't seen either since he'd risen.

"Andre, be reasonable."

"Don't tell me to be fucking reasonable. Listen to me: I think I have an idea where they'll be."

"You are claiming that one of our officers has kidnapped and intends to harm another officer of ours."

"Yes, I am, and I'm right."

"Andre crime and punishment may work like that in

your circles, but it doesn't work like that—"

He wanted to throttle Ivan. This was exactly why he loathed the Politia, and why his word meant very little in this network of supernaturals. They were so goddamn dense, clinging to their classicist beliefs even in the face of evidence.

Andre slammed a fist against the wall of his office. "Take down the following information, or so help me Ivan, I will have you wrung out to dry within the week."

"Fine," Ivan responded gruffly, "but no promises that our officers can get to it."

"Fuck you. When the crime is exposed, mark my words: I will make sure you pay for any inaction on your part."

Andre ended the call and threw the phone across the room. The Politia was out; this would be solely up to him.

He left his office to grab weapons and ammunition. He'd need all the arsenal he could bring along with him. Tonight, Andre would be fighting the devil.

"Morta," I whispered.

"In the flesh."

She was the fate that cut the thread of life; she was also the fate that was in the devil's pocket.

This was really effing bad.

Even tied up I managed to scramble away from her.

"You've made my life difficult these last few months," she said. "Not that I don't enjoy a challenge every now and then."

"What have you done?"

She patted my knee, and I tried not to flinch at her touch. "Let's just say that I've steered your life back on course."

Back on course? "Back on course from what?"

She didn't answer, and in her silence I thought of all the strange coincidences and unlikely situations I'd been in since I left Peel Academy. "How much of my life have you meddled with?" I asked, terrified of her answer.

"'Meddled with'? You court my wrath, using those words. I am a fate. I direct the flow of life. Everything that has led you here, to this moment, has been my doing."

"So the murders ... ?"

She made an impatient sound. "I am the fate of death—need you ask?"

"My involvement with this case?"

"Me," she said.

"My status as a demonologist?"

She guffawed at that. "Definitely me."

I sucked in my cheeks at the insult in her words. She'd been leading me like a lamb to slaughter.

She cleared her throat. "I'm not going to spend all evening discussing my actions. They mean little except that you are here now, about to fulfill your destiny."

I swallowed. "What are you going to do to me?"

"What do you think the fate of death is going to do to you? I'm going to deliver you from your flesh."

"I'M COMING WITH you."

Andre swiveled around to see Gabrielle's friend, Oliver, sashay into his room. Guess he hadn't been taken after all.

"No you're not," Andre growled, taking a menacing step towards him. There'd be no survivors tonight except him and Gabrielle—and perhaps Caleb, if the boy had also been taken. Andre sure as hell wasn't going to put another friend of Gabrielle's in danger.

"Yes, I am," the fairy insisted.

A growl of warning rumbled at the back of Andre's throat. "Don't push me, fairy. I still haven't forgiven you for touching her."

The fairy came right up to him, ignoring all the warning signs that indicated Andre was not to be reckoned with. "I know exactly how long Gabrielle and Caleb have been gone, and I'll only tell you if you take me with you."

Andre ground his teeth together. The audacity of this one. It was barely tolerable. "I can get that information from other sources." Like his servants.

"But you won't."

Andre's nostrils flared in anger. Now was not the time to test his patience.

Oblivious, the fairy plucked the map from Andre's hand. "So, where are we going?"

"What makes you think I'm going anywhere?"

Oliver lowered the map enough for Andre to see his raised eyebrows. He pointed to himself. "Fairy."

He'd made his point. Fairies were notorious for involving themselves in everyone else's business.

"How long were you eavesdropping?" Andre growled.

Oliver gave a shrug of one of his shoulders. A non-an-

244

swer.

Andre folded his arms, clenching and unclenching his jaw to keep his anger in check. "I will imprison you here if I have to. You are not coming with me."

The fairy dropped the map and leaned forward, his eyes glittering with interest. "How *does* she resist you?"

Andre turned from the fairy. He needed to stop talking and get his weapons strapped on. Back holsters for the twin blades that he favored in battle, and a belt to tuck in several throwing knives ...

Behind him the fairy shrieked. "Oh my God, I know where we're going! I always wanted to visit too!"

Damn it all to hell. "You are not going, fairy," Andre said, opening his closet to retrieve the supple leather gear. He began sliding the back holster over his shoulders when Oliver spoke again.

"This trip will take you hours to reach her. She could be dead by then."

Andre paused for the barest of moments. Gabrielle, dead. It was unimaginable.

"Take me with you, Andre, and I can get you there in twenty. All you'd need to do is drive us to a certain haunted forest."

Andre glanced over his shoulder at the fairy. "What, exactly, are you proposing?"

Oliver flashed him a mischievous smile. "I think you already know."

I'M GOING TO *deliver you from your flesh.*

That was quite ... blunt. And terrifying beyond belief.

"You don't need to do this," I said to Morta.

"Of course I do. I've been planning this for centuries, for millennia even."

"Please, there must be another way for you to get what you want. One that doesn't involve killing me." *Believe in us, believe in free will.* Andre's words ran through my mind.

She laughed and grasped my chin, pressing her fingers into my cheek. "You are Pluto's unwilling bride, through and through."

"I'm no one's bride," I ground out.

She ignored my response and instead patted my cheek. "Rejoice my dear, for tonight, you ascend. Tonight you become queen of the Underworld."

ANDRE PUSHED HIS car as fast as it could go, which was still pathetically slow. The storm continued to rage, and the roads were slick with snow and ice. What should've been a short drive to Hoia Baciu, the haunted forest on the outskirts of Cluj, was already taking much longer than usual.

This better work.

Next to him Oliver bounced to some song on his iPod, singing along.

Even if he and the fairy pulled this off, they still might be too late. And so help him God, if he was, there would be hell to pay.

Reaching over, Andre pulled out one of the fairy's earbuds. "You might as well play your music from the speakers," he said. He could hear the sound just as well from the fairy's earbuds. At least the car's acoustics would take away that horrible tinny edge to each song.

"Really?" the fairy said.

Andre glanced at him, then back at the road. He wasn't going to extend the offer twice.

But then again, the fairy wasn't one to turn down an opportunity. Oliver synced his iPod to the car's sound system, and a playlist titled "Kicking Ass and Taking Names," flashed along Andre's screen.

At that, Andre smirked. The fairy had style. He'd give him that.

The fairy cranked up the volume and whooped. "Evil bitches beware, we're coming for you!"

Andre's grip on the wheel tightened as he sped through a light, his smirk morphing into a sly smile. The thought of all the carnage to come ...

Evil beware, indeed. I am coming for you, and I am hungry for your blood.

"WHAT IF I don't want to become queen?" I asked.

"What you want matters little," Morta replied.

"Well, the devil can go screw himself. I'm not marrying him."

"Do not speak of him that way," she hissed.

Tou-chy.

"I'm not marrying him," I repeated.

"You are if you want your friend to live."

I went rigid. "Caleb? Where is he? *What have you done to him?*"

"He's safe, so long as you cooperate."

This all had the horrible echo of Samhain. But unlike Samhain, I didn't have Leanne to help me figure this one out, nor did I have Cecilia working behind the scenes to save my life. The devil had upped his game, and I was on my own.

"You are going to cooperate?" she asked.

I hesitated, then nodded. I couldn't do it again, couldn't allow others to sacrifice themselves so that I could live a bit longer before I met the devil.

"Why does he want me so badly?" I asked.

"You've been fated to be together for a very long time, and he's impatient to make you his."

Ugh, barf in my mouth. "Why would he care about me at all?" I asked. "He's the devil."

"He's Pluto," she corrected me, "and he is not all evil."

"Agree to disagree," I mumbled.

"It doesn't matter. Within the hour, you'll be his."

Chapter 25

"FUCK, SHIT, GODDAMNIT, bloody-fucking hell." Andre kept going.

There was an accident, a huge goddamned accident, blocking the one road they needed to take to get to Hoia Baciu. Even now he could hear the crunch of metal as cars ahead of him slammed on their brakes a second too late.

The fairy whistled. "That's not good."

Andre ran his hands through his hair. His options were limited at this point. Every moment they lost now brought Gabrielle closer to death.

He stared at the pileup in front of him. Even as he watched, he heard the skid of cars behind him, and the crunch of metal as they slammed into one another. The wreckage was only getting worse with each passing second. It was a small miracle they hadn't hit his car—yet. Other than completely abandoning his vehicle, he could only think of one alternative.

Andre opened his car door up and got out, crossing his fingers that no one would total his car before he had the chance to get back in it.

"What are you doing?" the fairy called after him.

Andre didn't bother looking behind him when he answered. "Clearing the road."

MY THROAT SEIZED up. Within the next hour? I began yanking against the ties, not caring that the enemy sat next to me.

"Don't bother," Morta said, "those bindings are enchanted. Only I can remove them."

Still I struggled. What other option did I have?

Morta sighed. "It's always got to be hard with you, doesn't it?"

"You don't know anything about me," I snapped.

"I know everything about you, mortal, and it's best you don't forget it. I am doing you a kindness, making you into a queen and a goddess."

"You can take those titles and shove them up—"

The air shifted, and then Morta's hand connected with my cheek, whipping my head to the side. The sound of the slap echoed throughout the room long before the pain blossomed.

"We're done here." The bed rocked as Morta stood up.

"Wait!" I begged. I wasn't ready to die.

Her footfalls moved away from me.

"Fate can't be the only reason he wants me!" I yelled after her.

Her footfalls stopped. "You're right, it isn't. You tip the scales in his favor."

Your lifeblood drips, the scales tip.

"In favor of what?" I called after her, dread settling into my bones.

The door clicked shut in response, and she was gone.

ONCE HE'D MOVED the cars aside, Andre got back into his own. Some idiot driver had ended up ramming into his car from behind. What was that, two accidents and a busted steering wheel all within a week? Even for him that was an impressive amount of damage.

But it didn't matter. Andre would wreck all of his cars getting to Gabrielle if he had to. He stepped off the clutch and shifted the car into first.

He could feel the fairy's eyes on his face.

"What?" he said.

"You moved those cars ... with your bare hands."

"And?" he asked, shifting gears.

The fairy raised his eyebrows and began fanning himself, his leg jiggling furiously. "Lucky fucking siren," he said, under his breath.

Andre gunned the engine, letting off only a little when the car lost traction. He cast a glance at Oliver. "Not lucky, fairy. Cursed."

"PLEASE," I BEGGED at the door, willing the fate to return.

"I promise to be respectful if you come back."

I listened.

Nothing.

I growled out my frustration. Damn my bound legs. I doubt Morta had even locked the door. Not when I'd have to roll my way out of here. Which was tempting ... but no.

I scooted up to the bed's headboard and leaned against it. Morta hadn't slipped the gag back on me, and that was a mistake I was going to fully exploit. She might be immune to my voice, but anyone else in the area wouldn't be.

I cleared my throat. Did I want to do what I was considering? If it didn't work, I might end up worse off.

Worse off than dying and marrying the devil?

I leaned my head back as a hum built in the back of my throat. Tendrils of my power snaked to the surface of my skin. The siren was awake, and she was a formidable monster when I embraced her carnal cruelty.

A smile curled along my lips as my power built. What I was about to do would be different from the glamour I'd used in the past.

Tonight, the siren was going to sing.

"STOP HERE," OLIVER said.

Andre pulled onto the shoulder of the road, and he and the fairy got out. He nodded to the back of his car, where he'd stashed extra weaponry. "Might be a good idea to arm yourself, fairy."

Rather than responding, the fairy leaned inside the car

and grabbed a gun from the back seat.

He held the gun up to the light, a gleeful smile forming along his lips. "Now I am one badass bitch," he said, posing with it. "Is it loaded?"

Andre nodded, leaning inside the car to grab the weapons he couldn't wear while he drove.

"I've never used one before," the fairy said.

Andre pushed away from the car. When he turned to face Oliver, the fairy was flipping the gun over in his hand, staring at it curiously. Giving a fairy a gun was a supremely bad idea—especially this one—but Andre didn't really have the patience to regret his decision.

He came around behind Oliver and positioned the fairy's hands over the gun, ignoring the lust pouring off the boy.

"Safety," Andre said, pointing to a switch near the trigger. "Keep this on until you're ready to shoot. Front and rear sight," he indicated to two eyepieces. "Line these up with your mark for better accuracy. And lastly, the trigger," he said, pointing to it. "I'm sure you know what to do there.

"This gun has eight bullets, seven in the magazine and one in the breach, so make them count. Try for close range targets and aim for the chest. Got it?" Andre said, stepping away from him.

"I think so." The fairy no longer sounded so flippant. Violence had a way of making men out of boys.

"I'll do my best to make sure you don't have to use that at all," Andre said, "but if someone tries to hurt you, don't hesitate to defend yourself."

Oliver jerked his head in answer.

"Good." Andre clasped him on the shoulder. "Now take me to my soulmate."

I OPENED MY mouth and something more than just words and notes came out. I couldn't see my skin, but I could feel it ripple as my essence freed itself.

Magic flowed out from my lips, arcane and powerful. Every instance I'd used glamour up until to now had been child's play in comparison. This, this was the true extent of my power, and it was terrifying.

The universe moved through me as I sang, and with each note I hit, I learned a new, impossible secret—how to seduce the unwilling, how to bring the proud to their knees, how to bring comfort to the desolate and leave the content wanting.

I tipped my head back and laughed even as I sang, the laughter fluidly weaving itself into the melody. I was getting high off the power. I might be tied up, but I was not the prisoner at the moment.

I listened for those humans who'd fallen under my spell, but I was met with ... silence.

"Nice try Gabrielle," I heard Morta say in the distance.

My voice faltered at her words. Nothing was happening, but surely something should be.

And then something did.

The smell of brimstone assaulted my nostrils as a being crept closer to my door. An unholy chill wrapped around my skin and seized up my windpipes. My voice painfully died away. The hollow sensation stroked my skin like a lover.

The being paused outside my door. My stomach clenched painfully, and my unseeing eyes darted under the blindfold.

Oh dear God and heaven above, my voice had garnered the attention of *something*.

After a pause, whatever lingered left, but not before it made me a promise.

Soon, Gabrielle.

DAMN, BUT ANDRE hated ley lines. The twisted, unnatural trees they passed were evidence of the snags in the fabric of this world. So was the strange, bloodied altar Oliver hoisted himself onto. The altar from the case Gabrielle was working on.

Oliver patted the stone slab, indicating that Andre join him.

In one fluid moment Andre lifted himself to the altar. He caught a whiff of an angelic being, and beneath that, a more familiar smell. *Gabrielle.* Her scent made him hiss through his teeth. Sometime recently she'd passed through here.

But now she was nothing more than a phantasm. And in a few more days, all traces of her would vanish from this place.

A fierce chill whipped down his spine. What did they call that? Revelers dancing over his grave? Whatever it was, it was a bad omen.

Oliver stretched out his hand. "Ready, Andre?"

In answer, Andre took his hand.

He'd die before all that remained of her was a scent in the wind.

THE STINK OF evil had barely left the hallway when I heard the click of two sets of footfalls. The door opened.

I almost choked on the smell of ash and roses. Two beings and only one scent.

"Oh lookie who's back!"

"Miss me?" another voice purred. The cambion from the club

I frowned. "I guess that depends on whether you're here to kill me or not."

"I heard your voice," she said. "Lovely. It will enchant our dark lord."

"Yeah, I don't think I'm happy to see you."

"All our preparations are ready," Morta interrupted, nearing the bed.

I heard the other woman approach the bed, and felt her soft touch as she grabbed my arm.

Morta hauled me off the mattress with impressive strength, and I felt the other woman adjust her stance to support my weight.

I didn't realize my feet were bare until they touched the cool floor. As for my wardrobe, the material swished around my ankles. A dress. Just like what the other victims wore.

What had Oliver said about virgins only being good for

sacrifices? Damn him, he'd jinxed me!

"I know you've figured it out," Morta whispered next to my ear.

I turned towards her voice.

"The myth of Pluto and Proserpine," she explained. "It really is a prophecy. A very old and very popular one. And it is a prophecy about you."

"But the details …" My voice trailed off as the cambion traced a finger down my arm. I grimaced as the sensation.

"The details matter not. That is what happens when a story outlasts several civilizations. Along the way word of mouth and cultural appropriation warp the details."

"Why was it so popular?" I asked before the two could haul me out of the room.

"Because it has to do with life and death," the cambion whispered into my ear, her breath hot against my skin.

"You were born of life but possess death in your blood-stream—you die even as you live. And yet in your death you'll live forever an immortal. You see?" Morta said. "You've been married to the god of death since your birth. Two sides of the same coin."

"But he's not the god of death. He's *the devil*." How many times did I have to say that?

"Best start thinking of him as Pluto," Morta said, "for I assure you his actions will conform to your beliefs. You want him cruel, he'll be cruel. You want his kindness, think of him as capable of it."

"Here we are," the fairy said.

When Andre opened his eyes, for a single moment he mistook his surroundings for the afterlife. The whiteness, the soft silence of falling snow—it was such a vast contrast to the vivacity of life as he knew it.

All around him stood tall trees. Cut between them was a snow-covered path marred with several pairs footprints. Several interwoven scents clung to the path. Supernatural beings. At least a dozen of them.

He stretched his senses. In the distance he felt a pulse of life and amongst it ...

"*Gabrielle.*"

He could feel her ahead of him. He almost fell to his knees; even with all his knowledge, he hadn't been sure she'd be here, and if she was, that she'd be alive.

He pushed forward. "There are at least twelve beings near Gabrielle, and we have to assume all are hostile. You should stay here."

"Oh hell no—I didn't come all this way just to be left out of the fun," the fairy said

Andre turned to give Oliver an appraising look. "This is not a game, fairy. People will get hurt. You will probably be one of them." Even as he spoke, he could feel his bloodthirsty nature rise.

Gabrielle never again wanted to see Andre massacre people. Tonight he was going to have to disappoint her.

"Argue all you want, Rambo," the fairy said. "I'll still be sticking to you like a nymph to a tree."

Andre didn't have time for this. He growled in frustration. "Fine," he said, defeated. "But once we get inside, you'll follow my orders."

The fairy's eyes twinkled with excitement. "Agreed."

They pressed forward once more, and as they did so, the trees began to thin out, and their destination towered over them. Made of marble and rock, conquests and cruelty, it was the perfect gateway into hell.

Bran Castle.

THERE WAS THAT reminder again, that belief trumped fate. Ironic that a Fate would be the one to tell me this.

"I'm going to cut the bonds around your ankles," Morta said. "If you try to pull some stunt on me, Lila will knock you out and carry you to your destination, and any remaining questions you have will go unanswered. Understood?"

Lila—I finally had a name for Creepy McCreeps-a-Lot.

I felt Lila stroke my cheek. "Please be difficult," she whispered in my ear, and I recoiled. I was beginning to think that Lila was here just to ensure my cooperation.

"Fine," I said to Morta, "so long as you answer more of my questions."

She knelt down at my feet and unwound the rope that shackled them together. "You do not get to make demands. However, I will entertain a few more questions, so long as it pleases me."

I didn't wait for more. "What kind of power would the devil possess by being with me?" I asked. The last of the rope fell away from my ankles, and I shook them out.

In front of me I heard Morta rise. "How does the end of the myth of Pluto and Proserpine unfold?"

259

Was she asking me? "Persephone's mother kills everything off until she gets her daughter back."

"After that," Morta said. "What is the end result?"

"Persephone gets to live half the year on Earth and half the year in the Underworld."

Morta took my arm once more. "That is the answer you seek," she said.

"What does that mean?"

Lila gave my face another caress, and her burnt floral scent assaulted my nose. Her lips brushed my cheek. "It means that you will be a creature that can freely travel between Earth and Hell."

WITH EVERY STEP Andre took, her scent got stronger. The smells of the damned seeped in along with it. Bran Castle had long been a place of pain. History knew the most public examples of it, but there were so many more that went unrecorded. Torture, rape, incest, murder—the place was saturated with it. Blood had fed the soil here. The place was stained with horror.

And somewhere in there Gabrielle was being held against her will. Silently Andre crept up the stairs to the entrance of the castle. His muscles twitched with the need to kick down the doors and unleash his fury, but he'd been in enough battles to know that brute force didn't often win, especially when outnumbered.

But the element of surprise, that could turn the tables. So rather than kicking down the door, he turned the handle. When he met resistance, he gave a deft yank, breaking the lock.

He pushed the door open, and then he and Oliver were inside.

My back went ramrod straight as a pulse of power thrummed along my skin. Andre was here.

But how? How had he found me when I had no clue where I was?

Morta gave me a yank. "Time to meet your destiny."

"Who even says that?" I asked, walking forward, but my mind was distracted. Andre had found me!

Together we crossed the room and slipped through the door. The hallway was chillier than the room I'd been in, and familiar dread churned in my stomach.

"No." I staggered and came to a stop.

"Move." Morta shoved me forward, but I refused to budge.

This place couldn't be real, but so help me God, somehow it was. I was back in the devil's home.

Even with Andre's soothing presence nearby, I began to shake, and my fangs descended. "Not here—I don't want to die here!" My voice became frantic.

I tugged on my bindings again, and began to struggle to get away.

"I warned you what would happen if you tried to get away," Morta said.

I couldn't die here; I refused to.

Power built along with my panic. At first I thought it was my own, but as the ground began to rumble and the sensation lashed against my skin, I realized it wasn't me at all.

Someone had officially pissed off my boyfriend.

As SOON AS Andre stepped inside, the connection between him and Gabrielle flared like a live wire.

"What is this place?" Oliver whispered. "The hall of horrors?"

The smell of decay and dried blood hit his nostrils. It came from all around him. From the leathery map that hung on the wall to the stained furniture. A fire crackled in a nearby hearth, but instead of emitting heat, it seemed to drain it from the room.

He turned to Oliver and pushed him into a nearby alcove. "Stay here," he said, his voice pitched low. He could hear the shuffling of feet in the distance.

"Not going to happen. Especially not next to this thing." He pointed to the marble statue of a horned being situated in the alcove. It had lifelike, inlaid eyes, and dried blood ringed its lips.

"Oliver, you agreed to follow my orders once we were inside. This is one of them."

"So you want me to stay here with this ... *thing*?" Oliver eyed the statue with obvious disgust.

"Yes."

"Fine, but I have a condition."

He didn't have time for this. "Whatever it is, it's yours. Now stay here."

"Deal." The fairy smiled, which probably meant Andre

had agreed to something ludicrous. Fucking fairies—you could always guarantee they'd take advantage of a situation.

"Oh, and if this thing eats me," Oliver added, "it's your ass I'm coming back to haunt."

Andre nodded absently, already strategizing his next move.

"Who even says that?"

Andre's head snapped up at the sound of Gabrielle's voice. Relief coursed through him at her insolent tone. It was an act, but it meant that she was alright for the moment.

He began to move towards the voice, winding his way through the castle nearing what appeared to be a turret.

Two women held a bound and blindfolded Gabrielle.

A sweltering rage burned inside him. If he let it, it would consume him. He stepped into the shadows and stilled, waiting for the appropriate moment to attack.

"No," Gabrielle choked out.

Andre closed his eyes when he heard the fear in Gabrielle's voice. *Don't lose control,* he willed himself. *Not yet.*

"Not here—I don't want to die here!" she begged.

As soon as he heard her desperate plea, Andre only had time to think of a single word before his rage consumed him.

Fuck.

MY CAPTORS STOPPED walking.

"Let her go," Andre's voice was sweet music to my ears.

The ground trembled violently beneath us, and I could hear metal clattering and glass tinkling.

Morta cursed. "It seems the vampire king has come after his mate."

Did they have no idea how close he was to losing it at the moment? They should be scared. Hell, *I* was scared, and I was his soulmate.

Air brushed against me, and the current between Andre and me throbbed; those were the only signs that Andre had moved.

Morta's grip was wrenched from mine, and I felt the ground shake as Andre slammed her into the wall. "You will die for daring to hurt her."

I didn't waste the opportunity Andre had given me. My leg shot out, and I kicked Lila. She gasped, and her hold on me slipped.

I pulled my foot back, preparing for another kick. "You do not want to fight, vampire," Lila said, glamour filling her words. "Gabrielle is in good hands."

The tremors racking the building softened.

I opened my mouth. "Don't listen to her," I said, pulling the siren into my voice. Poor Andre was getting majorly mind-raped right now. "She wants to—"

Lila covered my mouth. "Leave this place, vampire."

The trembling subsided, and I heard Morta suck in air. The current between Andre and I began to fade, which meant ... he was leaving.

I tried to shake Lila's hand from my mouth, but she held on. "Looks like your love is abandoning you," she whispered into my ear.

I screamed against her hand and yanked my head away from her mouth. Hate filled me. She'd glamoured Andre into abandoning his rescue mission.

Using as much force as I could muster, I head-butted the cambion. Her hold loosened on me, and I jerked my arm free of her hold. I began to run, almost falling when I realized I was moving down stairs.

"You stupid, little fool!" Morta was yelling at me.

Someone plowed into my back, and the two of us lurched forward. I fell, my head cracking against the edge of the stairs. I felt an instant of pain, and then I blacked out.

"ANDRE!" THE FAIRY hissed.

Andre ignored him, heading towards the front door.

"*What* are you doing?"

Once he passed across the threshold, his head cleared. Andre stopped, swiveled around, and locked eyes with Oliver.

That woman had glamoured him into leaving, and his only saving grace had been her vague wording. Otherwise, he would've left his soulmate to die.

The maps and antiques set on display began to shake.

"Uh, your hair's lifting," Oliver said.

"Give me your iPod."

"Hot damn," the fairy said, eyeing him, "are you going to blow?"

"*Now!*" Andre bellowed.

The fairy reached into his pocket and handed the iPod

over.

Andre placed the earbuds in his ears and turned the music on, cranking the volume all the way up.

"Stay here, fairy."

Oliver's lips moved, but Andre heard nothing over the music. And if he couldn't hear outside noise, then he couldn't get glamoured.

Andre smiled grimly, walking back through the house. Now there'd be hell to pay.

I WAS JOSTLED awake by the trembling surface beneath me. I blinked once and tried to sit up, but found my arms bound over my head and my legs bound at my feet.

Had I ... fallen and hit my head against the stairs? I frowned. It was suspiciously similar to the lie I'd told the coven during the trial, which probably meant it wasn't coincidental at all.

And now I'd managed to sleep through getting untied and retied. Just my luck.

The blindfold had been removed, so I could finally take in my surroundings. Candlelight flickered throughout the cloistered room. The smell of soil, blood, and death clung to the walls, but it was overshadowed by the scents of at least a dozen supernaturals. They loomed over me, cloaks covering their faces and bodies.

To my left Morta chanted in some ancient language. I couldn't see her face, but I'd recognize that voice from anywhere.

One of the shrouded figures caressed my cheek. I

ground my teeth together. Lila.

My eyes darted about, and it only took a moment for me to truly understand my predicament. I wore a white dress and lay on a wooden slab. I was going to die just like those other women. Except my expression wouldn't look peaceful like the others. Nope. Thanks to my immunity to glamour, mine would be contorted in agony and horror. No dignity for the dead.

The earth rocked again, but Morta's voice never wavered.

"Help me," I begged the cloaked figures, my skin flaring to life.

"Earplugs, lovely," Lila said.

Morta talked over us, her voice filling the chamber. The candles flickered, and the incantation came to an end.

The group stirred, and I saw a flash of metal pass hands.

"No, please," I said, thrashing in my bindings, "think about what you're doing."

"It's going to be alright, Proserpine. We're almost done." Morta lifted my head, and I felt the brush of twine rope as it passed over my face and hair before coming to rest around my neck. I closed my eyes. A noose.

When I opened them, the group loomed over me. I felt the noose tighten, and I began to choke.

I glanced at the shadowed faces that watched me. I couldn't see their eyes, but based on their smiles, they wouldn't help. They were excited to witness my death.

Two knives lifted, one to my side, and the other directly above me. I knew enough from the previous victims to know what was to come. A slash to my neck and a stab to my heart.

I began to struggle in earnest, but even with my supernatural strength, I couldn't break through my bonds.

Black dots began to smudge out my surroundings. *Losing consciousness.* My eyes completely clouded over, and I saw the knife above me start to move. In that second before I blacked out completely, I screamed.

I felt a slice of pain, and then nothing.

ANDRE DESCENDED THE stairs, his every step causing the earth to shudder beneath his feet. Bad techno music blared in his ears and somewhere below him he could sense magic building. The walls shivered, huge chunks of plaster raining down on him.

Dead. All who participated tonight, dead. He wasn't going to make it quick either. It would be slow and messy, and they'd be begging for mercy just like she'd been. And he'd give them the same chance they gave her.

The earth rippled out from under his feet, the tremors getting increasingly severe. He left the stairs and stalked down the hall.

The cord connecting him to Gabrielle flared, tightening his chest almost painfully, and then ... it was gone.

Chapter 26

I STOOD IN an empty bedroom.

I rubbed a hand over my neck. Had I died? Where was everyone? More importantly, where was I?

The same smells of blood and brimstone that had clung to the room I'd first found myself in lingered in this room as well, only here they were stronger.

Casting my hearing out, I listened for the sounds of my tormenters. Nothing. Not a single heartbeat. In the distance I thought I heard echoing screams, but nothing else seemed to stir in this place.

I eyed the bed, a hulking four-poster number carved with intricate designs. Skirting around it, I made my way to the window.

Outside I saw ... the castle grounds. I placed my hand to the glass. Everything was covered in snow, just like it had been in my dreams.

"Evening, consort."

My dress swished as I whipped around. Standing on the other side of the room, his hands in the pockets of his designer suit, was the devil.

ANDRE ROARED, UNCARING that the castle, which had survived centuries of attacks, was tearing apart from the shockwaves of his power. Anguish like he'd never experienced before now choked him.

He staggered, then fell to a knee. The world was red. Red with his bleeding heart, with his blood, with his tears. They dripped down his face, marring the ground in front of him.

The impossible had happened. Gabrielle, *gone*.

But she was his soulmate. She was supposed to live forever. With him. They were supposed to save each other.

He gripped his heart with his hand. Here was where he felt the cord most powerfully. But now, nothing.

They killed her.

Anger eclipsed his pain. He pushed himself to his feet, stepping over a rafter that had splintered and fallen.

He roared again, this time not in pain, but in rage, and the plastered walls running alongside him cracked. The entire castle seemed to scream in agony.

He could begin to smell the fear of the occupants trapped in the bowels of his place. They knew he was coming, which meant they knew they were never leaving.

They'd delivered Gabrielle to hell. Now it was his turn

to give them a taste of it.

I BLINKED, AND the devil stood in front of me.

Reflexively, I threw my fist out, aiming for his jaw.

He caught it in his own. "Now that is no way to treat your spouse."

"We are *not* married."

"You're right, we aren't—not officially anyway." The words were barely out of his mouth when he picked me up and tossed me onto the bed. I rolled across it and swung myself to my feet on the other side of it.

When I looked up, he again stood in front of me, smelling of brimstone and blood. I flinched. He'd moved faster than I could follow with my eyes. The devil's almond-shaped eyes appraised me.

"You want me to have sex with you?" I asked incredulously.

"That does seem to be an integral part of marriage, so yes, I do."

I tried to sidestep him, but he blocked me.

"That's never going to happen."

The devil's hand dropped to his stomach, and he undid the button of his suit jacket. "You could do this willingly, you know," he said, shrugging the jacket off and tossing it on a nearby armchair. He reached a hand to his wrist and unbuttoned the cufflinks. Then he moved to the other wrist and unbuttoned those.

"No, I really can't," I said.

The devil reached out, his hand cupped the base of my

skull, and his eyes dropped to my lips. "You're objection has been noted," he said, and then he kissed me.

BY THE TIME Andre kicked down the door and stormed into the dungeon, a grief-fueled rage had consumed him. Dust and plaster billowed around him as he stepped inside. The earth shook beneath his feet, the shockwaves rippling throughout the room.

His heart felt like it was imploding. Gabrielle, gone. *They will pay.*

The fairy's music still pounded in his ears, so he saw, rather than heard the cloaked figures' screams when they caught sight of him. They scattered, but there was nowhere for them to go. Andre blocked the only way into or out of the room.

He took another step into the room, his eyes scanning the crowd. *Kill them.*

He bellowed and the entire castle quaked. "You will all go down tonight and face your reckoning together," he said, his power amplifying his voice so that it vibrated the very walls around them. "And I swear by whatever god you all believe in that I when I join you, I will torment you in hell for all eternity."

Andre crossed the room and stood before the group. He could smell their terror. He grabbed the robed figure closest to him and yanked off the figure's hood.

A redheaded woman. Fear glittered in her eyes, but so did confusion.

She has no idea why I'm mad with grief. Grief for Gabrielle.

At the thought of her, Andre let the woman go long enough to withdraw his swords. Letting out a roar, he slashed an "X" down the woman's front. He saw her scream as her body was flayed open, and he smelled the sharp sting of fresh blood and entrails. It smelled like justice.

Unthinking, he moved onto the next robed figure and pulled the hood off. This one cloaked a bearded male in his late twenties. He performed the same brutal slashes and moved on.

Another robed figure tried to run. This time it was a blond male. A flick of Andre's wrists was all it took to mortally wound him.

He drew his lips back. "All who try to flee might as well run headlong into my sword, for you will die first." The group seemed to tremble at his words, and he was getting high off of it. The madness, the bloodlust ... it was all taking over; the more violence he meted out, the more violent he became.

It wasn't enough. These supernaturals were so ... weak. They were cowering rather than fighting. And yet they'd still managed to kill his soulmate.

The thought fueled Andre's fury. A fourth victim went down, then a fifth, and he still hadn't come across those two women.

"Where are you, you sadistic bitches?" he yelled. "Will you not face me? Or has your courage left you?" They would hide behind others to save themselves. "Afraid you'll be cleaved in two?"

Andre could smell one of them—the woman of ash

and roses. She was here in this crowd. He could pluck her right now. But he wouldn't. If Andre could help it, he'd continue to taunt her and the other woman until they were all that remained. He wanted them to be overcome with fear by the time he got to them. He'd drink it in, savor it like demons did.

They'd die slowest of all. "Cower all you want, you're not leaving ..." Andre trailed off as the sharp, irresistible scent of his soulmate's blood laced the air, distracting him. There was too much of it. No way a mortal could survive that kind of blood loss.

It stilled his hand and replaced his rage with something much, much worse. Sorrow. He needed to see her. Now.

He took a step away from the remaining crowd and pointed one of his swords. "Anyone so much as thinks about making a run for it, and I will make you wish I'd sliced open your stomach."

The group seemed to quiver at his words. He knew that amongst them those two women remained. Getting distracted now was dangerous while they were still alive. They might try to rise up against him.

The thought almost brought a grim smile to his face. If they did so, they'd lose. He'd incapacitate them, lock them up where no one would ever find them, and spend weeks torturing them before he finally let them die.

Some part of him even *hoped* it would come to that because right now, no one was putting up a fight. It felt less like retribution and more like slaughter.

Once again the seductive smell of his soulmate distracted him, beckoned to him.

Andre slid his swords into his sheath and purposefully turned his back to his enemies. His eyes drifted across the room. A primal cry left his throat as his eyes fell on Gabrielle's broken body.

Her hands had been tied above her head and her legs bound at her ankles. Trussed up and slaughtered like an animal.

Moving faster than human eyes could follow, he crossed the room and stared down at her. Gabrielle. Forever and always his soulmate.

He lifted a hand to her face, and stroked her cheek with the back of his hand. Even death couldn't ruin her beauty, but the soul that resided inside this body was gone. And their bond, broken.

A drop of his blood landed on her cheekbone, another just below her eye.

Out of his peripherals he saw movement as someone else entered the room. The fairy had decided to join the foray after all.

THE DEVIL'S LIPS moved over mine, and for a moment I forgot what he was and kissed him back.

I kissed the devil. Not that it had ever been in doubt, but I was so going to hell for this.

I pushed him away, coughing. It felt like I'd breathed in something sinister. The devil grabbed me, a hunger filling his eyes. This was going to end badly. He pushed me back onto the bed.

He lifted my leg ... and pressed a kiss to my ankle. Was

the devil being *gentle?* Hell had officially frozen over.

"*Wait,*" I gasped.

The devil dragged his eyes from my legs. "I've waited long enough, consort. You are mine."

I gazed wide-eyed at where the devil touched me. "I-I want a tour of the house!"

"No you don't. You're just trying to distract me."

"No really," I practically cried as his hands slid up one of my calves, "it's important to me that I know your home."

"*Our* home," he amended.

I waved my hands in the air. "Yes, yes—whatever." I'd do just about anything so long as he stopped touching me. And acting normal-ish. He needed to act thoroughly evil.

You want him cruel, he'll be cruel. You want his kindness, think of him as capable of it. Morta's words echoed in my head.

Please be capable of good, I silently begged him.

The devil's hands paused on my leg, and his mouth curved into a wicked smile. "You cannot outmaneuver me, consort. There is a reason I am known as the Deceiver."

That made me swallow. "Please," I repeated.

He stared at me, and I got the distinct impression he was weighing the benefits and the drawbacks of my request. "Why would I stop now when I have you on my bed, and I am minutes away from consummating this?" As he spoke, his hands drifted up my knee and began to caress my upper thigh.

I squirmed beneath him. "Because I am not leaving here anytime soon. Why rush what can be savored?"

The hungry look in his eyes deepened, and his hands stroked my skin.

I winced. It had been the wrong thing to say, but in all fairness, I hadn't practiced how I'd outwit the devil. Nope, I'd spent all that time with Andre learning how to physically defend myself against him.

I should've known that all the fighting in the world wouldn't save me from him.

And yet, the most surprising thing about this moment was the distinct lack of violence. "Why are you treating me so kindly?" I whispered.

He caressed my thigh again, and I shivered as my skin grew cold under his touch. His eyes drifted to my lips. "Perhaps I don't want my wife broken. I reign over enough mad souls as it is. Perhaps I want her fully lucid for all eternity."

I shuddered. Madness might be better than lucidity when it came to the devil.

"You're lying," I accused. Because if he was telling the truth, then that meant he wouldn't be violent with me. At least not to the point where I snapped. And that was definitely not the devil's style.

He smiled slyly, and his expression was full of wickedness. "Maybe I am, and maybe I'm not."

I stared at him, brows furrowed, until his hands began moving once more, caressing and kneading my thighs.

I gasped. No, this couldn't happen. I grabbed his hands. Fighting might not save me from the devil, but acting might.

"I want to see my room," I demanded.

"This is your room."

I raised my eyebrows. "If this is my room, then where are my things?" It took a lot of effort to keep my voice from shaking. To act entitled instead of scared. "I'd imagine that the devil's consort gets to have everything her heart desires?"

The devil's gaze narrowed. He knew I was up to something. "You will want for nothing."

"Then where are my clothes? And my shoes? And my makeup?"

"You will get all that and more, once you accept my wedding gift," he replied, a smile forming along his lips. He should not be amused. That usually was a sign that I was totally and completely screwed.

"Wedding gift?" I repeated, confused.

The devil studied my expression. His hands released their hold on my leg, leaving my own hands empty. I exhaled. "Yes, perhaps I'll give you my wedding gift before you give me yours."

I suppressed a cringe at the "wedding gift" he'd been planning on taking from me. He pushed himself off the bed and held out a hand for me.

Ignoring the proffered hand, I rose from the bed.

The devil captured my chin in his hand, forcing me to stare at him. "This is a warning, consort: I am the most dangerous creature to ever exist. I am the thing that monsters cower from, and I will not tolerate your insolence. So in the future, take my goddamned hand unless you want to see my darker side."

My body was racked with shivers as his eyes flashed,

and I felt evil closing in on me. I hadn't realized until now that he'd kept the darkness at bay. But now, with his anger, I felt it seep into me. How long before I'd lose myself in it? What would it do to me? The devil said he didn't want to break me, but how could he not if I was forced to always feel this?

I nodded and swallowed at the devil, not even pretending to be meek. The devil scared the courage out of me. His fingers lifted from my chin. They trailed up my cheek, and the malice drained from the devil's eyes. He was in control once more. "You wanted a tour of the house?" he said. "I can give you one on our way to your wedding present. Would you like that?"

"Yes," I whispered, my voice hoarse.

A smile touched his face. "Then so it shall be."

He steered me out of the room, and I almost sighed in relief. Anything would be better than what we were about to do.

I just hate it when I'm wrong.

ANDRE TURNED IN time to see Oliver taking in the scene before him. His eyebrows hiked up at the carnage, and then he caught sight of Gabrielle. Oliver staggered and grabbed the doorframe. His mouth moved, but over the music blaring in Andre's ears, he couldn't hear the fairy's words.

But he could see the fairy's grief. Oliver must've seen the blood or felt the death that clung to her body. Andre saw the ragged sob that came from the fairy's lips.

Andre's eyes closed again, and his body shook, his rage now usurped by his grief. She couldn't be gone. She couldn't. He refused to believe it.

His eyes snapped open as a thought crossed his mind. "Oliver," he said, "you can travel to other realms—you can get her, you can bring her back." He didn't have to hear his voice to know that desperation had entered it.

The fairy was shaking his head, and in the dim light of the room, Andre saw the glint of Oliver's tears. He began to speak, and Andre read his lips. "... so sorry ... can't travel to the Underworld ... unless ... Samhain. Even then, ... who enter ... can't leave."

Andre sagged against the altar, bowing his head as more bloody tears mixed with Gabrielle's blood.

Out of the corner of his eye, he caught movement. One of the cloaked figures was trying to escape. One of the bastards that had killed her.

They will pay.

He was on the figure in an instant, ripping off the being's cloak. Beneath it was a man who cowered at the sight of Andre.

Andre's upper lip curled, and he bared his fangs. "*You dare try to leave?*" he hissed.

The man's entire body shook, and he smelled ammonia as the man's bladder released. He could see his mouth moving, *begging.*

Andre's fury was no longer mindless—at least, not for the moment. He knew enough about grief to expect another wave to slam into him, and soon.

"Gabrielle begged for her life," Andre said. "I'll show

you as much mercy as you showed her." He kicked the man's knees in. The ridiculous techno music Oliver had programmed on his iPod drowned out the sound of shattering bone and screams. The man collapsed on the ground, his skin beginning to sweat. His face pinched together in agony.

Andre knelt. "I'd rip out your throat, except then you'd die too quickly. Perhaps if you hadn't killed my mate, I'd be more benevolent. Then again, humanity was always her thing, not mine."

He pulled out two of his throwing knives and slashed open the man's stomach, just like the others. Andre rose to his feet and kicked the man in the legs. Now *that* scream he could hear even over the music. Cold cruelty was always more satisfying than his mindless rages.

Andre glanced behind him at the fairy, who still stood in the doorway, his gun hanging limply at his side. The fairy's eyes were wide with shock.

"*This*, my friend, is why you should've stayed upstairs."

Chapter 27

"Game room," the devil said with a bored flick of his wrist as we entered it. We'd wound our way through the castle, the devil giving me the world's most half-assed tour.

Then again, considering the rooms' horrible contents, the less information, the better. Like this room, for instance.

I sucked in my cheeks as the smell of death wafted over me. It wasn't a game room in the sense of board games or a billiards table. Nope. It was a hunter's game room, and everywhere I looked, I saw relics of the hunted.

I was going to be sick. A unicorn's head was mounted next to a head of a dragon. The full body of a being with webbed feet and gills sat on display in the corner. Next to it was a centaur, posed to look as though it were rearing up. On the other side of the room a griffin rested next to a stuffed sphinx.

"These creatures are real?"

"*Were* real. Most are extinct now."

I caught sight of a wall dedicated solely to wings. Iridescent fairy wings were pinned to the wall right next to what looked like bat wings—very, very large bat wings. Other sets had plumage and came in deep, vibrant colors. There were so many pairs that they overlapped one another.

Intelligent beings had been caught, killed, and were now displayed. Perhaps when the devil got tired of me, I'd join them.

I shuddered at the thought.

"Enjoying the tour so far?" the devil asked, throwing me a glance. One side of his mouth curved up, and he gave me a knowing look.

"It's ... *unusual.*" Yeah, unusual and horrific.

We left the room and continued through the castle. I began to rub my arms as the preternatural chill sank into my bones. I was learning that was the chill that came from being in a place where God simply wasn't.

"Where is everyone?" I asked. We'd come across no one, and I still couldn't hear any voices.

The devil slowed until we walked side-by-side. "Gone," he murmured.

I pulled back to look at him and caught him just as his gaze dropped to my backside.

"For a guy who rules the Underworld, you sure seem awfully interested in ... life," I commented.

He flashed me a sinful smile. "Care to see the extent of my interest?"

The corners of my mouth drew down. There was innu-endo in that offer. Ew, ew, *ew!*

"Er, no." Before the devil could get all up in arms about my rejection, I changed the subject. "Where, exactly, is this home of yours?" I asked.

The devil's gaze drifted over my face and down my neck as we walked, but he didn't answer.

"Romania?" I ventured.

An amused smile touched his lips. "In your world it is."

I wasn't going to dissect that statement. I wasn't.

"It's a castle," I continued. "It's ..." I sucked in air. I glanced at him, wide-eyed. "Are we in Dracula's castle?"

"We are in *my* castle."

That was devil-speak for, *yes, we are in Dracula's castle.* Which would've been cool, except these were so not the right circumstances to rejoice. "Isn't this place a tourist destination?" I asked.

"Beings of both my world and yours do flock here," the devil said as we entered a hall.

"Beings of your world ... ?" A shiver ran down my spine when I remembered the shrieking I'd heard from some-where further inside the house. I shook my head to clear it. "*Are* we still in my world?"

"Your petty questions bore me," the devil said, reaching for my hand.

I bristled at his words, yanking my hand out of his reach.

In response, the devil pushed me against the wall and slid a leg between my own. He eyed my cleavage. "I warned you that I did not tolerate insolence. Since you're so deter-

mined to avoid my touch, it shall be your punishment."
He dipped his head and kissed the valley between my
breasts.

It took all my willpower not to punt his unholy ass
across the room. I'd already seen what the devil was like
when I pissed him off. But even as I held back, I knew I
couldn't forever. I'd end up living out my own personal
nightmare. I was in hell, after all.

He picked up a lock of hair and brushed it across the
exposed skin of my chest. My jaw tightened at the action.
"What I find strange," he said, "is that you haven't asked
about the wellbeing of the shapeshifter." His eyes flicked
up to mine.

I flushed at the reminder. I barely thought about Caleb
since I'd woken up. "Is he okay?" I asked, worry coating
my words. I ignored the stab of guilt I felt when I realized
that I'd rather know whether Andre was safe.

"Hmm, how badly do you want to know?" he asked,
peering at me. "I could tell you all about him and your
snaggle-toothed boyfriend—for a price."

I narrowed my eyes at him. "So that's how it's going to
be?"

"What did you expect? That I'd be some valiant, selfless
creature? I *am* the devil."

"Supposedly you are also Pluto, my husband," I said,
trying not to choke on the word.

The devil's attention snapped to me. He leaned in so
close that his torso pressed into mine. "Not *supposedly*. I
am your husband. I'm amusing your ridiculous questions
and interests right now instead of chaining you to *our* bed

because I'm trying to be *accommodating* and *caring*—vastly overrated qualities if you ask me. Those emotions have atrophied quite a bit since my fall," the devil said, leaning in closer to me, "so I suggest you tread lightly. If you don't," he snapped his fingers, "they just might disappear completely."

Holy shit. Nightmares really do come true.

"What are your conditions?" I whispered.

"That you accept and make use of my wedding gift immediately."

What sort of horrible present was it that he'd need me to agree to this? "And if I don't?" I asked.

"I will betray every last one of your secrets to those who'd wish you harm."

I furrowed my brows. What sort of secrets could harm me here and now?

"I'm not going to make that kind of deal with you," I said.

"Then perhaps we're wasting our time down here. Perhaps we should go back to our bedroom."

He was giving me a choice that wasn't really a choice at all.

"Fine," I snapped.

"Fine what?"

"I agree." I bit the inside of my cheeks as soon as the words left my mouth. What was wrong with me that I'd make a deal with the devil?

A triumphant smile spread across the devil's face, and I ignored how attractive his features were when he didn't look like he had gutting and flaying on his mind.

"Aw, consort, you like my form," he stated, drawing a hand down my arm. Revulsion had my muscles locking up.

"It's deceptive. Just like you."

"I'll take that as a compliment since I know you're not so stupid as to anger me right after I warned you of my wrath."

He stepped away from me and took my trembling hand. "Now," he said, beginning to walk again, "to answer my side of the bargain, Caleb and Andre are both quite fine—though I doubt the bloodsucker will hold onto his humanity much longer. Loss does that to a person."

My gaze darted to the devil, my mouth parting in horror. "You mean Andre's grieving ... for me?"

I touched my chest, feeling the aching absence of our connection. Yet somehow I was still aware, still lucid. I'd assumed the afterlife would feel like a hazy dream at best.

The devil only said, "More souls will enter my gates tonight, thanks to him."

I glanced away, my grief crumpling my expression. My heart flared to life weakly. Here in this place without God, love came to die.

"As for Caleb, it strikes me as odd that you haven't seen him since you woke."

"Perhaps I would've if I hadn't been bound, gagged, and *blindfolded*." But as usual, the devil's words had worked their way under my skin.

"Hmm," he murmured.

"What happened to him?" I asked.

We passed through a guestroom with walls the color

of dried blood. Judging by the old, metallic smell and the way my fangs descended—ew—that was exactly what it was.

"Well now this is what's unusual," the devil said. "The shapeshifter woke up shortly before you did in a small town about an hour from here. He's confused but unharmed."

My eyes widened at that. Grigori had dropped him off before delivering me to my killers? "What are you saying?"

The devil squeezed my hand, and I gnashed my teeth together to keep from ripping it away from him.

"Would it also surprise you to know that Grigori was not amongst those that watched you die?"

Now I did yank my hand from his and backed away from him. "Why are you telling me this?"

His eyes had a twinkle to them. "Because no one and nothing is as you think."

ANDRE LEFT THE broken man and prowled back to the altar, eyeing the cowering crowd. His rage, his inhuman rage, was being held in check by something even more primal—his grief-fueled instinct. And right now, it was telling him to stay by Gabrielle's side and protect his soulmate, even if her life had fled her.

And while he didn't understand it, he heeded it, approaching Gabrielle's bloody body once more. He took her hand in his, and another crimson tear dripped down his face when he felt the chill of her skin. The chill only death brings. Yet he couldn't leave her side, couldn't seem to believe she was really and truly gone.

Somewhere throughout the ages he'd heard about a species of bird that mated for life. If one of the pair was killed and their body left to rot, the other bird would inevitably come to it, day after day, trying to revive its mate.

He was that idiot bird. Not knowing when to quit. Not believing he could.

Andre's eyes flashed. He might be that stupid bird, but he was also a vampire; he *could* revive her. But her injuries ...

Don't think about it.

His eyes moved to the dagger still in her heart. He grasped the hilt and pulled it out, grimacing at the sucking noise the flesh made as it released the weapon. Déjà vu washed over him. He'd done the same thing only months before, when another dagger had missed Gabrielle's heart and embedded itself into her shoulder.

She'd recover like last time. *She must.* He had to believe this, or else he wouldn't survive this night.

He bit his wrist and held it to her lips. Only a couple drops of blood dripped into her parted lips before the wound stitched itself back together. That wouldn't do.

Someone stepped away from the huddled group. Andre gave the figure a sparing glance and growled low in his throat. The individual was shaking their head, their lips moving.

"They come any closer, you shoot them, Oliver," Andre said, nodding to the being. He couldn't see or hear the fairy's reaction, so he could only hope Oliver didn't choke up.

Andre still held the ceremonial dagger in his hand. The weapon meant to kill Gabrielle would now coax her back to life. He slashed the knife down his forearm. Blood gushed out from his wound, and he tilted is arm so that the rivulet of blood dripped into her mouth.

The cloaked figure blurred, and then they stood right before Andre. His lips drew back and he bared his fangs and growled low.

This filthy murderer dared to interrupt him?

Over the music, he heard the sound of a gunshot. The being in front of Andre didn't flinch, but someone in the clustered group staggered and then fell.

At least the fairy had hit *something*.

The being in front of Andre grabbed his wrist and yanked him away from Gabrielle. He stumbled from the force of their strength, and he howled in outrage.

The ground beneath them shook as Andre's closed fist snapped out and connected with flesh. The figure's hold on him loosened.

Save your soulmate, his instinct screamed at him

Andre threw another punch—one powerful enough to snap a person's neck—and jerked his arm from the being's grasp.

He ran back to the altar, dust and dirt sprinkling him from above. At the back of the room, another cloaked figure was inching forward. If they tried to escape, more would follow.

Not acceptable.

In one fluid movement Andre pulled a throwing knife from its sheath, aimed, and released it. He didn't have to look to know it sliced open the individual's throat. They'd bleed to death in a matter of minutes and join the other bodies scattered around them.

Turning his attention to Gabrielle, Andre grabbed the ceremonial knife once more. He opened another vein and let his blood trickle across Gabrielle's lips. *Need to revive her.*

And again that same annoying being yanked him away from Gabrielle too soon. He roared his rage. Around him the ground shook violently and the walls lurched. Some of the remaining cloaked figures grabbed for the wall while others fell.

Slowly Andre turned to face the cloaked figure, his hair beginning to lift. Never had he encountered a being that could deter him whilst he was on the edge of that mindless rage, and he could only think of one supernatural capable of that show of strength.

A deity.

"AH, HERE WE are." The devil gestured to a grand dining hall. He tugged on my hand, the action unsettlingly gentle.

Morta's words ran through my head again. I wondered if my perception had changed his behavior, or if his behavior was changing my perception. I rubbed my head.

"The dead don't get headaches in hell, consort."

When I dropped my hand, the devil gazed at me with open curiosity.

Stop being so nice to me. It was on the tip of my tongue,

but I refrained from saying the words because I knew that in response he'd say, *okay*, and then proceed to beat the living daylights out of me. Even if he was trying a different angle with me, he was still the devil.

The devil raised an eyebrow at me, as though he'd listened in on my thoughts, and a sly smile blossomed along his face.

I ignored him and glanced around me. "My wedding present is ... the dining room?"

The grin on his face grew. "Not quite." He released my hand and approached the dining room table. On it was a single object, a chalice made of gold and decorated with precious jewels. Something about it had me stepping forward.

My nostrils flared as I gazed at it, and absently I rubbed the area over my heart.

"This," the devil said, lifting the goblet into his hands, "is yours."

My eyes were riveted to it. The smell was heavenly. Whatever lay inside drew me in like a moth to flame, and I took several more steps towards the chalice.

"Why wouldn't I accept this gift?" I asked, wonder filling my voice. I couldn't look away from it to spare a glance at the devil.

"None at all. Here," he said, when I reached him, "it is yours, consort."

He handed me the golden cup, and I got my first good look at what lay inside it.

Blood.

Chapter 28

ANDRE KICKED THE cloaked figure, throwing all his unearthly fury into the hit. The kick blasted the being across the room. Their body slammed into the far wall, the impact shaking the castle. Dirt, dust, and chunks of stone rained down from the ceiling.

He didn't wait for the deity to recover. Lifting his hands to his shoulders, Andre slid out the two swords sheathed to his back and approached the crumpled being.

The figure's hood had fallen back, and beneath it he saw a petite woman with raven dark hair. It was the same woman who'd dragged Gabrielle to this room. One would never assume that she of all people was a deity. Too small, too dainty, her face too innocent. The most dangerous beings were wrapped in these sorts of packages.

"I've been looking for you, coward," he said.

He lifted his swords to her throat, and she looked at him defiantly. Her lips moved. "*I am ... fate of death ... cannot kill me.*"

"I choose my own fate." He sliced the swords across her neck, severing her head from her body.

He wiped his blades on her cloak and stepped away from her. He'd just beheaded the fate of death. She was immortal, which meant that she'd come back. And when she did, she'd most likely focus her wrath on him.

I'll relish the day.

Andre sheathed his swords and stalked back over to the altar, eyeing Oliver on his way. The boy still guarded the doorway, his expression shocked. His hands, however, didn't shake, and the stink of fear didn't cling to him. He'd survive the evening's horrors.

Grabbing a throwing knife from his belt, Andre began slicing his forearm open again. He wasn't going to give up on his soulmate, damnit, no matter how impossible the situation was.

He lifted Gabrielle's head, angling it so that his blood dripped between her parted lips. He was going to have to feed soon; he could only lose so much blood. Lucky for him there was a room full of blood donors. He glanced up briefly to glare at them.

He didn't need to. All around him, the Eleusinian Order was coming apart. The remaining members clung to one another. Some wept, others wailed, and somewhere amongst them, the woman of ash and roses still hid. Now that he'd killed a deity, they'd finally grasped just how screwed they were.

Andre's gaze dropped back down to his soulmate. "Gabrielle," he whispered, staring at her too pale face.

No response.

It wasn't working.

I BLINKED RAPIDLY, trying to resolve my revulsion to blood and my attraction to this liquid. "What am I supposed to do with it?" I asked. Stare at it all day? 'Cause I could.

"Drink it."

My fangs, which had descended at the sight of it, now throbbed, and my gut clenched painfully. I hadn't even realized I was hungry. Hungry for blood.

I hesitated. I'd never drunk blood before.

"What are you waiting for?" The edge in the devil's voice drew my gaze up to him. The face staring back at me looked calm, but there was an eager twinkle to his eyes.

"Why rush?" I countered. The smell of the liquid drew my gaze back down. It smelled like absolution, redemption, ... God.

I almost dropped the chalice, and the blood sloshed around inside. Angelic blood. "This was why the victim's blood had been collected."

"Yes. It's your wedding gift," the devil said. Did he sound a tad impatient?

"Why?" I asked, enraptured by the sight and scent of holy blood.

"What do you mean why, consort?" he said. "It is yours because it is the most rare and exquisite gift I could give you."

Angelic blood in the devil's domain? That seemed oxymoronic. And how did it get here? My hands shook as the wheels in my mind began to turn.

"So, the killers didn't drink the blood to absolve them of their sins?"

The devil gave me an amused look. "And why would they do that consort, when I can give them a place of honor in the Underworld?"

So the choice of victims and the way they'd died had to do with this wedding gift and nothing more. This strange and macabre wedding gift ...

My grip on the chalice wavered as realization hit me. Threefold death was symbolic, the death of three sides of human nature—the body, the soul, and the spirit. Complete and total death.

Which meant ...

I lowered the chalice. "This is food of the dead, isn't it?" I asked, my voice accusing. Food that would keep me trapped here, just like food had trapped Persephone in the Underworld

The devil snarled. "You agreed to make use of my wedding gift. You vowed it. Now drink, consort."

I stared at him and then the goblet, still hesitating. If the threefold ritual had actually worked, then nothing living resided in this blood. But there was something alive in this blood ... God. I could feel him in the liquid; I suspected it was what had captivated me when I laid eyes on the chalice.

I rubbed my heart again. *I* did not wish to be parted from Him. I definitely wouldn't call myself religious, but lately God had seemed synonymous with love, happiness, life—things I desperately craved. If I drank this, I'd be giving that up. Love, life, *God.*

"No," I said, my gaze rising from the chalice to gaze at the devil. I steeled myself for the devil's famed wrath. This was it; this was where I'd begin to fight, even if it was pointless. Even if I was stuck here for an eternity.

"You'd break your oath to me?" he asked. The earth around us trembled. Something far in the distance screeched.

"Shouldn't be too surprising that the Deceiver's wife wouldn't exactly keep her promises," I said.

Gabrielle. I cocked my head at the familiar voice.

My attention snapped back to the devil, my mouth forming an "O". I only had time to see the blur of movement before I was tackled to the ground.

"GABRIELLE," HE REPEATED. Still nothing.

It's not working.

Andre let loose an anguished cry and dragged Gabrielle's body off the altar and into his arms. He cradled her to him, sobbing as her torn neck listed back.

Another gunshot went off, but he didn't bother looking up. He still had a clear view of Oliver and the exit. If someone got that far, then he'd intervene, and he'd make sure they regretted their decision to flee.

He sliced his forearm open again and tipped the blood into her mouth. "Gabrielle, come back to me." His blood was all over her, and still he begged his body to offer up more. Hopelessness was beginning to set in.

And then he felt it. A spark of energy; the cord flared briefly. Andre sucked in a breath of air. His love was alive. *Alive.*

That was the only sign he needed. He dragged the knife down his forearm again, relishing the bite of metal because it was bringing Gabrielle back to life.

I GAZED UP at the devil, whose body pressed mine into the floor. Damn it all. This was the second time I'd been tackled this evening and the third time I'd found myself restrained. But ...

I'm not dead. I might not even be in hell. Where were we then? Purgatory? Limbo? Was there such a thing?

The devil held my wrists in one of his hands, and in the other he held the chalice. He'd managed to not spill a drop when he tackled me and wrested it from my grip.

"When were you going to tell me I wasn't dead?" I asked, the echo of Andre's voice lingering in my ear.

The devil's forearm pressed down against my windpipe, and in his other hand he held the goblet. He must've snatched it from me when we fell.

"Oh, but you did die, three times over," he said, his arm digging into my neck.

"No, I didn't," I rasped. That was why he had made me agree to accept his wedding gift. He had to trap me here because a dead thing would already be trapped.

"No one escapes a deal with me," he hissed. This close to the devil, I could see that the color of his irises flickered

298

like flames. "I will force you to drink this if I must."

Knowing that I had life in me still, I thrashed against him. How was I supposed to leave this Godforsaken place?

He laughed at me, raising the gooseflesh along my arms. "You will be unwilling after all. Don't say I didn't try to be a gentleman."

The devil began to tip the chalice, and I caught a glimpse of the scarlet liquid.

Gabrielle, come back to me.

My eyes widened even as I twisted my head away. Andre's voice. He was somewhere just beyond my reach. My heart throbbed painfully at the thought, and I felt ... I felt the cord that connected me to him.

"Look at me, consort," the devil snapped, "unless you want me to get that pretty face of yours bloody." Did I detect a hint of desperation in the devil's tone?

The goblet dipped closer to my face, the scent of heaven invading my senses, yet still I kept my head tilted away from the devil. He couldn't pin my hands, pour out the blood, and lock my head in place. He'd have to let something go first, and I'd attack him as soon as he did so.

I smiled as I spoke. "Face it, devil, you've lost this round."

"You think you've won?" the devil laughed. "You can never win against me, consort. I am the king of the damned."

He let my wrists go to snatch my chin, and that was all the opportunity I needed. I lunged up at him and dug my thumbs into his eyes.

The devil roared and the windows shattered with a

blast. The hand that held my chin now used its grip to slam my head into the ground.

I bit back a scream as tissue tore and bone cracked. My vision went hazy. My last coherent thought was, *Dear God, save me from this*, and then my vision went dark.

Chapter 29

My body jolted, and I sucked in a ragged gasp of air. Andre gazed down at me, his face and clothes soaked in blood. I stared at his face with awe. The sight was too gruesome for us to be in heaven, but because it included Andre, then I couldn't be hell either.

That meant I was alive.

Crimson tears streaked down Andre's face, yet he was smiling, laughing. He leaned in and pressed a kiss to my lips. "You came back," he murmured against my mouth.

I opened my mouth to tell him how much I loved him, but all that came out was a ragged choke.

The pain came a moment later. I squeezed my eyes shut and let out a wordless cry.

"*Gabrielle*," Andre said, pulling away.

Something was wrong with me. My neck ...

Oh God, my neck was sliced open.

"Gabrielle, you need to drink." Andre held up a bloody arm, and the blood, was his. What had happened to him?

His words sank in. Drink blood? But I'd just escaped that fate.

I turned my face away, wincing when I felt the agonizing burn of my neck wound.

"Please, Gabrielle," Andre said, his voice gentle.

I closed my eyes and grimaced. Even though my fangs throbbed, and my instinct screamed at me to take the blood, I didn't want to. Not when only a moment ago the devil had tried to get me to do the same thing.

With my eyes closed, my other senses heightened. I could hear the tinny sound of techno music blasting from earbuds Andre wore. Why would he be listening ... *To prevent getting glamoured.* Duh. Smart vampire.

But then, that meant that the cambion was still close by and still a threat.

"Where am I?" I asked. The scent of blood and ammonia hit my nostrils, and I opened my eyes. "What's going on?"

"You're still in the basement of Bran Castle, and you almost—"

"Oh. My. *Holy fucking smokes, Sabertooth!*" Oliver screeched. His footfalls pounded across the room, and then he fell to his knees in front of me, pulling me in for a bear hug.

I moaned as he jostled my wounds, and I swear I heard Andre growl in warning.

"Okay, okay, godslayer," Oliver said, letting me go. "I'm

backing off while you tend to your woman."

"Not ... anyone's ... woman," I wheezed. Andre's lips brushed my cheekbone, at that.

"Damn straight," Oliver said, and I heard him sniffle a little.

My eyes drifted to him as he stood and retreated to the doorway. *With a gun.*

Wait. What *was* Oliver doing here? And who was stupid enough to give him a gun? And now that I actually paused, I could hear moans and soft crying. Oh all that is on God's green earth, was the cult still in the same room as us?

"Soulmate ..." Andre said, pulling me away from my thoughts. My eyes flicked to his, and I only had a moment to perceive the hunger in them before his lips found mine again. The taste of him washed away the stink of the devil. It was the kiss of a desperate man. My skin flared weakly.

I heard the sigh of a knife cutting through flesh, and then Andre drew my mouth down to his neck.

Blood dripped from a wound there. I tried to pull my head away, but I was too weak. Andre brushed a hand over my hair. "Soulmate, you've already drunk my blood." I had? "But you need to drink a little more."

Gently he pressed me towards his neck. The wound there had already begun to heal, but my lips brushed against the blood that had pooled on the surface. As soon as the taste of it hit my tongue, my teeth sank into the flesh of his neck and instinct took over.

It tasted better than anything I could've imagined. A surge of endorphins rushed through me. My soulmate tasted like home.

My body shuddered as blood filled my system and my skin began to softly glow. Beneath me Andre groaned, and I smelled that wild, spicy scent of his. Pheromones. Guess I wasn't the only one that enjoyed getting bitten.

"I ... never realized just how repulsive blood drinking was," Oliver commented from behind us. "Though I will say, you two make nasty look *good*."

I ignored the peanut gallery. My wounds itched, and I could feel them stitching themselves back together. I pulled deeply from Andre's blood, and I felt him run his hand down the back of my hair, murmuring sweet things in Spanish.

The skin over my heart and neck sealed together. Very gently, Andre began to push me away from him. I made an annoyed noise in the back of my throat, which earned me a chuckle.

I released my hold on Andre's neck and blinked a few times, letting my bloodlust abate. I hadn't realized how close to death I'd still been until I'd gotten more blood in me.

I glanced up at Andre. "Thank you,'" I whispered hoarsely.

He gave me a tired grin, relief softening his features. He reached a hand up and stroked my face. "I love you."

When I tried to reach out to him, I realized my wrists and ankles were still bound. I tugged against them, and the bindings easily ripped apart.

I looked at Andre, my eyes surprised.

He raised an eyebrow, looking amused.

"They were enchanted," I explained.

He stared at my lips intently—reading them I assumed. "Look's like the spell's broken," he said in response. Then, as if he couldn't help it, he leaned in and brushed a kiss against my lips.

Above us I heard the sound of sirens, and I pulled away, letting out a shaky breath. The Politia were arriving.

I touched my neck. It still hurt like a mother, but the wound had closed.

"Let's get you out of here," Andre said, lifting me in his arms. It was only now that the altar was no longer blocking my view that I got a good glimpse of the rest of the room.

I made a noise at the back of my throat. It looked like a butcher shop in here. Except some of the bodies ... some of them still appeared to be *alive*. And now that I listened closely, I could hear whimpers of pain coming from some of them. When my eyes landed on Morta's severed head, I nearly lost what little food I had in my stomach. Andre had gone on a rampage.

In the far corner, what was left of my former attackers huddled together, crying and shaking. They didn't look quite so courageous now that the king of vampires stood in the same room as them.

When the group saw me and realized I was aware, I heard a few gasps. "She's alive!"

"The vampire brought her back to life!"

"The devil's consort lives!"

A few of them took a step forward.

"Move again, and I'll make you wish you were dead,"

Andre snarled.

I heard car doors slam and the sound of footsteps entering the castle.

He began backing up. "Time to go. Oliver?"

Some of the supernaturals with good hearing stirred amongst the crowd, restless at the thought of getting caught. Morta was probably supposed to take care of these details. Too bad the fate of death was now the dead one.

Karma was in fact a bitch.

A moment later the Politia swarmed inside the room, pointing their guns and yelling in Romanian. The group's hands went up into the air almost immediately.

Andre set me to my feet but kept one hand around my waist for support, eyeing the Politia like he dared them to pry me from him.

I leaned into him, still weak from my injuries, and emotionally battered from my encounter with the devil. I'd been so close to losing everything.

"You will not harm any of us," one of the cloaked figures said. I'd recognize that voice anywhere. Lila.

She stepped away from the cloaked crowd and removed her hood, her hips swaying as she walked. "You will let——"

Andre's hand slipped from my waist. A moment later he stood in front of her and wrapped a hand around her neck and lifted her off the ground. "You do not know how badly I've wanted to hurt you. And now you've presented me with the perfect opportunity."

I heard guns cock as officers trained their weapons on Andre. One of them shouted at him in Romanian, but he ignored the warning.

I shifted my weight. This could devolve real fast if I didn't do something. I took a deep breath, and called the siren up. "Don't listen to anything the woman says," I instructed the room, my skin glowing weakly. "Those of you who came here tonight intending to do me harm will willingly turn yourselves in. Officers, you will arrest the perpetrators."

Everyone except Andre, Oliver, Lila, and me appeared confused. The members of the Order weren't stepping forward to turn themselves in, but they also weren't trying to escape. The officers hadn't moved forward to arrest the Order members, but they hadn't stepped aside either. I was too weak to counteract the cambion's glamour.

"You will not hurt me," I heard Lila rasp. When I glanced back at her and Andre, she clutched the earbuds in one of her hands, and Andre's hold on her was loosening. I could see his trembling hand, the way his muscles spasmed.

No one could deal with her. No one but me. Well— there was Oliver, to be fair—but this was my battle.

I crossed the room just as Andre released her. She backed away from him and me, a smile dancing on her lips.

I grabbed two knives from Andre's belt while he stared at his empty hand. Stupefied. That was his expression; it was the same one that graced the faces of the other supernaturals in the room.

"Why don't you pick on someone your own size, Lila?" I asked, lunging at her with the knife.

She jumped away. "Sorry babe," she purred, "but you're

going to have to catch me first." Her form streaked across the room, and I bolted after her.

In front of the doorway out, Oliver squared his shoulders, spaced his feet apart, and pointed his gun at Lila. "Just say *no* to the hot, crazy ho." He pulled the trigger, and the sound of a gunshot rang out.

I screamed as a bullet tore into my side.

Oliver threw his hands in the air. "I got her! I got—oh *fuck*," he said when he saw me.

Behind me, Andre's angry howl raised the hairs on my arms. He might be dazed from the glamour, but he was becoming aware enough to know I'd just been shot. And once he came out of the trance, he'd be pissed.

Lila tore past us, pushing Oliver to the ground as she exited the room.

He yelped. "Not cool, wench!" he yelled after her.

"Move," I gasped out at Oliver as I trailed behind her, clutching my side.

"But sweets ..." he said, rising back to his feet.

I pushed him back down and darted out of the room.

Behind me I heard Oliver mutter, "I might've deserved that."

I ground my teeth together as movement jostled my new injury. It was the third time I'd gotten shot, and it was still just as blindingly painful as the first two.

I followed the scent of ash and roses through the castle, still gripping the throwing knives. Fat lot of good they'd do me at this point. My aim while injured would be crappy at best.

When I passed through the front entrance, I glanced

over the staircase at the barren landscape. Amongst the white snow, a small form was sprinting away from the castle.

Until my wound healed, I'd have a hard time catching her, even with my vampire speed. I tightened my hold on the throwing knives. If I decided to throw these at her, I'd likely miss, and then I'd be weaponless and she'd be further away.

Making a split-second decision, I steadied my breathing and focused on my target. I lifted my arm and took aim. *Move through the pain*, I chanted to myself.

I threw my entire body into the throw. I released the knife, biting back a cry as pain sliced through my side, and leaned a bloody hand heavily against the stone railing.

The knife embedded itself right between her shoulder blades, exactly where I'd intended it. Well, dang. That actually worked.

Lila cried out and fell to her knees.

Taking a deep breath, I pushed away from the railing and bounded down the stairs. I held my side as I ran, blinking several times to eliminate the black dots clouding my vision.

Ahead of me, Lila was whimpering. She reached over her shoulder and grasped the hilt of the knife. Letting out a scream, she pulled it out and tossed it aside. It took her several precious seconds to push herself to her feet, and I was almost upon her by then.

I let loose the second knife I carried, hissing in pain as I released it. This one embedded itself just below her ribcage. Chances were, it hit a vital organ.

Lila choked out another cry and fell into the snow once more. I picked up the knife she discarded and stalked towards her as she crawled away.

Lila moaned and glanced over her shoulder. "So ... fierce," she gasped out.

I leaned down and removed the knife from her lower back, and she screamed. Perhaps something about my visit with the devil had changed me, because I hardly batted an eyelash at my own cruelty. How our roles had reversed within a single evening.

"You want to know something?" she said, her voice weakening. Already her blood was pooling around her.

"No," I said, standing over her.

She flipped onto her back and winced. "I secretly didn't want you to die. You reminded me too much of myself."

"We're *nothing* alike," I said, staring down at her.

"We are," she insisted. "Beautiful, seductive—wicked."

She coughed thickly. Now that there was no one to glamour, she seemed fragile.

I knelt at her side and drew up one of the throwing knives. "You chose to be evil. I have not."

Even as she eyed the knife, she laughed weakly. "You will, though. You won't have any other choice. And the good guys? The ones you think you represent? They will hunt you down and steal your life from you. The saddest part of all is that they will think the world is a better place because you are no longer in it. *That* will be your legacy."

Her words chilled me; they felt too close to the truth. I placed the knife at her throat. "How about you worry about your own immortal soul right now."

I saw the whites of her eyes flash—saw true fear in them. Lila didn't want to die. The thought terrified her. "I already have a place of honor in hell," she said, her voice wavering.

I cocked my head at her. "Are you sure?"

This time I smelled rather than saw her fear. "I'll see you there, Proserpine," she promised.

"No, you won't." In one smooth stroke I slit her throat. "And my name is Gabrielle."

Chapter 30

Whᴇɴ I ᴛᴜʀɴᴇᴅ back to the castle, Andre stood at the entrance, watching me. My dark sentinel. He must've witnessed Lila's execution.

We stared at each other across the expanse of land, and then we were moving. I held my side as I ran, though the injury had mostly sealed up. My legs pumped furiously, and my weakened body screamed at me to rest. I promised it I would once I was back in my soulmate's arms.

We met somewhere in the middle. Andre lifted me in his arms, crushing me to him. I ignored the sharp stabs of pain that came along with his embrace. Instead I cupped his face and kissed him.

Our lips moved over one another's as though it were our last. I welcomed the warm sweep of his tongue as it invaded my mouth. There was a time this evening where I hadn't been sure I'd ever get this again. I rubbed my hands over his cheeks, smiling a little at the feel of stubble.

He groaned into my mouth and reluctantly pulled away. "I can't live without you, soulmate," he said, leaning his forehead against mine.

"That's funny, because apparently I can't die without you," I said.

I'd officially become one of those girls. The gross romantics. Screw it, I'd earned the right to be disgustingly cute with my scary vampire.

"I'm glad to hear it soulmate," Andre said, smiling. "So, so glad to hear it."

"WELL, MY WINTER break wasn't totally a bust," Oliver said, entering Andre's place behind us. "I got to shoot some foo's and help save the day."

"Yeah," I said, glanced behind me at him, "well one of those *foo's* just happened to be me. Still haven't forgiven you for that."

"Geez, I said I was sorry!" Oliver said. "I was trying to stop that trollop from escaping."

That trollop I'd killed. I swallowed at the memory. In response, Andre's arm tightened around my waist.

"Next time, Oliver," I said, "do us all a favor and aim."

Oliver narrowed his eyes. "Maybe my hands had a mind of their own. Maybe they wanted me to take out the more annoying of the two lusty women in the room."

Andre growled low in his throat.

"Oh, you do *not* get to get annoyed, Andre," I said.

313

"You were the one who gave him the gun."

Andre gave me an innocent look, as if to say, *Who moi?*

"That look doesn't work when you're covered in blood," I said.

Oliver glanced between the two of us. "Are you guys *finally* going to do the deed? 'Cause if you are, then Caleb and I should probably leave, lest you two destroy another house."

I glanced at Caleb. After waking up in a nearby town—right where the devil said he would be—Caleb had called in to the Politia. He'd been responsible for their arrival.

Since we met up with him at a Politia station, he'd been quiet. My guess was that he was suffering from some form of survivor's guilt.

"If you really must know, fairy, I'm planning on feeding Gabrielle," Andre said, giving me an intense look. "What happens after that is none of your damn business—unless, of course, you're interested in donating some blood to help her cause?"

Oliver cringed. "Um, *pass.*"

We stopped in the entryway, and Andre turned to Oliver and Caleb. "Then we'll see you tomorrow evening."

The two guys got the hint and headed off towards their rooms. Not that they needed any extra prodding. It was late, and by late I meant early in the morning.

I raised my eyebrows at Andre as he whisked me down the hall. "*We* won't be seeing them until tomorrow evening?" I asked, when we entered Andre's kitchen.

He set me on the counter, his hips pressed between my legs. His eyes looked haunted. "I'm worried that my blood may have sped along your transition. If it has, you'll probably have to start sleeping during the day."

I frowned. "I don't feel any different."

Andre's lips thinned, and he placed an ear to my chest. "Your heart beats twice as slowly as it did last night."

My lips parted in surprise.

Andre lifted his head and his lips skimmed my neck. Goosebumps rose along my skin.

"The smells of your skin are now much fainter—all but the scent of siren, which won't fade."

I tunneled my fingers through his hair, and tilted his head back to face me. "Please tell me that my body no longer has to die before I become a vampire."

Andre's eyes searched mine, and in them I saw remorse.

"Damnit," I whispered, my brows pulling together. "I shouldn't have asked."

"The truth," he said, "is that I don't know. When it comes to you, all the rules that govern the supernatural world get thrown out the window."

He clasped the sides of my face, his touch feather light. "*Are* you okay, soulmate?" he asked.

I shrugged. "I feel better."

He gave his head a shake. "I mean emotionally. A lot happened to you this evening."

He didn't know the half of it. I hadn't had a chance to tell him how the devil had kissed me, that he'd declared we were married, that he'd been a hair's breadth away from binding me to hell. I'd managed to spurn him again, which could not have made the king of darkness my biggest fan. Nope, I'd place lots of money that if he ever got the chance to touch me again, he'd make sure I knew exactly what hell felt like.

The sound of footsteps saved me from responding.

"Sir." One of Andre's men entered the kitchen, clearing his throat when he saw the two of us together.

Andre turned to face him. "What is it, Reginald?"

"The Elders waited for your attendance this evening. They asked me to pass along the warning that the next time you'll be charged with a misdemeanor for failing to appear in court."

Andre waved him off. "Let them know that I was indisposed, and that I will have to take off the next several days as well."

Without batting an eyelash, Reginald nodded and left the room.

I gave Andre a disbelieving look. "So vampire Elders kidnap me the first time they catch wind that I'm in the area, but you can just say you're indisposed, and they'll back off?"

Andre arched an eyebrow. "I'm the king of vampires," he said, as if that explained everything.

He moved away from me and walked over to his fridge, grabbed something from inside it. My breath caught when I saw what he held in his hand. Blood.

Andre came back over to where I was perched on his counter. "Here," he said, placing the bag in my hand and closing my fingers around it.

I grimaced at the thing in my hands. It was cold. "What am I supposed to do with this?"

"I was thinking we could play Hot Potato with it," Andre said. The side of his mouth quirked. The bastard was trying not to laugh.

I gave Andre a slitty-eyed look. "How do you even know what that game is?"

"Amazingly soulmate," he said, "I have learned a thing or two during my time on earth. Now do me a favor and at least give the blood a try. It even has a little straw so that my baby vampire doesn't have to get her fangs dirty," he said pointing to the top of the bag.

"Ha-ha—you're not funny."

He gave me a look that said he disagreed. "I want you to drink it."

"Andre, no." Ew. As if I hadn't seen—and drank—enough blood tonight.

He brought the bag to my mouth. "*Please*," he said, his eyes smoldering.

My hand trembled from exhaustion. I could do this. I'd shanked a bitch, dodged the devil, and survived death three times over. I was a badass.

Except when it came to blood.

"Let the record show that I'm only doing this because you asked nicely," I said. "See how far good manners go?"

Andre's lips twitched again. "I am amazed that in all my seven hundred years I hadn't discovered this asking-for-permission thing," he said, tucking a strand of hair behind my ear and letting his fingers run down my jaw. "It seems to be especially effective with the ladies."

"Hardy-har-har," I said, but I melted under his gaze.

He gave the blood bag a meaningful glance.

"Okay, okay, I'll stop stalling." I brought the plastic

straw to my lips and, drawing together my courage, I took a pull. As soon as the thick liquid hit my tongue, I grimaced ... at the temperature, not the taste. I also might've been little disgusted that the source of the blood was a plastic bag and not a big hunk of man.

This was so messed up.

In spite of my distaste, I didn't stop drinking until the bag was gone. Andre took it from me and gave me another. I felt like a kid drinking Capri Sun, sitting there on the kitchen counter, sucking my drink through a straw.

So much for me being a badass. This was totally ruining my image.

Once I'd finished a third bag, Andre declared I'd gotten enough color back to stop drinking.

"Don't you need to feed as well?" I asked him as he threw away the discarded blood bags.

"Once I know you're okay, I will."

"But you lost a lot of blood." Even now I eyed his bloody arms.

He came back over to me, a teasing smile tugging the corners of his lips. "Soulmate, I've fared far worse. I promise I'll take care of myself, but for now, let me worry about you." Andre didn't say it, but I could swear he was all sorts of pleased that I'd shown concern for his vampy needs.

He leaned in and placed his ear against my chest. When he pulled away his expression was grim.

"It's not speeding up, is it?" I asked.

"No."

I placed a hand to my heart. "But I can feel you here," I said, a happy smile drawing the corners of my lips up. It vanished when I remembered my time with the devil. "I couldn't when I was with *him*."

Andre's face looked pained. "I couldn't feel you for a while either." He placed his hand over mine. "Did he ... hurt you?"

I pursed my lips and chewed the inside of my mouth. "Not in the way you think. He kissed me and tried to do more, but it never happened."

Andre's hands gripped the marble countertops on either side of me, and I heard the rock groan.

"He kept insisting we were married," I whispered.

Andre's nostrils flared. "Not yet you're not."

"Why did I live?" I asked, searching his eyes.

Andre shook his head. "I don't know Gabrielle. The connection between us was gone. Severed. I swear you were dead. Perhaps the knife missed your heart? Perhaps the other fates interceded from afar? For all we know, it could've been divine intervention."

My head snapped up at that. "Does the big guy upstairs even do that sort of thing?" I asked, remembering my thoughts in those critical moments before I left the devil's presence.

Andre gave me a long look. "All the damn time."

LIKE ANDRE WARNED, I got sleepy as soon as the sky began to lighten. By then he'd fed, and we'd both washed off the remnants of our night from hell.

He took my hand. "If you want, you can sleep with me."

I glanced up at him. Was that vulnerability in Andre's

voice?

"Is it ... going to be weird?" I asked.

Andre ran a hand along the back of his neck. He was being bashful—*bashful!* "It might take some getting used to," he admitted. "When I sleep, I don't move at all—not even a heartbeat or a breath of air. It can be disconcerting."

As disconcerting as the evening we just had? I think not.

"I'd like that," I said, smiling shyly.

Andre flashed me a heart-stopping grin, and I realized that I'd managed to say just the right thing.

I was alive, with my soulmate, and back in the world of the living. Perhaps I wasn't so cursed after all.

Chapter 31

OH I WAS cursed all right.

I looked around me. I was back in the woods outside Bran Castle, barefoot and in that same stupid white gown.

"Dang it all, I thought I'd at least get a single night's sleep before having to see this hellhole again." And I do mean hellhole literally.

"You can never escape me." The devil's voice came from behind me.

I stifled my shriek and closed my eyes. My stomach clenched painfully and my hands began to shake. Fear pumped through my veins and my skin felt like it wanted to shed itself from my body. Anything to get away from the being at my back.

I couldn't say whether it was the devil or me that had changed, but we were back to our former relationship.

"It's both of us," he said, his voice calm and even. I wouldn't have thought him upset at all, except that I could feel the waves of malice rolling off of him.

I open my eyes and turned to face him. My hair stood on end. He watched me with barely contained rage simmering in his eyes.

"You broke your promise," he said.

"Yeah, well now you know how it feels to get tricked. Not very nice, is it?"

He moved faster than I could follow, grabbing my neck and shoving me against a nearby tree. "You need to learn your place. Trying to teach me a lesson will only earn you lots and lots of pain. And to my ears your cries will be sweeter than your music, siren."

My whole body trembled under his hand, my muscles seizing up only to spasm at random intervals. I clawed at the hand squeezing my neck.

"Because you are my consort, I will give you this warning: I promised that I'd betray every one of your secrets to those who'd wish you harm. And I will make good on that promise."

The clause of our earlier agreement suddenly made a whole lot of sense.

"Ah," he said, watching my reaction, "you finally get it. You will end up at my side one way or another. Did you really think that I'd let you go so easily?"

No, but I still thought I'd pulled off my grand escape.

"You, my little bird, have quite a few unsavory secrets, and tomorrow, they will be in the hands of those who'd wish you ill."

I swallowed. I had the kind of secrets that could get me killed, which was exactly what the devil wanted.

"How would you know my secrets and my enemies?"

He arched an eyebrow. "Is someone worried?"

"No." *Yes.* I lifted my chin. "Twice you've tried to kidnap me and force me into hell, and twice you've failed," I said. "What makes you think a little negative publicity will bring me back to you?"

A slow, sinful smile spread across the devil's face, and I knew—I *knew*—I was doomed from that expression alone. "I did better this time didn't I? Making you believe I was a gentleman. Maybe next time you *will* believe me. Maybe next time I'll mean it, too."

I eyed the monster in front of me. The devil was talking in riddles. Riddles that made me realize that I couldn't understand a creature as complex as him.

The devil's grip on my neck relaxed, and then he let me go.

I staggered away from him, shivers racking up down my body.

"Consort."

My body went rigid at his tone. I threw a glance over my shoulder.

The devil assessed me with a nefarious twinkle in his eye. "The apocalypse is coming, and you're a key player in it. Enjoy your final days as a mortal. Once they're over, you're mine."

I WAS IN Andre's jet when the news hit.

I'd stretched out along one of the couches, my head in Andre's lap, and I attempted to read a book while Andre played with my hair. My eyes *might* have fluttered shut once or twice, and I *might* have let out a contented sigh each time Andre's hand strayed from my hair to caress my cheek.

Since last night we'd been like this—constantly touching. Whether it was a product of Andre's blood running through my veins, our strengthening bond, or the fact that I nearly died, we'd come to some sort of understanding that we couldn't live—or die—without one another.

"How many times have you reread the sentence you're on?" Andre whispered. I could hear the smile in his voice. The punk knew what he was doing to me.

I closed the book and tried to swat him with it. He caught it and plucked it from my hands.

His face replaced the lines of text as he leaned over me. "I think you must've come back from the dead a little bit wickeder. The Gabrielle I knew never would've tried to bludgeon me with a book."

Just as I sat up and narrowed my eyes at him, he pulled out a small present from the bag sitting on his other side. "Now that I've got your attention, I wanted to give you your very late Christmas present."

My eyes widened. I glanced down at the gift, and then back up at Andre. "But I don't have a gift for you."

Andre cupped my chin and drew my face forward. "Then it's a good thing your presence is gift enough."

"You always have the perfect line, don't you?" I accused.

He flashed me a wolfish grinned. "It's one of the perks

of living as long as I have." He let my chin go and handed me the box.

I stared down at it.

"Open it," he encouraged.

I hesitantly slid a finger beneath the edge of the wrapping paper and began to tear through it. Under the wrapping was a thin cardboard box. I flashed Andre a curious look before I opened the lid.

Inside was a plane ticket to ... "Los Angeles?" I asked, glancing up.

"To visit your mother for spring break."

"But how will I explain this to her?" I asked.

Andre smiled. "Leanne's your cover. As far as your mother's concerned, her family is paying for you, her, and Oliver to visit California for spring break. I did mention that she and Oliver will be joining you, didn't I?"

A slow smile spread across my face, even as my eyebrows pinched together. "How could you have possibly known ...?"

The satellite flight phone next to Andre rang, interrupting my question. Andre winked at me, grinning, and I caught a flash of fang.

He grabbed the phone and brought it to his ear. "Andre," he answered.

I stared at the tickets. I'd finally get to see my mother. Somehow, Andre had known I'd been missing her like crazy. And he'd even included my friends in the gift.

As soon as the thought of my friends crossed my mind, I wondered if Oliver had already made it back to Peel Academy via ley line. Instantaneous travel was more appealing to him than flying in a private jet.

My thoughts drifted to Caleb. He was probably still tying up loose ends with the Romanian division of the Politia. I should've been there too, but I'd allowed Andre to bribe me out of the country early. Between getting kidnapped—twice—gagged, stabbed, shot, and nearly beheaded, I'd reached my physical and emotional limit. And that wasn't even counting my terrifying visit with the devil. Romania had officially lived up to all the spooky stories I'd read about.

Next to me, Andre's body froze, drawing my attention back to the present.

"This is a joke, right?" Andre said.

"Not a joke. Check the news."

Andre cursed. "Will do. Thanks for the heads up."

I sat up as Andre set the phone back in its cradle. "What's going on?" I asked, trying not to sound too interested.

A muscle in Andre's jaw feathered. "There's been a leak."

"A leak?" I repeated.

In response, Andre got up and grabbed his laptop. Sitting back down next to me, he opened it up and logged onto the supernatural community's news site.

When the front page loaded, I covered my mouth. On it was a spread, and yours truly was the top story.

Gabrielle Fiori: The Long-Awaited Anti-Christ

Anti-Christ. My eyes wouldn't stop returning back to that

word. Crap, could it actually be true?

Stories like this one had run periodically in the past two months, but they'd been so sensationalized that they were discredited almost immediately. But this ... this was a front-page story on *the* site for supernatural news. That kind of attention only came when the news was credible.

I leaned over Andre's shoulder and skimmed the story. It went on for pages, citing sources, pointing to evidence the community already had on me and discussing some ancient artifacts that accurately prophesized my fate. Some oracle had foreseen this whole shebang a long time ago. The prophecy had been scribed onto an ostrich egg in Teoian, the lost language of the gods. A month ago, cryptologists finished decoding the dead language, and shortly thereafter, researchers deciphered the ostrich egg prophecy.

How convenient.

Of course other mysterious artifacts had begun showing up over the last couple of months that validated the Teoian inscription. And if that wasn't enough, seers, psychometrics, and witches had been called in to shed light on the prophecy. Each one independently came to the same conclusion: Gabrielle Fiori was fated to marry the devil and bring hell on earth.

"Fuuuuuuuuuck," I drawled out.

At the end of the article were links to some related stories: "Gabrielle Fiori Soulmates with Andre de Leon: How the King of Vampires is Aiding the Devil"; "Gabrielle Fiori Prophesized to Lead the Vampire Genocide"; "Has Gabrielle Already Married the King of the Underworld?".

Only now did my dream from last night come flooding back. I rubbed my eyes. The devil really had divulged all of my unsavory secrets. And right now Andre and I were only staring at the secrets themselves. Who knew how many enemies were out there right now learning about them and readying to use them against me.

Andre let out a disgusted sound and cast aside the laptop. He stood and began to pace, rubbing his jaw.

I nervously twisted the ring he gave me round and round my finger. "Andre, there's something you should know."

He stopped to stare at me, his jaw clenching and unclenching.

"When I visited the devil, I made a deal with him."

"*Gabrielle.*"

I winced at Andre's tone. "I know, I know. But at the time it was either make a deal with him or do *the deed.*"

Andre's mouth thinned, reminding me that he still knew very little about what happened to me last night.

"So I made a deal with him, ... and then I reneged on it."

The muscle in Andre's jaw was ticking like crazy, but he stayed silent.

"One of his conditions was that if I broke my oath, he'd reveal all my secrets to those who'd wished me harm. As you can see, the devil made good on his promise."

Andre's face paled. "He revealed all your secrets?"

I nodded.

"And to those who'd use them against you?"

Well, to be honest, it looked like he revealed my secrets

to the entire world, but I nodded anyway.

Andre cursed and grabbed the satellite phone once more. "I need to make some calls."

I bit the inside of my lip and nodded. It was my turn to pace as Andre talked on the phone. I tried to not eavesdrop, but even still, phrases such as "devil's consort," "imminent death," and "wanted for future crimes against humanity" kept drawing my attention back to Andre.

When Andre finally ended the last of his calls, he dragged a hand down his mouth.

"What is it?" I asked.

"The House of Keys, my coven, and several religious groups are all actively hunting you at the moment. They want you—dead or alive. You've also been placed on hit lists by the more unsavory groups—Satanists, practitioners of the dark arts, possessed humans—the list goes on and on."

"More hit lists?" I croaked, my throat dry. Being on one was bad enough. Now I was on several?

Andre ran a hand through his hair. "The good guys want you gone, and the bad guys want to get credited with delivering you to the devil."

In the supernatural world, good and evil never agreed upon anything. Not until I came along.

That sucked gigantic balls.

"We need to get off the grid," Andre said.

"You mean ... go into hiding?" No school, no Politia, no freedom. The idea that my remaining days might be spent in some heavily fortified safety house frightened me. I'd just gotten a big enough taste of death to know that I wanted to enjoy life while I still had it.

But I might not get a choice either way.

Andre's eyes were pleading. "Please don't fight me on this, Gabrielle. I *can't* watch you die again. I won't."

I shook my head. "I'm not going to fight you. But … you're coming with me?"

Andre crossed the room until he stood in front of me. "We've already been over this, soulmate. Where you go, I follow."

I was going to be on the run, but Andre would be next to me the entire time.

"I need to go talk to the pilot about changing course." Just as Andre spoke, the jet dipped.

Our eyes met. Perhaps this was the normal turbulence. Perhaps it wasn't.

Andre went to the cockpit, and naturally, I followed, grabbing the wall as the plane dipped again.

"What's going on?" Andre demanded.

"We're being ordered to land the plane," one of the pilots said.

"Who's giving the orders?"

"The House of Keys."

In front of me, Andre's body went rigid. "You are not to land this jet," he said.

"Mr. de Leon, these are executive orders. I will lose my license if I don't."

"And you'll lose your life if you do."

I heard the man's delicate swallow, I could smell the sweat gathering on his neck as well as that of the copilot.

"Sir," the pilot said, "their orders state that if we don't

land the plane, they'll shoot us out of the sky.

I doubled back to look at the pilot. Did I just hear him correctly?

A long silence stretched on. "Fine," Andre said, "land the plane."

I rubbed my face. I was going to die in a matter of minutes.

"I'm sorry, sir," the pilot said.

Andre wasn't listening. He strode past me, heading to the back of the plane.

I walked over to the couch and sat down heavily, resting my head in my hands. "Why does everyone think that killing me is the answer?" I said to myself.

"Because they are idiots." Andre walked back into the cabin holding two canvas backpacks. "Here," he said, handing me one of them, "put this on."

I took it from him and eyed it warily. Now that I took a closer look, there were way too many straps for this to be *just* a backpack. Which meant ...

"Is this a parachute?" I asked, standing up. Dread pooled low in my stomach.

He wrapped his hands around my upper shoulders. "Do you trust me?"

"You want me to jump out of a plane," I stated. Only people in the movies jumped out of planes. Well, them and adrenaline junkies. But this was not comparable to skydiving. Not when we were up higher, flying faster, and people were after us.

Andre gave me a firm shake. "Do you trust me?" he repeated.

I blinked a few times, and then looked at him, really looked at him. "With my life."

"Good."

Andre glanced over his shoulder at the cabin. "If we stay in the air, you die. If we're in the plane when it lands, you die."

"No Andre, please don't sugarcoat it," I said.

His hands squeezed my arms tightly, his way of telling me to shut up. "The only situation where you live is if we jump."

"Please tell me you've done this before."

He nodded but looked away.

The jet dropped, and I grabbed ahold of Andre to steady myself. "Andre? How many times have you jumped out of a plane?"

His arms went around me, holding me to him. "Enough to tell you that you'll be safe."

"Will it hurt?"

"Compared to what you've been through? Not at all."

That wasn't exactly reassuring.

I took a deep breath. "Okay. Let's do this."

Andre handed me a pair of goggles and helped me strap the parachute on. Then he pulled a pair of goggles over his head and fastened his pack on. Once everything was secure, Andre instructed me on how to jump out of a plane, how and when to release the parachute, and how to control my landing.

"I'll be with you the entire time, so watch me for cues." He glanced over his shoulder at the front of the plane. "Give me a second to check how high up we are. If there's anything you want to keep, you better grab it now."

He walked over to the cabin, and I scrambled to my bag to grab my wallet. As I did so, a letter slipped out. I was about to put it back in my bag when I caught sight of Cecilia's handwriting.

> *Child of penance and pain,*
> *Dealer of beauty and bane,*
> *A coin's been flipped,*
> *The scales tipped,*
> *Nothing will be the same.*

Goosebumps broke out along my skin. It was the same letter Cecilia had sent me for my birthday, but the riddle had changed.

How was that possible?

"It's time to go," Andre said coming back over to me.

I shoved the card and my wallet in my pockets and followed him to the door of the plane.

"I can't believe I'm doing this," I muttered as Andre worked on opening an emergency exit located at the back of the plane. From the glimpse I caught out of a nearby window, the land below us was dark, meaning it was either wilderness, countryside, or water. *At least it's better than certain death.*

"Ready?" Andre asked, eyeing me.

I squared my jaw and nodded.

I might be wanted by the entire supernatural community and the devil, but they wouldn't get me. Not yet.

Andre flung the door open, and together we jumped.

Keep a lookout for the sequel

The Forsaken

Out now!

Be sure to check out the first book in Laura Thalassa's
new adult post-apocalyptic series

The Queen of All that Dies

Out now!

Be sure to check out Laura Thalassa's new adult science fiction series

The Vanishing Girl

Out now!

BORN AND RAISED in Fresno, California, Laura Thalassa
spent her childhood cooking up fantastic tales with her
best friend. Lucky for her overactive imagination, she also
happened to love writing. She now spends her days pen-
ning everything from paranormal romance to young adult
novels. Laura Thalassa lives in Santa Barbara, California
with her husband, author Dan Rix. When not writing,
you can find her at www.laurathalassa.blogspot.com.

CPSIA information can be obtained at www.ICGtesting.com
Printed in the USA
BVOW08s0123080915

416994BV00001B/8/P